Chasing The Dragon

BY NICK COLE & JASON ANSPACH

TYRUS RECHS:
CONTRACTS & TERMINATIONS
BOOK 2

Galaxy's Edge: CHASING THE DRAGON
By Nick Cole & Jason Anspach

Edited by David Gatewood
Published by Galaxy's Edge, LLC

Cover Art: Trent Kaniuga
Cover Design: Beaulistic Book Services
Interior Design: Kevin G. Summers

For more information:
Website: GalacticOutlaws.com
Facebook: facebook.com/atgalaxysedge
Newsletter: InTheLegion.com

A LONG, LONG TIME FROM NOW
AT THE EDGE OF THE GALAXY...

GALAXY'S
EDGE
galacticoutlaws.com

HISTORY OF THE GALAXY

IMPERATOR

0	The Pilgrimage
98	The Exploration
501	Savage Wars Begin
2000	Savage Wars Officially Declared Over
2032	Decay of the Republic

REQUIEM FOR MEDUSA

CHASING THE DRAGON

2047	Battle of Kublar

LEGIONNAIRE

The man was dying. But he was not alone.

That was the important thing. He wasn't alone.

Remember that. He did not die alone. Which is a bad fate—a bad death—in a galaxy that specializes in such things.

The man was surrounded by his family first, his wife and children. Then his friends. And finally his colony, small though it was. He had tamed this harsh yet beautiful alien world. He had survived where so many others had not, and because of him, so had his family. They had prospered.

Now, as he looked out on this life, the last of it that was left to him, he saw his wife crying. His children weeping. Especially the little girls. The boys too, in their own stoic way.

This was very sad for all of them.

Very sad for the man because he knew he was leaving soon. He knew he was dying. But that they would miss him meant that he had done at least one thing right in the galaxy, no matter how else it chose to remember him.

He was ready to go now. Except his mind just seemed to be hanging on for something. Waiting. Waiting for one last person to come and say goodbye.

The man had decided days before, when the dying began in earnest, that he would wait as long as he could. And so he had. Long ago he had been raised to think a thing before he did it. That thinking, that will, the determination was the iron that allowed one to go on doing even when the odds, the body, and the galaxy were against you.

The man had made up his mind to wait for the one he wanted to see one last time. And so, death too could wait.

All around him his family grieved. Death had made its appointment. It lingered by the door, waiting just as the man waited for a stranger to come and say goodbye.

01

THE MAN WITH NO HOPE STEPPED OUT ONTO THE ledge. He was sobbing. Ugly and hard at first, then gently as he resigned himself to his fate. Soft as the rain that lashed at his face.

The histrionics and terror that had gripped him for the past three months had faded. First with prescribed pharmaceuticals and high-grade, mood-altering biologics. Then with premium illegal drugs. The best, because the man on the ledge with no hope was incredibly wealthy. You don't invent the latest pleasure entertainment smart device that everyone simply has to have that year and end up broke. Not without some real bad luck.

He'd had no problem scoring the best finely chopped jade lotus to keep shoving up his nose and feeling like he was on top of the galaxy despite the facts of his situation.

His situation…

The man on the ledge had an estimated wealth in the trillions of credits due to intellectual property patents.

His circle of influence consisted of all the insider elites who shaped the culture that was the Galactic Republic that year. Who told them what to watch. What to wear.

What to think and who to vote for so that change, change for the better that was just around the corner, always just around the corner... could finally be achieved.

He dated models when he wasn't hiring high-end escorts. But that was just for the entertainment streams, because his passions had led him down some pretty dark alleys. And it was one dark alley in particular that led him, a man with no hope, out onto this ledge on a dark and rainy night.

Except there's one last aspect of his situation to consider. Security. In the months since the massacre on Cassio Station, when some crazed bounty hunter—*the* crazed bounty hunter—carved a path of blood and vengeance across the Reach to settle accounts, his situation had been all about security.

The best he could buy. Which was pretty stinking good. Because his was the last account that needed to be settled.

So he hired a state-of-the-art, high-end private firm with a hundred ex-legionnaires carrying lethal Fokke and Crowe high-cycle medium blasters along with a full suite of fraggers, bangers, and a variety of support weapons. Including two full dropships with air-to-ground-capable missile packages.

That was the man who gently weeps's level of security. Combined with the regular security that guarded this elite tower section of the Olympia District of a city devoted to tech dev and pleasure, the total force surrounding him had numbered at over a thousand.

And those weren't mere hired blasters. Every one of them was a highly trained security professional with military experience. Most with trigger time in the various conflicts the House of Reason had needed to address in recent years.

But that wasn't enough.

The corporate cabal that had formed around the man's brilliance—his genius—and who traded heavily in the stock that was the man with no hope on a ledge on a dark and stormy night… they simply could not suffer a loss. Not the loss of him. And so, as the man slowly lost his mind, the cabal cut him off and insulated him in hopes that this "situation," as they called it, would pass. And that their stock would come out of it a new man with new ideas to sell.

They hired him a trainer. Two trainers and a nutritionist. All of these professionals were also ex-military and carrying blasters. They'd spend their lives, in theory according to digital contract, to save their client's.

But he was just fine with the jade lotus and the darkness of his film room. Watching action movies and surrounding himself with expensive and stylish blasters he thought he knew how to use.

If it ever came down to it.

To protect their investment, the cabal even cut off his net access, dialing it down to a highly protected channel that served the thirty-six-story tower where the man on the ledge was the only occupant. Unless you counted the guards. But that was enough for him to get his action flicks. Watching them as they flashed in the dark. As impossible heroes did impossible things right after delivering just the right hardened phrase.

In those moments the weeping man lied to himself and said he'd somehow come through this. That it wasn't really a death sentence. That the thing he did on Cassio to the girl—the machine—he didn't even do it. He only tried. He tried. He didn't go through with it.

And so he told himself that it wouldn't come back on him.

Three months before, they'd warned him that the crazed bounty hunter was looking for him. That's when his fellow elites surrounded him and buried him here. Protected by the best money can buy.

"No one will ever get you here," they said.

The man with no hope, the man on the ledge gently sobbing, screamed out into the dark and stormy night from the thirty-fourth-floor hangar deck. The one only he had access to. The one the security forces had mined in case the bounty hunter came in hot and fast in some tricky dropship. Or HALO-jumped from the dark skies of Minaron.

One last time, the man flicked on the holo feature on his smart ring. The device that stored his most precious files. Where he kept the darkest secrets only for himself.

The things he'd hoped would make him happy and never really had. Which was what he'd said each time he found some new lust to throw himself into.

Maybe this will make me happy.

Each dark fantasy made real.

The warning had come during his enjoyment—or at least his consumption—of one of the tamest of these fantasies. As he watched Antonio Becerra mow down right-wing insurgents in yet another installment of the *Justice Warrior* film franchise, an innocuous little file download had appeared in the flickering dark of his movie room. Drop file. Coming off one of the devices in the room.

Someone was sending him a secret message.

And after all these months of isolation and fear, this contact—this uncontrolled contact with some stranger—was received with unexpected welcome. At first. The man who at that time still had hope thought, *Maybe this will make me happy.*

For the umpteenth too many a time.

Then the man who would soon be on the ledge opened the file and saw the holo message from Tyrus Rechs. That crazed bounty hunter he'd been running from since Cassio Station.

A bounty hunter in old Mark I Legion armor. All battered and scarred.

A voice of iron and gravel spoke from the miniature blue-hued holo. A real man who stood in stark contrast to a galaxy forever chasing its tail and changing its mind.

"I know who you are, and I'm going to kill you tonight," promised the hologram of Tyrus Rechs.

That's when everyone got good and scared.

The first security teams flat-out walked away when they heard the name Tyrus Rechs. No sense in getting killed for a guy who probably deserved it. And even if he didn't… no sense getting killed. Replacements were hurriedly hired and not told who was coming for their client. Only to protect him.

I know who you are, and I'm going to kill you tonight.

The man with no hope on the ledge of the thirty-fourth-floor hangar flicked on the holo feature on his smart ring and watched the holographic figure of Tyrus Rechs promise death one last time. Violent, painful death for what the man had done to the girl becoming a machine.

Turns out she was some kind of a friend to the killer. Back luck.

And so the man with no hope stepped off the ledge and out into the open air.

It was a long fall onto the rocks jutting from the deep dark of an ocean filled with almost-prehistoric predators. Minaron was a violent and toothy world. But that death was far better than what he'd imagined waited for him at the hands of the crazed bounty hunter who never stopped until all the accounts were settled.

That's what they said about Tyrus Rechs. That's what the falling man had gathered about who Tyrus Rechs really was. What he did. And how badly it had ended for almost everyone in his path.

This way was better.

The long fall was better.

02

Tyrus Rechs lowered the high-powered laser-designator rifle and disconnected the uplink from his bucket as he watched the dark figure fall from the thirty-fourth floor over half a mile away.

"How'd you know?" asked Gabriella in his ear.

"Know what?" muttered Rechs. He stripped the rifle and tossed pieces of it in a nearby pile of refuse. The homeless who lived on the outskirts of the Olympia District would search through it tomorrow. Maybe they'd get some credits for the after-market tech. Probably they'd just get themselves some trouble.

"How did you know he'd jump?"

Time to leave. Rechs was walking quickly now. Needed to reach the hangar bay and get going fast. Already massive klieg lights were scanning the storm clouds over the Olympia District in the distance—bone-white searchlights shooting up into the midnight blue and boiling clouds. The rain was not intense, but it was enough to keep everyone along the swollen sides of the favela under cover and dry. Huddling under their makeshift tents and drinking hot teas and lotus-infused elixirs.

Hoping tomorrow might be their lucky day. Hoping to be of service to the bright and shining luminaries who lived beyond the massive walls of the district that kept the haves free of the have-nots.

Sirens rose up in the night, and already the two drop-ships from the security company, Dark Skies Solutions, were hovering over the tower. Searching the waters that surrounded the fantastic glittering offshore towers where the rich lived and played.

For now they would think he was inside their perimeter. That Tyrus Rechs had done it up close and personal. They wouldn't be able to imagine the chain of events that had started from bouncing a data package off some low-level device inside the building. That the data worm that ran the package had found the desperately lonely and isolated man and offered to share a file.

A tech guru, and a lonely frightened one at that, couldn't resist a look. A peek at some new pleasure. And then he'd gotten the simple holo-message and its promise.

"I know a jumper when I see one," said Rechs into the ether of his bucket.

There was silence from Gabriella on the other end of the comm. He didn't care what she thought. The galaxy was a hard place. Stick around and you'll see enough to figure people out occasionally. And Rechs had stuck around for a very long, long time.

"This ends it then?" she asked as Rechs made the main thoroughfare through the favela, walking quickly. This way led back to the supply hangars built along the trash-strewn swamps of the mainland. The broad street was the only viable option back. The favela was a danger-ous place with over a hundred desperate local gangs con-trolling synth, lotus, and every other vice. Rechs didn't have time to pay their "passage taxes" or get involved in a dispute.

"It does," whispered Rechs after a long moment. The Medusa account was settled in full. You could tell just by the corpses.

He heard her sigh on the other end of the comm being fed to him from his ship. "Rechs, something else big is going down."

"How big?"

"Big enough that you've just been moved down to number two on the unofficial wanted list of the House of Reason."

"Really?" asked Rechs with an uncharacteristic dry chuckle. "And who's the lucky dead man who beat me out?"

"The guild isn't sure, really. All we know is that our contractors—your fellow bounty hunters—have all gotten unofficial contact requests for an open termination contract on someone codenamed *The Dragon*."

"That's unusual?" Rechs rarely concerned himself with the details of guild protocol.

"It's more than unusual. It's downright strange. They've bypassed the guild altogether. Which, you know, happens when someone with credits wants *one* hunter. But this went to everybody. And the bounty is huge. Ten times the one on your head. Whoever this 'Dragon' is, they want him dead. And very badly, Tyrus."

"Sounds like it."

"And here's what bothers me..." she almost whispered to herself.

"Uh-huh."

"There's no credible tag for any criminal, bounty hunter, or operative known as 'the Dragon.'"

"I can think of at least ten different dragons off the top of my head. It's not exactly an original name."

"They thought of that. There's a do-not-kill list with most of the hunters, gamblers, and pirates you'd think of on it. Don't kill the *dragons*, kill the *Dragon*. In other words, this particular Dragon doesn't exist, officially."

"And why does that bother you?"

"Because maybe it's you. Maybe they've re-tagged you as 'The Dragon' in hopes of getting people dumb enough to come after you to actually take the bait. Wild thought… I know. But… they could be that desperate. Going up against Tyrus Rechs is a death sentence. No one wants to try."

"I'll—"

The two dropships hovering in the distance turned, banking hard and away from the towers. They were coming straight for Rechs. Bright searchlights lanced out into the poverty-stricken streets where the party never seemed to stop despite the squalor.

A slitherne offered him a good time, her voice purring and her tentacles crossing her more than ample chest and hips that contrasted with her ironically tight frame and rock-hard abs. "Oma-se!" she gushed. "Warrior need love-love?"

"Lyra… fire up the engines," muttered Rechs into the comm.

That's when the blaster fire started.

"Tyrus Rechs!" shouted one of the legionnaires who'd been hiding along the street, disguised as pilgrims from some desert world where denizens hid underneath black robes and cloaks to avoid blistering suns. More legionnaires were already throwing off their disguises and firing.

"Spotted," Rechs told Gabriella, and dropped behind a long-abandoned sled.

She could no doubt hear the whine and ricochet of close blaster fire across the comm. "I have no other bounty hunters in the area for assist, Rechs. Dammit... you're on your own." Her voice was peeved and coldly matter-of-fact. Like she was mad at him for being in this situation. "I wish you would've..."

Her voice trailed off. She wasn't mad at him. She was mad at herself that she couldn't help.

"It's not your fault, Gabriella. Gotta go!"

And then Rechs was moving along the dark street where neon holograms offering food and sex swirled out and away from grimly lit stores where music thumped and thundered.

The rain was beginning to fall in earnest as Rechs pulled his hand cannon, firing to keep the legionnaires back and their heads down. He didn't like killing them. In some weird way they were still his children. It was he, Tyrus Rechs, or whatever similar name he'd gone by at the time, who had formed the Legion over fifteen hundred years before. Not that any of them knew that. Or cared. And these were probably legionnaires sucked into the decay that was Nether Ops. Not the most loyal, or filled with esprit de corps.

But they were still killers. Just like every legionnaire.

Just a few feet away, Rechs saw the scantily clad slitherne crouched next to a dumpster that had been rolled out into the street and set on fire. The look in her almond-shaped alien eyes was pure horror at the sudden hurricane of insanity. The squad of legionnaires was advancing down the street toward Rechs—and thus toward her—at a trot, shooting anyone who got in their way. Those who could scatter bolted into the run-down buildings and dark alleys that fed the main thoroughfare of the favela. Those who couldn't, or who didn't want to chance the horror of those places, ran along with Rechs. Surged around him like a river. Hoping the fight would stick somewhere behind them.

"Stay down," Rechs told the slitherne. "They're after me. Play dead if you have to."

But she was too frightened. She stood and ran, her goods bouncing and her curves undulating seductively even by the hellish light of the burning dumpster.

One of the legionnaires targeted her and pulled. She went down with a blaster bolt smoking in the center of her back.

That confirmed it. Nether Ops kill team. Bad guys who liked to kill for the sake of it.

Rechs stood and fired back with the hand cannon on full auto, catching one of them on a five-second dash for cover. The hand cannon spat six rounds that smacked into the scumbag's armor and left great, big, fifty-caliber smoking holes. The legionnaire staggered into a pile of garbage, mortally wounded.

In return Rechs got a volley of blaster fire that was close and accurate. And it all would've hit if he'd stayed where they wanted him to. But he was already low-crawling for the far side of the dumpster, which suddenly exploded after one of the Nether Ops members tossed a fragger into it. Fire and burning debris, including a few shards of white-hot metal, spread out across the night. Screams went up, and local gang members began to fire with their junkie blasters, tricked and dangerous, at the intrusive legionnaires.

Big mistake for those guys, thought Rechs.

Kill team members might be bad guys in Rechs's galaxy-view, but Nether Ops didn't pull them into a team unless they'd been more than proficient in the business of killing.

The squad hunkered down, returned fire, and sent an anti-armor missile, that had most likely been brought along to take down Rechs, against the building the gang members were firing from. The smoking round collapsed the whole facade, sending debris sliding out and across the street even as a secondary explosion gutted the building.

Overhead the dropships were circling below the storm. Throwing hot searchlights across the walls, alleys, and fleeing people.

Rechs hoped the two factions—the private security and Nether Ops—would fight it out. But more likely, they'd team up on him. That seemed to be his luck of late.

A gunner from a cargo door of one of the dropships opened up on the street Rechs moved down, already dodging kill team fire and keeping abandoned sleds and kiosks between him and his pursuers. The gunner's high-powered heavy blaster fire tore up everything, including the fleeing aliens and a bot jabbering in arcane Plutonica. And the pursuing kill team was not afraid to burn through charge packs, filling every conceivable space with fire.

Rechs was chased into a blind alley, just barely getting out of the line of fire. He hugged wall and fired back at a soldier preparing to pop a fragger. The guy spun away and dropped behind cover, wounded.

Rechs ran through his comm descrambler, pulling up their scrambled feeds. Nether Ops didn't use the L-comm; they had their own thing. Not as good, but good enough that Rechs's algo couldn't hack in. He'd need to get ahold of one of them and run a hard decrypt with fiber-wire. But in this situation—a running firefight with all of them pairing up while shooting and moving—pulling that hack looked extremely unlikely... at best.

03

CAPTAIN HESS SWUNG AWAY FROM OVER THE SHOULDER of the door gunner pumping out blasts into the streets below. He had all his elements tagged, and they were closing in on Tyrus Rechs. But they weren't alone. The sky was crowded with private security trying to get their own angle on the bounty hunter.

"Tell those other birds to get out of here or they'll be shot down!" Hess yelled to his pilot.

He gripped the overhead handhold inside the dropship's cargo compartment and uplinked with the commander of the two Republic Navy destroyers on station in the space above Minaron.

Nether Ops, and really Captain Hess, who'd become a sort of true believer high priest in the Cult of Killing Rechs—a cult that possessed the inner sanctums of some of the most secret chambers of the House of Reason—had bet the bounty hunter would surface here on Minaron. Even they knew the tech mogul who'd just thrown himself off the tower was unfinished business for Tyrus Rechs.

It was foolish of the bounty hunter to have come above ground so soon.

"We have the target pinned on the streets, Commander," shouted Hess. "But I'm not taking any chances. Get your fighters up. If he reaches his ship, we'll need to cut him off before he makes the jump to light speed. I've dealt with this one before."

The other door gunner opened up afresh on Rechs below. The fleeing civilians who were mixed in and among the action below were only so much collateral damage.

At the thought of his last encounter with Tyrus Rechs on Cassio Royale six months ago, Hess's eye hurt. Or rather... where his eye should have been.

He'd been hit in the firefight in Grand Central Square on the now-dead station. Taken a shot from someone right in the bucket not long after launching a Dragon X missile in an attempt to save his own life. The high-powered blast had taken off the bucket in pieces and melted others onto his face. His left eye had been destroyed. An abundance of skinpacks had been needed.

His dreams of one day sitting in the House of Reason had gone up in smoke. Not with the way his face looked. Not now. There was no amount of plastic surgery that could make right what Tyrus Rechs had ruined. He would always be just a little... off. You could always tell. And that was enough when you were up against the galaxy.

Hess leaned forward, watching the battle play out on the streets below. Half hoping they'd capture Rechs. Half hoping they'd kill him. If it came to it, he was willing to call in an orbital strike on the entire port just to get the man he'd sworn would pay.

That would be messy.

But the House was getting nervous. Extreme measures had been authorized.

As a last resort, of course.

***

Rechs sensed the rush coming.

One of the kill team carrying a heavy repeater opened up with suppressive fire at max output. A streak of blue blaster fire tore up the duracrete all around Rechs, along with several abandoned vehicles. A small meat-on-the-street kiosk exploded; some gas tank used for cooking must've taken a hit. The Nether Ops B team rushed in from Rechs's left flank, moving fast but not firing, hoping to get close under the cover their comrades were laying down.

So Rechs charged.

Straight into the line, firing for all he was worth. The hand cannon rang out in concussive staccato bursts of dumb slug fire. He dropped three legionnaires and possibly punctured another hugging for cover behind an abandoned taxi sled. Then he was in and among them. Mixed right in their line and firing point blank as he crossed through.

He ran straight into the hulk of a massive legionnaire. The man tried to bring his N-4 to bear, but Rechs moved too quickly, and the weapon crashed against Rechs's armor, its butt shattering. Still, the sheer force of the blow stopped Rechs's forward rush, and he was sent reeling.

One of the dropships overhead spun hard on her reversers, trying to take up a new engagement track, but for the moment denying the door gunner a target.

The big leej came after Rechs, faster than the bounty hunter was able to check him. Rechs saw stars when the armored gauntlet the man used for a fist smashed hard into his bucket.

A tossed fragger rolled right into the space Rechs and the Nether Ops soldier were fighting in. It bounced off an old sign that advertised cheap stim, landed in front of a parted-out old taxi sled, and skittered toward them.

Rechs grabbed the big leej's head and yanked it down to meet his incoming knee. Then he pushed the helpless man down onto the fragger and leapt over the taxi.

The explosion sent steel needles into the hapless legionnaire.

The taxi shifted as Rechs went over, but it still blocked the part of the blast the big leej's body hadn't.

Then Rechs was scrambling to his feet and engaging more of the assault team's hunkered operatives. Firing when he had a shot. Spending brass to keep them low when he didn't.

The dropship made a close, screaming pass, shooting up everything with little discrimination. Sooner or later, that thing would tag him. Rechs decided to break contact and run.

He raced to the far sidewalk, smashed into a door at a dead sprint, and tumbled inside a ramshackle structure leaning at the edge of the port. Already he could hear the descrambled comm transmissions of the legionnaires shouting orders to follow. Shouting for the dropship to stop firing so they, too, could cross the street without getting dusted.

Now it was a chase.

There was no time to turn and shoot as blaster fire pursued him into the darkness of the old building. It looked to be some kind of abandoned apartment complex that had probably never been anyone's first choice of living quarters. The sort of place you ended up in only because it was better than sleeping on the streets. Barely.

Dark shadows were the most illuminated part of the room; utter blackness took the rest. Rechs switched over to thermal and saw dozens of squatters huddled in alcoves and along the walls, their sleep interrupted by the firefight that the House of Reason had brought to their slum.

Rechs ran for the far wall where a deep darkness lay; some chunk in the wall had been torn out and now lay open like the mouth of an urban cave. As he sprinted toward it, the first elements of the kill team were already entering the room and taking wild shots. That brightened the room, revealing broken furniture and shattered light fixtures hanging from the ceiling.

As Rechs flung himself through the hole into the darkness of the inner structure, he switched from thermal to low-light imaging—the tunnel he was moving through was instantly revealed in blue starlight lines—and looked to his HUD for an idea of what was happening outside.

His drone telemetry fritzed out, and for a moment the real-time tactical analysis of the location surrounding his hit went out. It came back, then went out again—this time completely. A message appeared in his HUD.

Drone destroyed.

So much for that.

Overhead the dropships could be heard swimming through the skies or hovering above the building.

Rechs dashed through the midnight catacombs of the gutted building, weaving through a labyrinth of rooms, past smashed and dirty windows occasionally illuminated by bone-white searchlights.

His pursuers weren't letting up. They were perhaps a room behind him.

They're legionnaires, Rechs told himself. Even though they'd gone over to the dark side of Nether Ops for whatever reason, they were still the one percent of the one percent of the one percent the galaxy had to offer. They were the ultimate killing machines. The line that could never be broken if the Republic was to survive.

And they weren't just pacing Rechs... they were closing in for the kill.

Sudden red-hot blaster shots crossed the darkness, illuminating the dingy walls and ancient graffiti like comets streaking down the long-abandoned halls of the universe.

The one thing Rechs feared at this point was hitting a dead end and having to put his back to the wall and kill as many of them as he could before they killed him. Or before they called in air support to shoot up the block and level the building. An orbital strike against the whole city only to kill one man.

But it wasn't a dead end that Rechs reached.

It was a cliff.

He came to the rear of the massive sprawl and found that the back of the building was just... gone. The creaking floor came to an end, its crumbling edge hovering over the desiccated levels below. Rechs stood at the blown-up back of the building on an elevated cliff, and from here, he could see the entire city below.

The main level of the city had been constructed as a central hub that connected to the glittering tower islands off shore. All around the outer edges of that hub had been the favela that Rechs had been racing through. A place where all the hopeless flotsam the galaxy created washed to shore, hoping that, by some extreme stroke of unreasonably good luck, it might one day be elevated out of crushing poverty.

And Rechs stood at its end. In view of the impenetrable fortress towers where the rich hid and played. Elites who left only when they chose to.

Like the guy who threw himself off when he heard you were coming for him.

Somewhere, way down there, was the docking port where the *Obsidian Crow* and all the other vagabond freighters waited to leap away and be free of this oppressive world of playgrounds and slums.

Of haves and have-nots.

Rechs merely had to get there without being shot to death.

04

RECHS RAN ACROSS THE LAST ROOM OF THE CRUM-
bling old building on the edge of Minaron's upper deck
as blaster fire careened behind him. Legionnaires were
swarming onto the wide, uppermost level of the ruin,
shooting red-hot blaster bolts out of the shadowy darkness. They looked to Rechs like angry demons in their
charcoal-dusted leej armor. Demons come from the outer
dark to take the infamous bounty hunter once and for all.

So many others had tried. All had failed.

Rechs activated the jump jets on his ancient Mark
I armor, lifting him off the battered and debris-strewn
duracrete floor in a whirlwind of blast and grit. The pursuing Nether Ops kill team fired into the sky after him,
bolts sizzling against the storm as Rechs rocketed off into
the night.

He cut his burst short and bounded down onto the
next level like an insect hopping through a forest. All in
a downward flight to reach his ship and leave this painful
payback contract behind him for good.

He was able to clear three levels this way before the
dropships swarmed in from above, departing from their

search and engagement patterns over the top of glittering Minaron. It would just be Rechs and the ships now—the kill teams had been left behind. Modern Legion armor, including the upgraded stuff the kill teams were rocking, wasn't jump-capable. It was cheaper for the Legion to employ the Republic's many sleds and shuttles; this wasn't the Savage Wars anymore, where credits didn't matter so much as basic survival.

The dropships dove in like raptors, angling in on Rechs's bounding leaps from rooftop to rooftop as he descended the city's vast step-levels. Gunners opened up disciplined burst fire whenever a momentary targeting window opened up. The shots all missed Rechs, who was moving like a ball of lightning—but the exposed civilians down below weren't as lucky. Rechs thought it a shame that they were dying because he had come here to finish off the man on the ledge—more accurately they were dying simply because he was on planet, regardless of his reasons—but Tyrus Rechs wasn't the one doing the shooting. He would sleep just fine.

Rechs expended more jump juice to streak past open docking bays and along the sides of raw cargo refineries. He rocketed over hanging dwellings that swayed and sighed like tortured prisoners in the gusts of the storm and the cobalt night.

Finally, he crashed onto a rain-slick catwalk between two ramshackle comm stations and ran, the dropships hovering as the pilots tried to figure out which way to follow. The comms towers would give him cover for a moment.

"Three-Two!" shouted Rechs over his bucket's comm. "Three-Two, this is an emergency. I need you to warm up the omni-cannon and switch on the Nubarian bot."

A dropship came in close to the towers, dangerously close, and the gunner opened up from the swing-mounted N-50 inside the cabin. Heavy automatic blaster fire struck the railings and power conduits around Rechs, sending a light show of sparks showering out into the storm-tossed night.

"Three—"

"I am here, master—er, I mean, Captain. That is what you want me to call you, correct? I would advise against booting up *that* little bot. He seems rather psychotic. Need I remind—"

"Three-Two!" Rechs shouted. "Do it now!"

He leapt out into the void at the end of the comm tower catwalk, twenty stories up the sloping side of Minaron. Jump juice was low, so he made the effort with only brute strength and some servo-assist, flying out across the dark chasm and smashing through the flimsy wall of some tumbledown apartment tower that would never pass core-world building code.

That probably shouldn't have passed mid-core code.

Rechs rolled into a family's living room as their wall came apart, letting in the wind and rain from the dark outside. The family was sharing of a meal of a local crustacean soup known as *pengicheula*, but they stopped, spoons halfway to mouths, and stared in disbelief at the armored stranger who had just landed in their midst.

The man—a husband, a father—stood. "My wall!"

As if on cue, the dropship reversed her thrusters and came in close to hover by the gaping hole Rechs had created, pivoting so the door gunner could fill the room with overwhelming blaster fire.

Rechs saw a husband and wife with six children. Doe-eyed with mouths open in disbelief. Not one of them was aware that they were seconds from being riddled with blaster fire. A war crime that would be hushed up with all the usual payoffs.

"Not today!" grunted Rechs. He pulled his hand cannon from its locking thigh holster, switched to full auto, and nailed the door gunner several times before the man could line up his shot. The gunner landed on his back on the cargo deck of the dropship, mortally wounded.

The pilot checked his six and then went for the yaw thrusters to bring about the other gunner on the opposite door. Rechs took a few steps forward and unloaded in successive concussive bursts on the pilot's canopy, smashing the glass just above the pilot's flight helmet. Freaked out, or message received, the pilot chose life over target acquisition and rocketed away from the ramshackle tower.

Rechs immediately threw himself through the gaping hole in the wall, leaving the family safe and in one piece, albeit utterly soaked from the wind and rain.

Five levels down and fifteen stories up from the docking bay where the *Obsidian Crow* was berthed, dropship number two, apparently weary of tracking Rechs's frantic bumblebee path down the face of the cobble-work city, loosed one of her missiles as Rechs ran along the top of a gas refinery.

Rech's HUD warned him that he'd been acquired for lock by an air-to-ground missile live and loose. He was not in the best place to be.

Without needing a voice command, the armor's ECM generator attempted to break the lock, succeeding at the last viable moment. The missile sidewindered off into the night and exploded harmlessly out across the skyline.

But the dropship likely had more than one air-to-ground missile.

Rechs ran along the top of the octagonal refinery tank as the dropship stabilized her altitude and readied to fire again. Emergency and hazard lights washed everything in bloody red and extreme-caution yellow.

Switching course at almost a dead run, Rechs made for the edge of the tank, taking a straight line that would unfortunately speed up the pilot's missile lock. The bounty hunter fired at the pilot as he moved, hoping to rattle him. Get him to fire short or wide. Or not at all.

Then Rechs was leaping. All too well aware that what jump juice was left was precious little. And that the next stop was fifteen stories down.

Flying out into the darkness, feeling the clutch of gravity, Rechs stabilized his hand cannon with both hands and aimed for the repulsor intake of the dropship.

Most combat dropships have graphene baffles that are activated if the ship's micro-sensors identify incoming fire. Ideally, the baffles lock in place to shield the intake for a brief second, ablating the energy blast—and then shutter open again afterward, allowing the dropship to maintain lift uninterrupted. The repulsor intake is the most critically vulnerable system of the dropship design. Losing even one of the two mains is an almost guaranteed splash. Auto-rotation might still save the crew... but that's hardly a guarantee.

Rechs wasn't thinking about that or any of the science of lift versus weight. Or of ablative graphene baffles. He simply knew, from ages of warfare and exposure to war machines, where stuff was weak.

Equipment changed. But destruction was constant.

Shoot the intake repulsor just like you did during the assault on Hatreides VII during the Synth Wars. It'll go down.

A bright line of gunfire and ricochet drew itself across the wing and repulsor housings of the dropship before Rechs landed three shots inside the intake. The graphene baffles activated as intended, but they were designed to deflect energy-based blaster fire charged around a minuscule bolt. They weren't designed to stand up to a depleted-uranium fifty-caliber slug fired from a hand cannon. Kinetics excelled in places where energy failed.

The baffles shuddered and disintegrated, sending even more debris into the energy-converting repulsor. Which immediately malfunctioned and exploded. Oily black smoke mixed with the inky night as Rechs, now in freefall, descended away from the wounded dropship.

No doubt the pilot was now frantically switching to damage control and auto-rotation procedures instead of worrying about that missile he had intended to fire.

And Rechs was falling at ninety feet per second. Heading for the hard duracrete of the giant hangar docks that served Minaron's freighter traffic.

05

Rᴇᴄʜs ᴏʀɪᴇɴᴛᴇᴅ ʜɪs ꜰᴇᴇᴛ ᴛᴏᴡᴀʀᴅ ᴛʜᴇ ɢʀᴏᴜɴᴅ ᴀɴᴅ expended the last of the jet's jump juice in an attempt to slow himself down. He knew it wasn't enough. The old Mark I armor would have to absorb the damage. And what it couldn't, Rechs would.

He hit the wet and hard overhanging roof of a berth and felt all his wind leave him. His next breath was sharp and pained. A few broken ribs for sure. And he was rolling. Rolling down the steep sloping face of the overhang toward the main docking passage that ran along the outward-facing freighter berths.

Each rotation of his battered body inside the armor was like a series of rabbit punches to his screaming midsection. But he bit down on that and did everything he could to hold on to his hand cannon. A weapon he'd carried for as long as he'd worn the armor. He didn't want to lose it. He liked that gun. A weapon almost singular in a galaxy full of cheap knock-off blasters that killed people just as dead as the overpriced models the Republic armed its servicepeople with.

The bounty hunter splayed himself out flat, attempting to arrest his slide. But Mark I armor is heavy, and its weight carried him down the overhang's face until he felt his legs slide over the edge, the start of a drop that would end twenty meters down. Rechs stubbornly held on to his hand cannon as his free hand grasped for something to hold. He found nothing, but still managed to catch a small and ironic break: the momentum of his slide sent him just across the gaping drop and into a far wall, part of a symmetrical twin of the roof berth he'd just fallen from. He hit hard against it and dropped onto some shipping containers. This fall was much less than the twenty-meter drop that had menaced him before.

The containers collapsed in slow motion, dumping Rechs onto the wide, concrete floor of the sublevel.

He landed on his hands and knees, feeling at first as though something more than his ribs had been broken. But he was all right. Smashed. Bruised. Beaten. But all right. Nothing else screamed snapped or fractured in that endless horrifying moment when such things reveal themselves and take precedent over all else in the mind.

"Attention!" bellowed a message from the station AI. Yellow hazard strobes sent swimming lights across the deeps of the curving hall. "Minaron Security Services has advised the Port Authority that a situation is in progress. All berths are locked down until further notice. Please seek shelter at this time and do not attempt to interfere with security operations. Attention…"

Rechs checked the big numbers on the outward wall of the passage, looking for lucky number fifty-two where the *Crow* was waiting. Behind these numbers freighters waited to be loaded and set free, jumping away to all the foreign and exotic destinations of the galaxy. Or sometimes disappearing forever.

Docking bay seventy-eight.

Rechs's ship was still a long ways off.

The bounty hunter stumbled forward, ignoring the pain as he forced himself into a trot.

"Mast—uh, Captain Rechs."

It was G232, formerly "Fancy Pants," the bot Rechs had rescued from a falling ore freighter six months ago before the shootout on Cassio Royale. He'd had every intention of setting the thing free. Or even selling it, if that was what it wanted. But in the six months since what the news networks had called "a deadly gang shootout" with "the infamous criminal Tyrus Rechs" instigating a "massacre," Rechs had avoided the larger systems and more populous stations where the bot could be freed or sold. He'd had to avoid attention, even going dark on an old dead drop he used to call the Dog House. Other than a quick trip to have a coder perform some special work, he'd lain low, only darkening the airlocks of lonely old sensor stations along the less-used runs out toward the edge of the galaxy. Places like that had little use for an admin and protocol bot. And so Rechs had kept the bot, which seemed content to serve there as well as anywhere else.

The problem was that Rechs didn't like having anyone do anything for him. He rarely needed it and felt that the bot would make him soft. Make him reliant. So the bot often merely waited in the central lounge of the *Crow*, its optical receptors looking up hopefully whenever Rechs passed through on his way from his weapons workbench to his rack. Which were generally the only places he occupied—besides the flight deck when the *Crow* was in jump. Not that the old souped-up freighter was large enough to have many places to get lost inside anyway.

And on those occasions when Rechs passed the bot, he tended to look away. The hopefulness and helpfulness the thing emitted, the wish to somehow be of service… it bothered Rechs, for reasons he couldn't quite place. It made him uncomfortable.

So he hid from it. From G232. Which even he admitted was ridiculous.

"Is the bot in the omni-gun?" grunted Rechs as he heaved himself past bay sixty-five.

"As I have stated, Captain, this is very unwise. The homicidal runt is advocating blasting the walls of the berth to—and I am quoting here just so you know it's not me making these insane little threats—'to unlimber the guns for use on the savages.'"

"Good," muttered Rechs. "Do it."

The little Nubarian bot was a relic from the last days of the Savage Wars. A gunner's mate on one of the big dreadnoughts, the bot had seen action at Morrae, the Reef, and the Battle of Oaen System. Rechs had needed someone to operate the *Crow*'s lone defensive gun, the powerful omni-cannon, when running from pursuit. He'd hoped the ship's AI, Lyra, would take more of the flight duties, leaving him free to man the gun as needed, but for some reason she was hesitant to do much beyond run the systems and engines. Actual helm and flight made the new AI skittish. And for various reasons… Rechs didn't want to push her. So he'd purchased the Nubarian bot from a salvage yard at a junk station out along the rim run to Sychar, if only just to handle the gun.

"I don't think that's 'good' in the least, Captain. Imagine the consequences if—"

"Things have gone completely dumpster-shaped. The likelihood that those two destroyers in orbit are going to intercept our departure is fairly high. So buckle up and—"

Blaster fire smashed into a service pylon just outside bay fifty-eight. Local station security in riot armor had deployed, and a team ran straight into Rechs coming off an intersecting tube.

"Still," continued the indignant bot over comm regardless of the screaming blaster fire in the background, "I would like to register…"

Rechs tried a few shots with the hand cannon. While nothing was broken, something was definitely sprained. In the time since his fall, the muscles had stiffened, and working the hand cannon felt like trying to chew while on oral deadeners.

"Relaxers!" grunted Rechs to the suit's HUD as he tagged the affected area.

The armor's medical suite pumped him with a local muscle relaxer. Until it kicked in, he hugged wall and fumbled for a banger to toss.

G232 was still at it. "… bots are here to assist. Not to destroy. I find his wanton disregard for life… unseemly."

Rechs tossed the banger at the security team in the tube and waited for the flashbang explosion. Then he did his best hobble-run down the passage toward bay fifty-two.

Security types weren't usually much of a threat, but anyone with a blaster was potentially lethal. Fact. And if the station was working with Nether Ops, then that security team would alert whichever elements were nearby to intercept.

Rechs checked the algo worm he'd left inside the Port Authority. All bay doors were locked down, but that was an easy thing for the worm to deal with.

"Worm," said Rechs into the ether of the comm.

He got an acknowledgment squeal from the embedded hunter-killer algo.

"Activate breach and disable all the locks. Fry the tractor."

But at that moment, the worm's status switched to inactive inside Rechs's HUD.

Someone had found it. Found it and nailed it.

"Plan B…" muttered Rechs as he approached the massive blast doors that guarded bay fifty-two.

Behind him he could hear the boots of more security teams converging on his position. In sufficient numbers, even local security types became a serious threat. But if this was like all the other times, their orders would be to capture, not kill. Because the House of Reason wanted him alive—for now.

"Three-Two!" shouted Rechs, as badly aimed blaster fire chased him into the shifting darkness of the yellow strobes that undulated across the corridor. "Tell the little bot to target the bay doors and fire!"

G232 was slow to respond. "This will surely be a violation of the flight safety and standards regulations that govern this—"

"Do it!"

Rechs slammed against the wall.

Another security team, coming from the opposite direction and seeking to cut the bounty hunter off, arrived a few bays down. The two squads of local security had Rechs pinned down.

"There he is!" yelled the new team's sergeant. "Blast him!"

So much for being captured alive.

Then the little bot fired, blowing the mechanisms of both doors to shreds. As well as much of the duracrete frame and wall that guarded the bay.

The security team that had moved to intercept was in the middle of a charge, firing at Rechs, sensing the opportunity for all those secret millions the House of Reason had been quietly promising everyone for the capture—or, apparently, kill—of Tyrus Rechs. Dreams of wealth beyond imagining must have occupied their last seconds before the ship's blaster, a powerful one, designed for ship-to-ship warfare, disintegrated the doors and sent molten duracrete fragments flying out across the passage. Smoke and steam filled the corridor, and Port Authority emergency damage control klaxons began to wail.

Overhead extinguishers filled the passage with a white chem-cloud.

Now! Rechs yelled to himself, forcing his battered body to move to the opening.

The bounty hunter passed the dead and mangled security team in their fancy armor lying amid the melted slag and blasted rock where the doors had once been. Amazingly, one stunned security guard stood there virtually untouched, ignoring Rechs and examining his own body as though he couldn't believe he was alive. As though he'd hit the lottery of all time.

Rechs ran past him, into the bay, and straight for the boarding ramp of the *Obsidian Crow* as more blaster fire came from farther down the passage.

The muscle relaxers were finally kicking in, a bit late for Rechs's purposes. The pain wasn't gone, but it was fainter now, calling out like some friend that promised a meeting soon.

Lyra had the engines already warm and filling the bay with dull shimmering waves of ridiculous power. Vent cables and power hookups had been auto-disconnected.

Rechs slammed his gauntlet onto the boarding hatch controls, bringing the ramp up behind him and sealing the ship off from any would-be boarders. He ran for the flight deck, peeling off his helmet and his gauntlets, and threw himself into the captain's seat. As his fingers swam across the controls of the *Crow*, G232 came to stand in the entrance to the flight deck.

"The little devil is carrying on about wanting to shoot more savages, sir. Really! I do advise that we shut him down and add an inhibitor restraint for good measure. His murderousness knows no—"

"Secure for takeoff, Three-Two. This is gonna get hot, and we still have to get by those two destroyers in orbit. Tell the little maniac he's going to get all the target practice he wants in the next thirty seconds."

"Oh my…"

Rechs had the *Crow*'s three landing gears up, repulsors engaged. He pivoted the ship for departure from the bay. Beyond the impervisteel-latticed windows of the center-mounted cockpit, fresh security troops stormed the bay, shooting at his ship. Then the view swam away and Rechs saw nothing but open sky. Dark and stormy though it was.

A second after that he punched it. The *Crow* roared away along the lower levels of Minaron.

06

"Captain, I'm tracking three Repub interceptors, Lancer class, coming in from above." Lyra's warning came in her increasingly-as-of-late cautious tone.

Rechs swiveled away from the deflector array panel and took control of the *Crow*'s yoke and throttle. "Set up a jump calc. Nearest executable."

"Computing now," replied the ship's AI.

A moment later three fast-moving Lancers, twin ion engines screaming blue murder, shot down out of the upper atmosphere's dark cloudscape. Forward blaster fire smashed into the *Crow*'s deflectors, triggering an alarm bell and starting a light show across the energy management panels at the back of the flight deck.

"We're hit!" shrieked G232 indignantly.

Rechs flicked off the power management alarms and reoriented the deflector shields for a chase. The Lancers, fast but taking forever to turn after the intercept burn, picked up his tail and gave chase through the turbulent upper atmosphere.

"How long till jump?" Rechs growled impatiently.

"Unless you are going to climb and get us clear of the atmosphere, Captain, the jump metrics are suboptimal," said Lyra. "I'm really not comfortable with these numbers."

Over the ship's internal comm the little Nubarian bot currently occupying the omni-cannon gun cupola yowled in Signica, the binary programming language of its technical-class build.

"He says…" G232 began in his role as human-bot interface. "Oh dear. He says we are to call him Death, destroyer of worlds."

The powerful blasts of the omni-cannon surged across the ship, smashing into one pursuing Republic Lancer and vaporizing it. Debris spread away from its expanding explosion.

"He can call himself whatever he wants as long as he keeps up that kind of shooting," said Rechs as he fought to keep the freighter out of the blaster sights of the pursuing interceptors.

"Oh, please, master," erupted G232, "don't encourage him! This sort of thing in a bot never leads anywhere good. I can assure you."

The *Obsidian Crow* hurtled through canyons of dark gray clouds to break out into a clear field of sky. Behind it, a Diplomat-class destroyer descended through the storm, dropping a hornet's nest of fighters into the running contest to bring the rogue freighter to heel.

"Unidentified freighter!" barked an authoritarian voice over the ship-to-ship comm. "You are currently eluding pursuit from Republic forces. Back off your thrusters and prepare for tractor lock and boarding."

Rechs switched off the comm.

Back in the omni-cannon, the little Nubarian bot was ululating and whooping through electronic beeps and sudden beatbox giggles at the target-rich environment as more and more fighters joined the chase. Rechs knew enough Signica to understand at least that much.

"Lyra, I need a jump point in the next thirty seconds. We're not reaching orbit," Rechs said matter-of-factly.

Nothing came back other than G232 telling the Nubarian bot to stop crowing at each Lancer it managed to knock down. "No one likes a braggart!"

A swarm of Lancers swam in at the *Crow* from a different heading, their colored markings indicating a second squadron had joined the chase. Rechs brought in the yaw destabilizer on one engine and pushed more power into the opposite. The *Crow* rolled three hundred and sixty degrees, presenting a much less stable profile for targeting as she passed through the swarm of angry oncoming fighters.

One of the pursuing Lancers from the first squadron smacked straight into two of these oncoming Lancers. The two squadrons' flight leaders were clearly not communicating with each other.

The digital war whoop of the little bot in the omni-gun seemed to indicate the maniacal thing was taking credit for this accidental collision and increasing its kill count.

"Captain," announced G232, who had been quizzically interfacing with the sensor panel while fighters erupted all across the cockpit's forward view. "Sensors are telling me that big ship up ahead is preparing to engage her capture tractor. I'm not a pilot, of course, but if they succeed while we are at maximum throttle—as you now are in your reckless press forward with little regard for our collective runtime—then we shall be ripped to pieces at an altitude of thirteen thousand, four hundred and ninety-one meters. If you like, I can compute our rate of fall and time to impact with the planet's surface below, though factors such as rapid decompression, current momentum, and the explosion of the reactor may alter my calculations significantly."

"We're going in," said Rechs through gritted teeth. "If we get close enough, they won't be able to get a lock."

The *Crow* pulled up hard, streaking straight toward the midsection of the slender destroyer looming in the background of the sky battle. Rechs noted that they no longer built them the way they did back during the Savage Wars, when he and Casper needed every ship they could get to be able to stand up to the Savage cruisers, and even then they would take a pounding in a toe-to-toe broadside that might include upwards of a hundred heavy blaster turrets, PDCs, SSMs, and main ion guns. And woe to anyone who got in the way of an Iowa-class battleship and her main gun.

Pulling out of her collision course with the bigger ship, the *Crow* raced along its hull. Massive portholes the size of several decks revealed crew and techs turning away from their internal tasks to watch the rogue freighter streak by. Collision klaxons were surely scrambling damage control teams within the behemoth. But any amazement the crew might have held at the sight of the old freighter twisting and turning to avoid blaster fire likely turned to horror when the Nubarian bot working the omni-cannon unloaded a blue streak of fire, ripping up the destroyer's un-defended hull. The ship's captain—probably a point—had failed to engage shields. Had been too busy telling the comm operator to order

Rechs to pull back on the throttles and submit to boarding, search and seizure. Confident that this would happen. Because it always happened. Because the authority of the Republic was unquestioned.

You get lazy like that when you've never been in a real fight, thought Rechs. *Guy's probably never been punched in the face.*

"Captain," began Lyra, her voice rising above the whooping power management system crying out damage from incoming blaster fire, "I have the jump calculated. We can depart for Roaxshell, but the safety parameters are only—"

But Rechs had tuned out the AI as soon as he heard the words "jump calculated." He watched until the jump window controls went solid green, then immediately engaged them, and the starfield turned over to a hundred thousand lines of starlight.

***

Republic destroyer *Cooperation* watched the tiny freighter leap away, helpless to pursue. A plot on possible locations would yield at least a dozen worlds... all of which could be just as easily jumped away from in the seconds after Rechs arrived.

Hess, who had arrived to the bridge from planetside in time to watch the bounty hunter's little stunt, stood disfigured among the bridge officers. He sneered and swore a silent oath.

Tyrus Rechs would never, ever, escape him again.

Today was the last time.

The swarm of fighters out there beyond the bridge realized they were pursuing a ghost and slowed to maneuver speed. The target was long gone from this system.

07

Lost in hyperspace, Rechs turned toward weapons maintenance. That was always his first priority. Then healing, and finally, rest. Those responsible for Medusa's death had all been dealt with. He could go quiet for a while.

He stowed his armor in its rack, cleaned his weapons, ate the first thing he pulled out of the galley's cupboard, and slept. He was hungry again when he woke up hours later, so he got up, ate something more, then took a seat in the captain's chair on the flight deck, just watching hyperspace while he pretended to run a basic systems check.

"Is something wrong?" Lyra asked in the silence that was the background hum of the engines. So much white noise while traveling among the stars. You stopped noticing unless you thought about it. And there was always the ghostly, almost inaudible howl of hyperspace below everything.

G232 was aft in the lounge. The bot, in its spare time, liked to read things off the web. Mainly academic articles about the ruins of the Ancients. And the tiny Nubarian gunner's mate bot, endlessly fascinated with the ship's weapons—*any* weapons for that matter—was still by the workbench, where it had watched Rechs silently clean his weapons. The bot had sighed some digital sigh each time Tyrus had selected and cleaned some new killing tool that looked even more wicked than the previous.

There's definitely something weird about that bot, thought Rechs. But... it was a more than capable gunner. And it didn't want much, or cost much, in the way of power.

"I said, is there something wrong?" asked Lyra one more time.

"No," he answered. "Nothing."

It was odd talking to her. Hearing her voice. Knowing who the AI was based on. Knowing the AI viewed itself as something different. Something not her. Not the woman he'd once known.

AIs could be temperamental. Could even turn schizophrenic.

Give the install time to settle in, he reminded himself. It was the same advice he'd given himself after every one of these stilted conversations she'd attempted.

In time she'll...

... come back?

... understand?

But deep down, Rechs knew that only one of those things was possible. For an AI based on a dead person, only one was possible.

"Am I not running the ship to your liking? Is there something wrong with my parameter decision matrix that we can improve upon? I'm here..." There was a pause. Then: "I'm here... to serve you... Captain Rechs."

Tyrus waited.

Waited to see if she'd come back.

But after a long pause, he decided that now wasn't the right time. The AI was still insecure about its new place in the universe.

So he thought of something else. Something that had been bothering him. He would share it with her and let her feel like she was helping him. That might... help.

"It's something else," he began. Rechs was not a sharer. Not used to revealing anything to anyone. "That's bothering me."

He felt her waiting. Listening to everything within and without him in order to... better serve him.

"Gabriella told me there's a big contract, bigger than the one on my head, being offered on someone tagged 'The Dragon.'"

"Why does that bother you?" asked Lyra.

Tyrus paused. Asking himself anew the question he'd been vaguely aware of during the whole of downtime after the op he'd just pulled.

Why does it bother you?

"To be honest... I don't know. But there's something familiar about this. Something I should remember. And for some reason... I can't."

"You've lived a very long time, Captain. Obviously, some memory loss is to be expected given your extreme age."

Tyrus knew this. He'd even had himself checked out a couple of times when he'd noticed several drops of common memories he should have never forgotten. The name of an old ship he'd flown for twenty years. His father's first name. The state he'd been born in on long-lost mythical Earth.

Usually the forgotten details were mundane. The battles, the deaths of comrades, the killings, the victories, the losses… those stuck around. So did the systems, weapons, bombs, and all the tools of killing. Those things were hard-wired into him. He *never* forgot those things. Even if he wanted to. And if he could have chosen right then and there to choose what to remember, to mark down what really mattered, he knew that somehow the right choice would be to forget all those things of war and death, and keep the memories of the good and simple life.

That was the right choice.

But it was not him. It was not Tyrus Rechs.

He'd been built for war. For conflict and killing.

And sitting there on the flight deck, something happened. Some tumbler fell into place. Something. It wasn't an epiphany. It was more like the snatched line of a half-remembered song heard a long time ago.

"Project Phoenix."

"What is that, Captain?"

Rechs didn't answer. He was trying to untangle the meaning of those words for a long while as hyperspace howled in its low keening moan and vast interstellar distances were crossed almost effortlessly. But the more he thought, the more he tried to hold on to it, the less of it there seemed to be. Like it no longer existed.

Occasionally the big questions got lost in his mind. Things he'd wondered about. Things he was supposed to remember. Things that would save the galaxy from itself.

Like tracking down an old friend who'd gone off looking for something he never should have. Waiting near the edge. Waiting for his return.

Then what…?

Then the thing you were made for.

But right now, sitting on the flight deck and watching the static light of hyperspace shifting slowly all across the void beyond the ship... right now, that was not the thing that was bothering him. It was something about what Gabriella had said in the moments before everything went to pieces back on Minaron.

The Dragon.

It was a tag. A tag that was common but unimportant... except for one unique and familiar instance. And that one needed to be remembered. But no matter how hard he tried, or didn't try, he could not coax the memory from within.

Nor could he forget it.

There was something very important about the Dragon.

And a program he'd once been part of. Back when he was a general. Back during the Savage Wars.

Doomsday.

That was the next word, after *Dragon* and *Project Phoenix*, to appear in his mind.

Doomsday.

To: Lt. Col. ████████████████
From: ████████████
Re: Assignment Subject 33

Subject 33 has become eligible to transition from the Project into the Legion. Testing in the 99+ Percentile, the subject is a solid 1111111. Subject 33 greenlit for advanced training.

Subject 33 issued identity as ████████. Ordered to Legion Academy for Basic Training and application to Legion OCS. Testing to determine schools pending, but highly recommended for Pathfinder, HOLO, and Sniper before first unit tour and application to the Q-Course for Special Warfare. Observers in place at all levels.

████████████

Lt. Col. ████████████████
Section 19
Project Phoenix
Asymmetrical Warfare Command

08

AFTER ARRIVING AT THE JUMP POINT IN ROAXSHELL, Rechs set the *Crow* to cruise through the empty system while he jumped on the nets and dove into what he could find on this "Dragon."

Which wasn't much. At least not of the real deal. The one he couldn't remember.

But there *were* rumors, if you knew where to look. At best they were half-truths. Most were probably outright lies. Yet they were there.

The Dragon wasn't Rechs, as Gabriella had feared. It wasn't some clever trick by the House of Reason to re-target him and engage the overly optimistic into taking a crack at the unofficial bounty they offered. The Dragon, according to the dark webs, was a terrorist bent on violent overthrow of the Republic.

Other reports claimed he was the instigator of something known as the Avivo Massacre a few years back. A whole colony at galaxy's edge had been wiped out. Executed and nailed to crosses. Some hung upside down. The colony disappeared overnight, and now images, shot by adventurous chroniclers, showed the remains of the small colony sinking into the wastes of a vast salt desert.

Digging deeper into the incident, Rechs found an odd connection: the colony was an authorized importer of Sinasian goods. To get such a permit was exceedingly rare, seeing as how all Sinasian worlds were currently off-limits.

Rechs sat back and remembered that little nightmare.

The Sinasian Conflict.

Thirteen years of brutal warfare. No holds barred. No friendly forces. Everyone an enemy. The Sinasian worlds had sided with the Savages at the darkest moments of the war, and the Republic had sent in three legions to quell them.

Rechs's own had been part of that. And only his legion had survived the conflict.

Now the Sinasian worlds had been reduced to an almost pre-industrial state. Forbidden the use of all advanced tech and weapons. Forever at the mercy of the Republic for daring to stand with their greatest foe.

Rechs went back to tracking down rumors about the Dragon. The misinformation piled up. Either because every bounty hunter wanted to throw every other bounty hunter off the trail, or because in lieu of hard information, people just tended to make things up.

There was a rumor that a secret cabal within the House of Reason wanted the Dragon alive, to lead a revolt. To become a dictator and rule with iron fist. All to this secret cabal's benefit, of course. Another rumor said the Dragon was a fiction, a mere distraction to draw fire away from the ongoing disaster of a dozen brushfire conflicts raging along the edge of the galaxy. Conflicts where the Legion was spread too thin. That part of the rumor, anyway, was true: the Legion had repeatedly allowed itself to be drawn into conflicts that members of the House of Reason had a personal financial stake in. It was all there to see if you opened your eyes and knew where to look.

Finally Rechs tapped into the Dark Ops clouds using some old credentials that had been kept valid by friends on the inside. He couldn't get too far without attracting attention, but he got far enough to look at some intel on Nether Ops, the House of Reason's version of Dark Ops. The naughty stepsister of Dark Ops was prepping its kill teams for the hunt. Entire groups were being switched off mission and trained up for something big. Whether that was to find and kill the Dragon, or some other mission… that was beyond Rechs's access. Had he tried to hack in, a dozen monitored-at-all-times warnings would have triggered within the first nanosecond of the attempt.

He sat back and stared at the screen as all the data he'd pulled floated across at random. Artsy photographs of the remains of the colony massacre, haunted and forlorn, stared back at him.

The little Nubarian gunner beeped somberly next to Rechs.

"Grim, huh?" said Rechs.

The bot did not respond. After a moment it rolled away.

The question, Rechs thought to himself as he studied the entirety of the little he'd managed to collect on this Dragon, was whether a lot of people, leejes too, *his* leejes, were going to get killed trying to bring this target in, or…

Or…

Or what?

Because there was definitely an "or." Another option. One no one was considering.

He needed more information before he made his choice.

And he knew of two guys that would have access to the intel he needed to make that call.

"Lyra. Boot up the nav comp and set course for Breakers World."

Doc and Chappy were supposed to be running down a Hool hit man there. They always left him a sitrep on a digital dead drop in code.

They'd know something.

Order of the Centurion Testimony from SFC Evan Kowalski Concerning the events during Operation ███████

SFC Kowalski: We got the call about oh-two-hundred. Repub artillery up on ███████ was getting hit hard by the Jumwara. No one expected that. This was ███████. All jungle fighting out along the islands. No one expected the sharks to get all up in there on the ███████ where we had our battery overwatch and attack our fire support. Least of all the marines who were providing…

Investigator's Note: SFC Kowalski, though every inch the legionnaire, has a small tic above the right eye when we talk about the engagement and the events of Operation ███████.

SFC Kowalski: L-T Kong comes in and tells us to jock up. We headin' up that way. Now remember, according to the sharks and the House of Reason, we ain't even s'posed to be on ███████. That was part of the ███████—which I'd like to point out they never honored in the least. Like I said… we ain't even s'posed to be on ███████ when we get the oh-dark-hundred someone's-in-trouble call. Fifteen and we're on the pads ready to board the drop. That's QRF duty, sir. No questions. Just go in and save someone's bacon.

Investigator's Note: SFC Kowalski stubs out his third cigarette since the interview began. Recommend psych eval. Possible PTSD.

SFC Kowalski: So we're on Reaper Four-Two and the other half is on Four-Three. Plus we got two gunships ridin' scatterblaster. And don't you know it… it's a trap. Sharks ain't overrunnin' the position like the marine commander on the ground was screamin' at everybody. They're shooting from the rocks across the valley. So Four-Three goes in to drop her leejes and gets hit by an anti-armor round fired from upslope of the base. Up in some rocks the other side of which is the sheer face of ████████. See, that was the trap. The sharks, which are supposed to be amphibians that stick close to the shores of that hellhole, well, they did the impossible and come up the side of ████████ and attacked our guns from above. Except they waited until we showed up to go with the main attack. Until then they was just makin' everyone mad. So, like I said... Four-Three is hit real bad and she goes in smokin' and spinnin' and puts down on a field of rocks near the gun batteries and not far from the marine bunkers.

Investigator's Note: SFC Kowalski stops the narrative at this point to light yet another cigarette. His hands are shaking. He notices that I notice.

SFC Kowalski: Oh, that's just 'cause my electrolytes are low. I need to drink more water.

Investigator's Note: We pause while he is brought a fresh glass.

SFC Kowalski: You... you seen those sharks up close, sir? They're not like in that movie where one of 'em chases all those teens around on that sailboat on that world... *Deep Thunder* or whatever. That one in the movie is big like a monster. They're like... like us in real life. Which kinda makes 'em scarier. About as tall. More slender than I thought they'd be. But it's that face. That shark face that's just looking at you with beady, soulless eyes. And all them teeth. It's like looking at a nightmare. 'Cept you're wide awake. You ever see one, sir? Up close and all?

Investigator: The only Jumwara I saw on Far Station were already deceased.

SFC Kowalski: Well, that ain't the same thing. But never mind all that. This ain't about that. This is about L-T Kong. Listen. I always knew he was high-speed low-drag. Sinasian and all. Or at least half. He never said much about himself either way. But the L-T is squared away, and if this is about giving him the big medal, well, he deserves two.

See... we wouldn't've made it off that mountain if the lieutenant hadn't ordered us to land. Gunships, they started workin' the rocks them sharks were comin' out of. And I mean by the hundreds. In seconds we realize this is the real deal. This ain't no IED roadside ambush. This is a battle. And battles on ███████ is few and far between. Real ones where you shoot until the other guy's dead. Sharks'll just drop back into the waters and go deep. Might even take your buddy with them. You know about that, right? They do that. Don't listen to the reports. That really happens.

Investigator's Note: SFC Kowalski stares off into space for quite a while. Just smoking and seeing something he does not describe. I won't hazard a guess. But it seems to have left an impact.

SFC Kowalski: So we set down and pull the wounded off Four-Two while the gunships deal with the sharks. One gunship takes a hit, and that kills the gunner. They wave off and head back to base. In no time the other gunship is low on ammunition and making her last pass. The artillery base is under attack and the marines have gone into their bunkers. Problem is, Four-Two can only carry so many. So four of us, myself and the L-T, and

Guntaar and Myrone, we stick right there on the rock field so that Four-Two can get the wounded back.

It ain't even dawn yet and it's gonna be a long day. By six, just as the sun comes up, the sharks blow the wire and take down a gun tower. Then they're inside the camp and goin' to town on the marines. We interface with the on-site commander and he requests an evac from the Navy. Now mind you, we're bein' shot at from the other side of the valley, we've already lost two birds, and the sharks are inside the camp and they've got a base of fire in the rocks above us. And this is high-altitude stuff. This is above nine thousand feet. It's cold. Air's thin. Marines don't have our armor so they strugglin' and all.

Anyhow... we can't get the marine commander to stick. She wants off the hill, and she outranks us as an artillery company commander. Lieutenant Kong decides we gonna help 'em. Since I'm Pathfinder qual'd myself and Guntaar set up an L-Z that's not under direct fire to get the marines' birds in, L-T goes forward where the fighting is and takes the other gun tower. Did I mention there were two? First one got dropped by a suicide. Blew the wire and deactivated the minefield. That's where they're comin' through. So the L-T and Myrone—he was new, by the way. So new you could smell it. They retake the other gun tower and they start dealing out death on the sharks.

By noon we got the marines off the mountain, and bonus, we detonated the artillery they were just gonna leave behind. But Myrone was dead by then, and the L-T can't get back through the base or the bunkers to reach the last dropship because it's crawlin' with sharks. They good with a blaster, but up close and personal they like to use the teeth. They'll bite your arm clean off, leej armor and all.

Investigator's Note: SFC Kowalski holds out his arm and traces his fingers across the point in the armor between seams where the arm can be severed by a bite.

SFC Kowalski: I try to get the pilot to go in close, but he won't do it, and now, thinkin' back about it, I don't blame him. Those marine birds is thin-skinned. They'd-a shot us down and we'd all be dead.

It's things like that, remembering times when you were so convinced you were right, that bother me now, sir. 'Cause I wasn't. I wasn't right at all. Pilot was. L-T too. He tells us to dust off and clear the mountain.

I say, "What you gonna do, L-T, if we leave you?" I said that, but there's no answer. None. So we lift off on the last bird out of Dodge—wherever that place is—and we circling the base from a good distance with the door gunners just shootin' up the sharks who are all over the place by then.

That's when I see L-T runnin' for the bunkers. He's runnin' and shootin' and killin' every one of them monsters. He's in and among them and movin' like one of them ninja movies they used to make all those years ago. Back when I was a kid and I didn't know nothin' about nothin'.

That's when we get the clear-out order from the Navy. ████████ is gonna hit the mountain with everything she got.

I think…

Investigator's Note: SFC Kowalski, big, tattooed, the very definition of a man and a legionnaire, begins to weep. He tries to hide it. But the tears escape his massive hands.

SFC Kowalski: I think I lost my mind a little at that point. They… they had to restrain me. Restrain me 'cause he was about to die down there all alone. And… and that just ain't right. I'da thrown myself outta that bird so that young L-T, and he weren't no point that's for damn sure, but I'da thrown myself out just so he… so he didn't have to… y'know. Go that way and all. Alone.

They tranqed me. Last I saw was from a distance. Them main guns from ███████ hitting the side of the mountain and just burning everything to high heaven.

Investigator's Note: SFC Kowalski wipes the tears from his eyes and lights his last cigarette. He's calmer now. The twitch is gone. But this man definitely has PTSD and needs help. Referral for mental nanite reconditioning to follow this meeting.

SFC Kowalski: So yeah, I know we weren't supposed to be there. But Lieutenant Kong deserves the Order. That's for sure. And that's all I have to say about that. We wouldn't-a got off that rock if he hadn't held the gun tower long enough to get all the birds in. Then, when it was time to go, he stayed. And he didn't give up. He kept killin' 'em, and I know he was headed toward the marine bunkers. Tryna make it there and hunker 'cause it was him that called it in. That's one thing marines do well… they can dig. If he made it there… he coulda lived. Y'know?

Investigator's Conclusion: This account has been verified at all levels. As ordered, I did not inform SFC Kowalski of Lieutenant Kong's survival of ███████ orbital strike on ███████. I did, however, inform the SFC that the award for the Order of the Centurion would, in all likelihood, not be awarded publicly, if at all, due to the sensitive nature of Operation ███████. I further informed SFC Kowalski that he was never to make mention of this interview or the events of that day.

09

Breakers World was one of those lawless places where everyone watched everything because everything was information that could be sold to someone else. It masqueraded as a scrap yard for all the old rusting ships the galaxy had ever seen crawl along its length and lanes, but in reality it was one of the darkest nests of low-down trash and outright psychopathy the galaxy had to offer those willing to make a buck.

And Doc and Chappy, two Dark Ops operators who'd gone in there to ferret out a Hool mercenary who specialized in high-level military hits, were knee-deep in it somewhere. Most likely getting ready to pull a snatch and boogie.

The word on the Breakers street was that the Hool had been offered a contract to get close to the Legion commander on Acheron in the hope of taking him out on behalf of the Mid-Core Rebellion, a new player who was just starting to get some juice in the galactic scheme. Dark Ops couldn't let this happen, especially in-conflict. The death of a Legion commander didn't look good for anyone. So Dark Ops made it abundantly clear that the Hool was target number one for the time being.

Doc and Chappy were a rare two-man capture team. But they worked well together, and being the stuff of legends, they had pretty much earned the ability to do whatever they chose to do with the time they had left in the Legion. And what they'd chosen to do was track the Hool hit man all the way to the rock called Breakers World.

Or at least… that's what their most promising lead suggested. Whether the Hool was *actually* on Breakers World still needed confirmation.

This was all information Rechs had pulled from his secret foray into Dark Ops dataspace. He didn't care much about the Hool, or even the sector Legion commander whose life was in jeopardy. He cared about Doc and Chappy, though—and they would have the lowdown on the Dragon. They would have the information Rechs needed to decide whether to get involved.

What do you mean, involved? asked that other voice inside Rechs's head that sometimes threw out the hard questions. Whether Rechs liked it or not.

Do you mean kill?

Maybe, thought Rechs as he brought the *Crow* in low from the wastelands that ran for hundreds of kilometers around the main hub of Breakers World, *both reasons are the same*.

Maybe.

The question hung there, unanswered, and Rechs knew it wouldn't go away. Such questions never did, despite the answers one gave. In the end, there would be only one choice. The one Tyrus Rechs felt was right. And that usually meant it would be the hardest path to follow.

He drifted the *Crow* into an old route known as Heaven's Highway. The name was a joke. It was the secret flight path into the main hub, affectionately known as Hell Supreme. That name was not a joke.

The skies over the capitol of Breakers World were watched by almost every intelligence agency and criminal cartel within the galaxy. But drone and satellite coverage were difficult due to the constant screeching sandstorms creating low visibility on the surface. So the electronic eyes in the sky mostly watched the city, not the wastelands—and not the secret path that led through them.

Spreading away from Hell Supreme in almost every direction were thousands of ships, many verging on the colossal, beached upon the red oxidized-iron sands. When the skies were clear, which wasn't often, three tidally locked bone-white moons stared down on these fields of ancient destruction. And through these rusted behemoths lay the secret route into Hell Supreme.

But the problem with Heaven's Highway was…

"Salvage pirates!" shouted Rechs over the comm at the little Nubarian bot, who for some reason had chosen not to charge up the omni-cannon. Probably because Rechs hadn't told it to. But he was telling it now. "Shoot them!"

There wasn't much chance of hitting the pirates inside the twisting, turning, junk maze of old hulls and massive skeletons of ancient drive systems. The run started deep in the wastes of the Breakers, via a dune-covered entrance that was an old thrust nozzle from a massive Savage colony ship. Who knew how long ago that thing had been abandoned there for salvage?

Rechs had taken the *Crow* into the old Savage ship hard, racing through the orange twilight of an approaching sandstorm visible through massive sections of missing hull plating that served as witness to a thousand years of dead ships. He'd followed marking lights left for those who aimed to run the ruin—the lights of Heaven's Highway—before shooting out from underneath the bow of the massive ship and beginning the tortuous labyrinth through unused parts and sand-blasted destruction. Any element of which could have brought the *Crow* down hard in the sand if contact was made.

G232 watched with interest from his place just inside the flight deck hatch. "This doesn't seem like a designated approach for starships, Captain. Not that I'm in any way qualified to make such an observation."

Rechs was too busy flying the dangerous approach to respond. It was full reversers hard on the rudder and yoke to make a hairpin turn in a corridor that opened out onto a channel of ancient piping from some long-salvaged synth hauler from the early days of the robber baron boom. Before Herbeer had become a prison world.

Rechs flew its dark length, switching on the *Crow*'s landing lights in the orange and shadowy dark rather than trust his sensors alone. He never let his speed drop.

"The rate at which you are flying this vessel seems counter to safety and continued runtime. Just pointing that out, Captain Rechs."

"Noted," said Rechs, not bothering to explain that time was of the essence. And perhaps wondering why the idea of explaining things to a bot even occurred to him. A major sandstorm was due in Hell Supreme within the hour, and if flying Heaven's Highway was bad now, doing it in zero visibility with the sensors going haywire due to the incoming sand as gale-force winds pushed the *Crow* off her flight track… that would be tantamount to suicide.

No thanks.

The freighter leapt away from ancient dark synth pipes and crossed a dead field where Maragni nomads had built an encampment within the salvage. Several of the hooded figures scattered at the sight of the speeding freighter, while others took potshots with long-barreled rifles.

The *Crow* throttled back only slightly as it entered the humungous maintenance elevator section of an old first-gen Republic battle carrier. Victory class. It was here, just inside the massive hangar deck now gone as dark and deserted as a mausoleum at twilight on Hell's Eve, that the salvage pirates finally showed themselves and jumped Rechs's ship.

Flying light, tri-hulled interceptors—fighters from some local navy long gone—they came at him from all directions at once, firing blaster shots to disable the *Crow*'s repulsors and force her to set down on some abandoned deck. There they would have the upper hand.

The first series of shots ravaged the *Crow*'s general deflector array, forcing Rechs to back off the power, rerouting engines for defense.

"Light the scum up!" Rechs told the little Nubarian.

Rechs had always hated pirates. From way back. Few things in the galaxy bothered him as much as pirates did. They really were the bottom-feeders of the galaxy. Rarely did he pass up an opportunity to make life miserable for them, or just end their lives altogether.

With the bot now filling the volume of the cathedral-like hangar with the omni-cannon's bright blue fire, Rechs turned all his resources to finding a way out of the little trap set for him inside the massive hangar deck of the old Victory-class battle carrier.

The rules that governed Heaven's Highway insisted that a way through be provided. Otherwise how would the cartels be able to get their goods in? Tolls were paid to the pirates, of course—but a way *had* to remain open.

Turning sharply to avoid hitting an old skeletal docking arm, Rechs spotted a gaping hole in the deck that had to lead down to the lower decks of the carrier. He couldn't quite remember there being other hangar decks aboard these old battle carriers; in his ancient memories, the lower decks were stores. Not that it mattered. It seemed the only way out.

Rechs killed the thrusters, pulled back on the yoke, and executed a perfect roundlet. The *Crow* climbed and then fell over on her starboard engines to point straight down at the deck of the massive hangar. He angled for the ragged-cut hole and flung the ship down into its darkness.

Tri-hulled interceptors on full burn screamed in after him, flinging blaster fire in every direction.

His deflectors recharged, Rechs throttled forward, knowing that a dead end would amount to a very short trip inside the tight quarters of the ancient stores section. He flew through the darkness, the *Crow*'s running lights caressing a first-generation corvette that had been left inside the main shipping dock. Ahead lay the exit from stores in the form of a series of savage torch-cuts through the outer bulkheads of the big ship. With no other choice, Rechs took that channel and raced off, just barely ahead of the pursuing pirate fighters.

He ordered the Nubarian bot to cease fire. The omni-cannon was useless inside these tight quarters. A hit on the fast and agile fighters dancing all over the aft deflector of the fleeing freighter would likely cause just as much damage to the *Crow*.

The pirate flying the lead interceptor managed to lock on with a grappling tractor. Within seconds, two more had secured themselves to the *Crow*'s outer hull. The fighters were too small to reel in such a big fish, but that wasn't their intent.

"Captain!" said Lyra with more than a little alarm in her voice. "We're being boarded!"

Ahead, the run straightened out into a wreck-covered channel that, although not easy to navigate, was a far cry from the twisting labyrinth Rechs had already been through. He only had to avoid the occasional collapsing spars that had fallen across its length—a feat that could be managed by most competent pilots.

"Lyra, take the controls."

He received no answer.

"Take over, Lyra!"

"I really don't—"

"Do it, Lyra, unless you've got a way to physically manifest yourself so you can kill all these boarders cutting their way into you!"

Rechs scanned the controls and waited for the ship to show that it had taken over.

"All right," Lyra sighed, devoid of confidence.

Something in the back of the ship boomed—like a localized explosion.

Rechs flung himself up from his chair. His hand cannon was in the shop with his armor, but he always kept no fewer than three blasters in the cockpit.

For situations like this.

He grabbed two. One for each hand. High-punch Pit Demon barkers he'd picked up from a blastersmith on Gilador. As he ran down the curving corridor leading away from the flight deck, he felt the ship slow from reckless to merely fast.

"Lyra!" he shouted. "Keep our speed up! We've got to beat that storm into port!"

"But Captain—"

"Keep the speed up!"

The first boarder had attached to the forward upper hatch—and had blown it open. A Tennar stalked down into the hab quarters of the old freighter. This wasn't one of the two-tentacled humanoids who sometimes served in the Repub Navy, but one of the big eight-tentacled warrior males. Drug-fueled misogynists who ruled from a declining patriarchy around their submerged volcano temples. Not even their fellow Tennar could get along with them. Often they left their water world to become criminals, unwilling to adapt to a Repub society of equality.

Rechs fired at the new arrival with one of the barkers. Two rapid-fire shots left great, big smoking holes in the pirate's chest. He was dead even before he hit the deck.

But more of the tribal Tennar followed, orange-skinned with all eight tentacles moving like pythons, clutching and grasping their way in or bearing lethal weapons ranging from blasters and wicked combat knives to wrenches and spanners.

Rechs fired, again and again.

Two more dead Tennar.

He reached the underside of the hatch and shot one more as it came down. He fired five times as he moved aside to avoid being hit by the falling, flailing thing. He put two more in its head when it hit the deck with a *thump*.

And then he felt a tentacle wrap around his throat like a whip. Instantly his air was cut off. He had to fight that age-old reflex to drop everything in order to simply get more air. That screaming banshee at the fear-racked front of his brain, demanding oxygen.

His mind railed as his body turned and fell, dragging the wild-eyed Tennar male down onto him. *Breathe!* his mind roared. *Breathe now or you'll pass out and die.*

The only problem was… he couldn't.

Instead he pulled both triggers on his blasters for as long and as hard as he could.

The Tennar's body flew up and apart with the powerful impact of each bolt until finally the pirate released its hold. A limp tendril uncurled and slithered away from around Rechs's throat.

Gasping for air, Rechs clawed his way to the ladder leading up to the hatch. He pulled himself through the tube that connected to the outer hull, and continued into the pirate's interceptor. The ancient fighter smelled of old leather and dust mixed with burning ozone and melting plastic.

Rechs grabbed the docking handle and pulled, releasing the fighter. Then he dropped back down into the docking tube, watching the interceptor as it tumbled away and smashed into a trailing pirate ship. Both exploded across the waste of crimson dust–covered wrecks.

On the *Crow*'s outer hull were two other pirate ships. Neither had breached directly; instead the pirate boarders were making their way toward the omni-cannon, and its access hatch, via mag boots and tethers. Lyra came online to tell Rechs that one of the Tennar had been smart enough to fire an energy disruption gun into the omni-gun cupola, temporarily shorting out its ability to swivel and acquire targets.

The wind, filled with gritty sand, tore at Rechs, scouring his flesh, as the *Crow* rocketed through the junkscape. He shielded his eyes and spotted the pilots, both waiting behind in the cockpits of the interceptors. He changed blaster packs, raised a blaster, dialed it up with a flick of his thumb to full charge, and fired at the first pilot. And while he didn't hit the pilot—aiming was impossible in this sand-laden hurricane—he did manage to smash the cockpit glass.

A moment later the pilot disconnected the grappling gears and tractor hook. The loss of friction allowed it to lift off, dragging the tethered breach team with it. The boarders seemed for a moment almost to float above the speeding freighter, shouting distantly up at the pilot, horrified at what was happening, what was about to happen.

Rechs turned his blaster on the second ship.

But its pilot wasn't waiting to be fired upon. He was already emergency disconnecting, spinning up his ship's engines... which immediately sucked in the breach team from the first ship.

The second ship's two ion engines blew in unison. From Rechs's perspective, it looked as though the ship was dropped to the bottom of a great well as it lost motive power while the *Crow* raced away from it.

The first ship, down its wingman and both its boarders, danced away from Rechs. The pilot pressed his luck and made to fire its main blasters at Rechs, who was still sticking halfway out of his own ship, but the Tennar never had the chance to pull the trigger. A collapsed spar that had fallen out over the course of Heaven's Highway slammed into the ship at the pilot's distraction. At the speed the ship was traveling, annihilation was instant. Parts and components, both machine and organic, exploded in every direction while the *Obsidian Crow* raced away.

Med File Incident Report
Q-Selection Candidate 901

Upon medical inspection after the ten-day land nav exercise in the Panamanion jungle and mountains, Candidate 901 was found to have fractured his navicular bone near the intermediate cuneiform. Candidate 901 stated that he suspected something may have broken during the low-altitude jump insertion at the very start of the exercise, but chose not to report this as he (correctly) assumed this would have disqualified him from the rest of the exercise.

Instead Candidate 901 walked up mountains, crawled through jungles, and waded through swamps with a broken foot. All with a full pack, rifle, and combat load. He did not at any time remove his boot, because his foot was so swollen he feared that he would not be able to get it back on, making him unable to complete the mission.

It is this Chief Warrant Officer's medical opinion that Candidate 901 is either too stupid to be a Special Operator and must be immediately disqualified from selection, or he is too hardcore *not* to be a Special Operator and should be successfully cleared for Advanced Warfare School.

Either way, you people are too crazy to be assessed by sane and rational professionals such as myself. I'm a warrant officer close to retirement and so I can speak the truth regardless of whether anyone wants to hear it or not. It's good that Dark Ops exists. Someone needs to keep an eye on dangerous lunatics such as Candidate 901 and the people I submit my reports to.

CW4 ███████
Q-Course Chief Medical Officer

10

THE *CROW* SET DOWN IN THE CENTRAL STEWS OF HELL
Supreme. The swirling winds swept red dust, oxidized
iron, and coarse sand over everything. The local automated weather system advised that the sandstorm was a
cat-three in development. Rechs had no idea what that
meant and where three stood in relation to cat-four or
any other higher number. Out in the unincorporated
worlds that had been flung across the galaxy, the local
rules were often made up and purely that. Local.

The bounty hunter was in his armor and down the
boarding ramp within ten minutes. The sandstorm had
thankfully provided enough cover for Rechs to egress
Heaven's Highway and get into Hell Supreme with little
notice, setting his ship down in a quiet hollow made by
piled wrecks of starships. He was guessing that if Doc
and Chappy were going to pull a snatch, they'd do it
right now during the storm. The cover and confusion of
the duster was perfect for such operations. But that also
meant they'd already have gone dark. Rechs wouldn't be
able to raise them on the general comm. He might be
able to eavesdrop on the specially encrypted team comm,

but he couldn't bring himself to do it. That channel was sacred and inviolable during the critical phases of any Dark Ops operation.

He'd need to find them in person.

And since he knew their target, Rechs planned to find the alien and simply wait for the team to show. Once he had line of sight on Doc, he could ping his bucket with a laser comm and let him know he was in the AO.

Tyrus Rechs carried his usual assortment of weapons, along with a medium-engagement Lurpa sniper rifle that he'd favored of late. Chances were that he would watch whatever was going down from afar through the weapon's scope. Anything up close and personal would be met with his favored choices of the hand cannon or carbon-forged machete. Maybe even the bandolier of fraggers if things got too sticky. But the odds were that observing a Dark Ops takedown of a high-value target would be done through a scope. The rest was just in case things got interesting.

G232 was left with strict instructions to keep the ship locked down and to monitor comms in case Rechs needed him. Rechs didn't like leaving that option open. Didn't like to even *think* about needing someone. But he gave the bot the orders all the same.

Entering the stews surrounding the central warrens of Hell Supreme, Rechs noted that despite the fierceness of the storm, there was still traffic on the streets. An odd assortment of service and utility bots, each intent on some errand, made their way through the harshness of the oncoming sands, and Rechs passed small collections of huddling humanoids, their rendezvous set amid the storm to do trade or far more nefarious business under the cat-three's natural cover. Glowing optical sensors mixed with the chitterings of strange languages in the dusky wan light of the end of the day on that harsh world.

"I need to buy some info on a Hool. *The* Hool, as it were." Rechs tossed a five-hundred-credit chit into the midst of some chattering humanoids. One of them picked the money up and, just when it seemed like he would keep it without a word, pointed to a lone Ootari explorer standing by himself. The insect-like alien had ventured far from its strange and fungal world to be all the way out here.

It cost Rechs another fifteen hundred credits to get the info he was looking for. He could have gotten it for less, but time was of the essence.

Mohsaffa Huranzadi, the most wanted Hool in several of the surrounding star systems, had been seen of late in the Bottom of the Barrel cantina out in Battleship Row. Rechs accessed the local net, which was unreliable at best, and got a semi-serviceable map that would interface with his nav. The bar was located beside the ruins of a Repub battleship from early during the Savage Wars. A small-arms bazaar had set up in the shadow of the rusting hulk, and the cantina was located along its portside length.

Standing out of the wind, in a shadowy alcove, Rechs waited. He'd beaten them to the location. Now he only had to wait.

***

An hour later, the skies were clearing and what little of the atmosphere that could be seen was starting to appear. Rechs was concerned, or would have been if Doc and Chappy weren't such consummate professionals. But the op should have happened by now.

Rechs had been watching the sands swirling around an old crane that had once been used to pull plating for salvage off a battleship that rose several stories over the main street. Since even that venerable old alloy was no longer rated for any kind of service, the battleship had been left to decompose, and the crane alongside it. As he was still the first one at the scene, he decided to risk leaving his alcove for a better vantage point.

Ten stories up, half the length of the crane, Rechs had a nice view of the cantina below. And he'd arrived to his overwatch location just in time. Through the scope of the Lurpa blaster rifle, he found the extraction team's observers. There were two. Rechs wasn't sure if they'd been there the whole time, obscured by the storm, or if they'd just arrived. One of them was on the street, and the other was inside a split-level shop across from the Bottom of the Barrel cantina. Rechs watched until he was content that they hadn't made him, then expanded his search.

He spotted a paneled sled parked on a side street a block down from a bazaar that sold cured meats and a large array of anti-personnel mines. Because sometimes you got hungry when laying an ambush. It was a non-descript utility vehicle, but something about it twigged Rechs's intuition. He kept an eye on it.

A few minutes later a shrouded figure, dressed like any one of the dozens of salvage nomads that wandered the Breakers, stepped from the sled. He walked around it once. To Rechs, the man looked like a disguised Dark Ops legionnaire, and the walk-around smacked of a last-minute check.

"It's going down now," Rechs muttered to himself. "But where're Doc and Chappy?"

The two veteran operators should be the ones taking the Hool down, neutralizing the target, and getting it ready for transport. Hools were too dangerous for anyone without a lot of experience to handle. And there would be two other teams besides the extraction team, if everything was being run by the book. But that was the book Rechs had written a long time ago. Maybe they'd thrown it out and written a new one. Who knew?

Rechs scanned the lonely street once more. There was no sign of an overwatch team in all the locations where they should have been.

And that's when Rechs saw the blaster fire and heard the reports. He moved the rifle toward the flash and scanned the street around the sled. The fire could have been related to any number of a dozen other seething quarrels waiting to be settled at the conclusion of the sandstorm. Storms the locals called devil winds. According to native legend, the storms were dark, howling demonic spirits roving the lost sands of this world, keening over some long-forgotten wrong lost to the galactic twilight.

But Rechs didn't find any thugs taking things outside to settle up with blasters. Instead he watched two cloaked figures drag the disguised legionnaire into a nearby alley. A moment later one of the figures re-emerged and slid behind the wheel of the sled. And the two observers were gone.

Rechs tracked movement from several points across the compass. Small groups of humanoids and vehicles—definitely technicals—were on the move from out of the ruins of the old battleship and the lesser wreckages that lay alongside it. Within seconds it was clear that they were all moving toward the Bottom of the Barrel.

Blaster fire sounded from inside the bar. Rechs didn't catch it, but the Mark I armor's audio detection systems did. A rapidly developing firefight. One that was getting out of hand.

Rechs moved the scope to cover the bar. If Chappy and Doc did it right, they'd be exiting, expecting over-watch to have their backs and extraction ready to go. Instead they were about to walk into the noose of an ambush.

"First things first," muttered Rechs. He centered his scope on the driver's side of the paneled sled. The windows were dark. Of course they'd be that way for the op. And maybe if Doc had had the time, they would also be blaster-proof.

Rechs pulled the trigger all the same. He used a full charge pack.

He'd had a good sight picture on the approaching sled, and the blast melted the window and probably blew apart the driver from the torso up. Full charge shots with a rifle like this did horrible things to bodies.

Without fanfare, the sled slowed and made a half-hearted left turn into the hull of the battleship along the street, just a block down from the cantina.

Rechs moved the scope across the developing battle-field. There was still no sign of Chappy or Doc, and the ambush had now coalesced into three elements, coming from the three major streets that led onto Battleship Row.

Rechs chose the target he thought might best help the Dark Ops team get through. He engaged the group coming in the moment he had a new charge pack in. He blew off the head of a Hasadi sand raider. As the dead raider's partner scrambled for cover, Rechs drilled him through the chest. The man collapsed behind an old rusting destabilization field container module, but Rechs was pretty sure he was down for the count.

Firing a blaster sniper rifle had its advantages. Effective range and accuracy, because there was no bullet drop, was a big factor in the why-to-use column. That was why the Legion were switching to the N-19s despite the dead giveaway on position. Which was a big strike against. But then, Legion snipers had a whole company of legionnaires to keep 'em safe.

Rechs had no such luxury. But he was making it work for what he wanted to accomplish.

All three elements of the ambush quickly got wise to the counterattack as Rechs continued to fire at targets of opportunity. For a moment, the noose was stopped. If the extraction team came out on the street right now, there was a chance for them to get clear. Even if Rechs needed to be a target for the collective shooting gallery that was the junk-laden streets below.

The bounty hunter had both cover and height. The old crane had been built to cover the workers inside from the brutal winds and sandstorms that swept the planet at random times. And Rechs was able to move about on this level of the crane, finding new vantages from within its fastness to fire down on the attackers.

He nailed a vuline, a real go-getter wearing tactical gear and sporting a Maas subcompact blaster with all the bells and whistles. Rechs sent him spinning down onto the street a hundred yards from the bar. As he scanned for another shot and considered shifting position, he spotted Chappy moving out of the bar with his primary, engaging targets on the street all around him. Doc followed with the captured target.

The Hool was bagged, and he was held by a shock-and-rod collar, with ener-chains in place. Doc was using one hand to work the rod that connected to the collar, and the other to fire his blaster pistol.

These two were still expecting a ride out of town, but they had to have known things outside had gone sour when they heard the shooting. At least that had given them some warning. If Rechs hadn't been there to *start* that shooting... they would have walked unawares right into a trap. It would have been a massacre.

Rechs tapped the side of his bucket and sent a laser-designated message straight at Doc. Then he centered the scope on a human who looked more scumbag than hired blaster and pulled, blowing the guy's legs out from under him. The heavy blaster the creep had been carrying went clattering out across the rough street.

Rechs got a **Connected** message. Doc had recognized the incoming encryption and okayed it for contact. Only a few who ran L-comm knew Rechs's identifier. Doc was one.

"Your ride's blown, Doc. Get off the street!"

"Copy that, General. Which way?" Doc was a generally talkative and friendly guy when he wasn't busy being a cold-blooded Legion life-taker, but in this firefight, it was all business.

"Alley. Straight across the way," directed Rechs, looking down from his vantage on the crane. "Keep moving for two hundred yards and then hang a right."

"Acknowledged."

Rechs set to making the ambush pay while covering Doc and Chappy's egress from the street. Blaster fire rang out in an epic shooting spree as Rechs kept on firing. He rarely missed, and when he did, it was usually intentional—to keep someone pinned, or to freak them out enough that they'd try to get clear of his ranged fury. In those instances, he let them run and then tagged them in the back a second later.

He liked to call those kills… motivational. As in a warning to the rest: *Keep back or I will kill every last one of you to get my leejes off the OBJ.*

"End of the alley," huffed Doc, the adrenaline making the operator breathy.

"They're moving to cut you off," Rechs said, still observing the movements from above. "Lost a team behind the buildings… south end of the street. Proceed with caution next two hundred meters. Putting eyes on an exit in thirty seconds."

That meant for Doc and Chappy to keep moving along the exit route. In thirty seconds Rechs would check, give a status update, and tell them if it was clear to proceed—and if not, he'd tell them what obstacles they'd be dealing with.

Rechs returned to firing at the two elements he'd pinned in front of the bar where the snatch had taken place. Some of them attempted mad dashes for the entrance to the alley the two operators and their boss had disappeared down. They died trying.

Rechs fired dry, then scanned the street as he slapped in a new pack. A speeding sled was coming straight for the crane. It was probably remote operated and loaded with explosives. This was the ambush's response to Rechs on overwatch.

Rechs fired at the sled, tagging it once. That didn't slow it in its collision course with the base of the salvage crane that lay alongside the beached wreck of the ancient dark battleship.

Thirty seconds were up.

Rechs repositioned, fully aware that the crane was about to be destroyed—with him in it. He put eyes on the alley's exit Chappy and Doc were approaching with their prisoner. A technical sled arrived, mounted with a surplus heavy N-60 blaster oriented straight down the alley at the two legionnaires.

The gunner pulled the charging handle back, his head centered inside Rechs's scope. Rechs could hear the whine of the approaching kamikaze sled as the vehicle throttled to strike the base of the crane.

Rechs pulled the trigger smoothly and shot the gunner center mass. Nothing fancy. A kill was all he needed right now.

And a kill was what the bounty hunter got.

The explosion below went off like some giant child's firecracker, ripping through the superstructure of the crane in an instant. Metal groaned as the main lifting arm began a long slow collapse out in front of Rechs's position inside the control housing. Rechs was thrown back against the engine winch, then smashed into an old rusty plate wall. The entire crane was falling. Going over on its side onto the scavenged skeleton of the old battleship.

Still holding his rifle, Rechs pushed himself away from the wall and ran toward the exit from the control housing. The floor was getting steeper by the second. He felt he was looking almost straight up by the time he launched himself from the crane and into the night.

He activated his jets and flew out into nothingness.

The crane smashed down over the side of the old ship with a titanic groan, sounding like all the china dishes of a giant's cupboard shattered in succession.

11

THE AMBUSH WAS BROKEN... WHATEVER IT HAD BEEN. Given what the Hool was supposedly up to, Rechs might even have been engaging the MCR. A first for him. Regardless, Doc and Chappy had escaped the kill zone.

Rechs was relayed the link-up coordinates to meet the two Dark Ops operators a few streets over. Another sand-blasted alley shrouded in darkness brought them together.

In Hell Supreme, there was no law. No emergency services. So the city was ominously quiet. As if the sound of the massive crane falling on top of the old warship had struck some attentive note all were supposed to heed.

"Everyone all right?" asked Rechs as he came down the alley. "Anyone wounded?"

The two operators were watching opposite avenues of approach into the twisting confines. The Hool lay like a sack of feed against a wall, but it was still dangerous. Its quills were full of toxins, and it didn't take much of those to put a man down.

"Negative, General," answered Doc. "Low on charge packs but otherwise okay."

Rechs handed out what he had left from the rifle, slung the weapon, and pulled his hand cannon. He gestured at the Hool. "What about him?"

"Oh, him?" asked Doc with a wry tone. "Tried to squirt on us. So I gave him five thousand to get him compliant, and twenty once we stopped. Hools can take a lot of stun, but not that much. If the scumbag dies… well, it's no big loss to the galaxy. But we said we'd bring him in, so…" Doc swapped packs and charged his sidearm.

Chappy, as usual, remained silent.

They set off with the Hool stimmed and tranqed at the same time, moving quickly to get to the assault frigate disguised as a freighter that Dark Ops used for covert missions.

"What happened to your team?" asked Rechs.

The three men and their prisoner were threading a small night bazaar that had come out in the aftermath of the storm showing no concern over the blaster fight and crane collapse minutes earlier. The mystery meat vendors and arms dealers didn't seem to mind the passing legionnaires in charcoal-dusted armor accompanied by a bagged Hool and what they probably took as a freelance merc in old and battered Savage Wars armor that must have seemed to them almost museum-quality. Bounty hunters and scavengers came in all shapes and sizes out here. A blaster, armor, a prisoner… these things were nothing special to see.

"No team this time, General," answered Doc. "Everyone's been pulled to hunt down an HVT that's got the House of Reason's knickers all up in a bunch."

"Forced," grumbled Chappy over L-comm.

"Forced?" asked Rechs.

Doc sighed. "That's actually the more accurate term, General. 'Forced' is a good way to put it. But we didn't want anything to do with it, so we picked up this little op. Sort of something we could go hide out on until everything blew over."

Rechs could feel the dark cloud that had fallen over the conversation. The two veteran operators didn't like what they were being asked to do, so they'd faded. That was how it had to be sometimes. You took the fade or you stood up and got court-martialed with retirement just ahead.

That was a tactic that the point officers the House of Reason had seeded throughout the Legion had been running as of late, to keep from paying veteran NCOs their much-earned reward for hard years of service. Rechs had heard that a *lot* of court-martials had been coming down the chain lately, with the standard reduction in rank to private and a bonus dishonorable on top of that—if they could make something stick. Even now Rechs felt himself grinding his teeth at how his leejes were being treated. The Legion should never have allowed the point program to get started. It would be a disaster.

But then, no one in the House of Reason would've cared what Rechs had to say about it.

A dark cloud of silence settled over the L-comm, and they didn't continue their conversation until after they had reached the disguised assault frigate and gotten the Hool settled in a cryo coffin for containment and transportation. It was only then, when the three sat around cleaning their weapons, that Rechs, still wearing his armor save for the helmet, asked for more details on the House of Reason's HVT.

"Who is this that everyone's being pulled for, that sent you out here with just a few leejes as backup?"

Chappy and Doc looked at each other quizzically.

"Leejes? Where?"

"The kid at the panel sled?"

Doc made a face. "Oh… that guy. He wasn't a leej. Just some local blaster we recruited to drive. Told him we'd hunt him down and kill his family if he didn't show."

Chappy made a small snort and returned to cleaning his sidearm, which had seen a lot of use in the bar, and even more in the hot desperate seconds as they made their escape. The alley leading away from the Bottom of the Barrel hadn't been clear. It had been a run-and-gun series of engagements in the dark. But the two operators had handled everything with skill and professionalism. They'd fired dry on their primaries and moved to their backups, and they'd left a lot of dead bodies on their way to getting clear with their prisoner.

"For a while there," Rechs said, trying his best to make conversation—something he didn't exactly excel at, "I was worried you weren't going to make it to the green zone."

"The takedown inside the bar weren't no picnic, either," said Chappy with another disgusted snort, this one without the good humor of the last. "Hoolie didn't want to go peaceable. Turned into a regular old firefight until Doc lit the place on fire. Then ever'body got all afraid of burning to death!"

Doc gave a sanguine smile. "Fire does clarify people's thinking, Chappy. It's a real attention-getter. Especially when you're willing to burn it all down with yourself inside. I felt that needed to be added to the discussion of how serious we were about taking in old Mohsaffa Huranzadi in and all."

Chappy looked warily at Doc. Rechs got the feeling Chappy had not been totally on board with the fire.

Rechs brought the discussion back to what he wanted to know. "So what's going on then? Who's so important that backup and a full takedown team can't be spared?"

Doc's eyes narrowed in contempt at the issue, but he kept his thoughts stowed as he set to cleaning the carbon scoring from his blaster with an almost furious intensity.

Rechs sat there, arms folded. Waiting.

Doc paused to look at Chappy. After a moment, Chappy nodded, as if giving some green light.

"After you… *got out*, General," Doc began.

Left, thought Rechs. *Left you all like some bad parent who just drove away one day. Really, isn't it that?*

"After the Savages were defeated at Ontong Bay," Doc continued. "After all that, and after what had happened on that raid to rescue the diplomat's daughter… the Legion got involved in a little conflict on Psydon. I don't know if you heard much about it… being off in Dark Ops and doing who knows what while we were still in the regular Legion."

"I heard. Came close to doing some ops on planet."

Doc nodded. "All right then, well, for clarity's sake, I don't know how much you actually heard."

"I heard it was bad and got worse." Two harsh years of jungle fighting with a determined and homicidal enemy.

"Yeah," said Doc slowly. "It was pretty bad. Leadership was a big problem. And I don't mean the points—they were brand new, not a factor. I don't mean our Legion officers, either. It was the House of Reason. Psydon was the first time the House of Reason really got down to micro-managing a conflict. Lanes. Avenues we had to use that were conveniently TRP'd and full of IEDs any basic could have told them would be right there. Ambushes we were forced to walk into just to see if someone from a nearby village would take a shot. Bases in the middle of nowhere but ever in range of constant, nightly artillery fire. Calling in before we could engage. Just dumb, dumb, and *real* dumb stuff that doesn't have any business being part of a fight, which is what a war is—two sides out looking to get into a good old-fashioned gunfight. No politics. That's for back home. Okay… that's my rant… and so I'll get back to the story. This really isn't my story. It's Chappy's. But he doesn't like to talk about it.

"Anyway, we both got platoons, and for a time I was over with the Red Devils, and we were fighting up there in the Aachon for this hill. Another story. Well, Chappy here, since he doesn't mind me telling the story any further…" Doc looked to his friend. "Because if you do, pal, we'll just stop there and let it go."

Chappy grunted. As close to an affirmative as he was likely to give.

"Okay," said Doc. "You'll get the drift, General. Chappy was part of a long-range recon patrol team that got hit hard. Aftermath of the battle is that Chappy finds himself in a prisoner-of-war camp up above the lines of skirmish. Politics says we can't get him out. The doros that own that land won't let us in as long as they're 'neutral' to the central conflict. Never mind that they're allowing a POW camp inside their tribal lands.

"I guess the House and its blithering diplomats were trying to get them to come over and all. And until they did, we can't hit the camp. Did you ever hear of the Phoenix program? Hearts and minds and all that?"

Rechs narrowed his eyes. He had heard of it, but couldn't remember any of what he'd heard.

"Part of Dark Ops?" Doc said. "Teach factions within our enemies to fight and hopefully flip 'em? Only highly motivated true believers need apply?"

Rechs nodded. He knew part of this, once. But only a very small part. Nothing... *sensitive* in the least. But he started remembering. Putting a few more things together in his mind.

"Anyhow, so Chappy sits in there for a couple of months. He sits through the beatings, interrogations, starvation... those are the good days. Bad days are worse by orders of magnitude.

"A province away there's an operation underway called Wooden Horse. The House of Reason has Dark Ops trying to flip a local affiliation of doro chiefs to their side. Guys who are half in and half out of the war. And that's no easy task either. The doros' special Red Band hit squads are out killing entire villages just on the strength of rumors that they're leaning Republic. That was a dedicated rebellion, Psydon. The galaxy really hasn't seen anything like it since.

"But there's a couple of villages the dog-men don't have a lock on. High up in the mountains. Auwaroo tribes. And that's the first time, in my personal history, that we hear of the Dragon.

"Dragon is real deep in it. Red Band is trying to kill him. The doros have a price on his head. And the wilderness up there in the jungle highlands ain't exactly hospitable. And throughout all this, the Dragon is all alone. He's been sent in to train up a counterinsurgency to fight back in the doro rear. That's Phoenix. High-speed, low-drag. Real crazy monkeys.

"So Dragon gets wind that most of the prisoners in the next tribal province over are being moved deeper into hostile territory and that any window of the Legion being close enough to extract them and get them back to our lines is closing. So he goes for it. All on his own. Executes a raid after a three-day march deep into a territory swarming with Red Bands. If half the stories are true about what he did to the dobies, then he's not so much a legend as a nightmare.

"Anyway, at oh-dark-nothing he hits the camp hard, again, all by himself, and the doros think it's a whole battalion of legionnaires coming through the wire to get their buddies out. Except it's just him. And get this: according to Chappy, he wasn't even using a blaster. Not until later. Not until it got real hot. Nah, he's in and among them and carving them up with a knife. Moving like a ghost. He's even using a—and I kid you not here—a bow and some arrows.

"Within a few minutes, the dog-men are shooting at *each other*. So. Dragon gets Chappy and three others out of there. All of them are half-starved, but somehow he gets them down the mountain in what turned out to be an all-night running gunfight in the jungle. How many, Chappy?"

Chappy studies the blaster he's been cleaning. Or at least it looks like he's studying the weapon. There's a faraway look in the operator's eyes. Rechs guesses that Chappy is somewhere—some*when*—else.

"Two, maybe two-fifty that night. Can't take credit for but a few, myself. We was all but useless by then."

And that's all Chappy says about being a prisoner of war for two months and then a long night of death coming down the side of a steep jungle mountain pursued by vicious caninoids baying for his death. As if anything else that happened in those mist-shrouded highlands was beyond the ken of words to convey.

"Long story short, General," continues Doc, "the Dragon is the target. That's who the House has everyone chasing down. Crimes against humanity, supposedly. That's why Chappy and I are here, and everyone else is somewhere else. Because the Dragon the House is describing, the HVT that they want more than any other… that ain't the Dragon Chappy says pulled him out of that lice-infested jungle hellhole. And if Chappy says the Dragon is square, then he's square. And we aren't tracking him down."

"Nope," mumbles Chappy to himself quietly as he stands and racks his blaster. He returns to Rechs and Doc. "Not gonna happen."

■■■■■■

To: ■■■■■■
From: ■■■■■
Re: Letter of Reprimand for Operator 901, codename ■■■■■■

On ■■■■■■, Operator 901 disobeyed direct orders and undertook an unauthorized mission against Allied Forces in the region of ■■■■■.

Immense damage was done to the ongoing indigenous diplomatic efforts within the region, and it is conceivable that Operator 901 has aided the enemy war effort by deciding for himself how that war should be prosecuted.

House of Reason officials have asked that Operator 901 be court-martialed and reduced in rank. They have further indicated the need for a five-year sentence on Herbeer to dissuade other members of the Phoenix program from conducting operations that are at cross-purposes with the House of Reason's goals.

I, Legion Lieutenant General ■■■■■■, having the sole prerogative in this matter, have declined the House of Reason's request and instead am issuing this letter of reprimand as a written warning for Operator 901's offenses.

As none of this can ever enter the official record, both parties have decided that this letter will serve as the only record of this incident.

■■■■■
Project Phoenix

12

Rechs had time to think on the long walk back to the *Crow*. To decide what should come next. To search his head and try to put the long unused pieces together. With its gathering gloom, its rusting bits of metal singing in the strange breezes, this salvage waste seemed made for contemplation.

In a way, Rechs's mind was like this place. The wrecks of two thousand years of galactic travel, spreading away in every direction like some cosmic car crash that never seemed to be finished with its destruction. Every bit of it washed and scoured by countless sandstorms.

Rechs watched as an old salvage marking pennant picked up and began to shift. There was another storm coming in.

Project Phoenix.

The Durance.

After the hell of that world, he'd been lost for two long years. Two years when the Republic, and the Legion, needed him most.

Lost on a planet called Raven.

"Curse you," muttered Rechs at himself as he approached the looming *Crow* among the piles of junk and wreckage. The coming storm was already sweeping lost bits of paper and trash this way and that. The old metal creaked and keened in the breezes that whipped frenetically along the worn paths.

"Everything is just a picture."

A picture of a field of ravens and children, thin, dark, and strong. Streaking out through a forest in the rain on a gloomy afternoon. Causing those ravens to suddenly take flight. Except they weren't ravens. The birds were indigenous to that world. Like ravens, but with larger wings. And their eyes... almost intelligent. Almost knowing.

That was the image of Raven.

And when he thought about the Durance...

That was one of the few places Rechs didn't like to think about much. But the Durance, and his absence from the galactic scene... that was the reason for Phoenix.

For the children.

The landing lights of the *Crow* were on, made misty by the flying grit of the storm and turned yellow by the tired atmosphere of the place. They beckoned Rechs to the boarding ramp of an old freighter that had gone far across the reaches of the galaxy. It had not been his only ship. He'd had others. He thought he could still remember most of them.

Rechs climbed the ramp, feeling tired but knowing he wasn't. It was just the memories of old times best left forgotten. Coming to stand around him like mourners at a grave. Coming to remind him how truly ancient he was despite all the outward evidence to the contrary. Coming to taunt him with the concept of time passing faster than anyone ever thinks it will.

That was why he felt tired.

The memories.

He shrugged out of his armor and told Lyra to start pre-flight.

"Is something wrong... Tyrus?" she asked. Not merely as the ship, but almost as the girl he'd once known. The girl the AI was based on. The girl becoming a machine. "You seem bothered."

How does she know?

"It's nothing."

He stepped into the shower and stayed there for a long time.

When he came out, the *Crow*'s engines were warm. He could feel them through the deck plating, through the superstructure of his ship.

"It's nothing?" she asked, picking up the conversation as though no time had passed. She sounded disembodied, almost ethereal. Like a ghost.

Because she was.

If a ghost is a memory, then she was a ghost. Except that the AI speaking to him didn't know that it was a ghost. Or a memory. It only knew that it existed. Like some child that can't picture the world as any larger than the field it plays on in the afternoon. Thinking that such is the size and shape of all that the world contains.

Tyrus threw on a pair of cargo pants and a tight-fitting shirt. He'd be flying now. Making the jump to light speed. Another long one. Days in that howling darkness. And then he'd have to break into a place the galaxy didn't know about. A place called the Graveyard.

A place of truth, where the records of what really happened lay buried.

Rechs needed the file on the Dragon. Needed to read about all the things and incidents that had made him who he was. Needed to know what had turned him into something that needed to be hunted.

Taken out?
Or...
Saved?
Or both?

Rechs needed to know where he could find that little raven from Project Phoenix. After the Durance. On a dark planet in a lonely forest long ago. When a child had come into the forest dark and had seen Rechs watching. Standing among the trees. Watching them play their games.

A lost ball had only been his interaction with them. And only one of them at that. Rechs had picked it up and given it to the silent, large-eyed child. And then the boy had run to tell the others of his... tribe... about the man in the forest.

The man watching in the rain.

***

Graveyard 13 was what some deep inside the Galactic Republic called the lonely, nearly undetectable station out in a no-name system conveniently left off most stellar charts. But Doc had pointed Rechs in the right direction. And according to Doc, it was a place where the Republic buried the truths they didn't like. Because even the House of Reason with their constant revisionism knew that the truth needed to be kept around somewhere... just in case it could one day be of use.

Occasionally, according to Doc, Dark Ops broke into a Graveyard to poke around for background information on ops they were supposed to pull. Ops called for by the House of Reason. It wasn't unusual in the least for the House to want something done, but be unwilling to tell everything they knew to the people they were sending into harm's way.

There were several Graveyards. To the extent that they were recorded on stellar charts at all, they were known by mundane monikers.

Signal Array Tk-247.

Emergency Repair Facility Alpha Nine.

BM-32904.

Sensors would have detected that these stations were unmanned. Bot-run stations that served some useless function across the reaches, byways, star lanes, and even the edges. Little would anyone realize that they were vast storehouses of a precious resource. More precious than synth. More precious than all the highly sought-after commodities that people of a hundred different socio-political elements would be glad to knife each other over on any given day.

The truth.

The Graveyards guarded the truth. The uncomfortable, and often unfortunate, truth.

Doc had pointed the way to this particular Graveyard because it was where the Project Phoenix records were stored—and thus where Rechs believed he could find information on the individual codenamed the Dragon. There was a connection there. The Dragon. Project Phoenix. Rechs knew that much. But little more.

His memory was yet another graveyard.

Doc also claimed Graveyard 13 had proven vulnerable to a certain type of infiltration. Ironically, Nether Ops considered this Graveyard one of their most secure, and had given such assurances to the House of Reason.

Graveyard 13, officially designated Tracking Station Delta-309, was hidden inside the ring of a super gas giant in an uninhabited system. Deflector shielding allowed the station to remain inside the maelstrom, swimming through a sea of cosmic dust that blocked its external communications and prevented it from being detected unless you knew exactly where it was. Once a week, the station had to surface in order to send and receive traffic requests for information from those with the proper security clearance, but otherwise it remained shrouded in the protective guardianship of the gas giant.

The station was actually little more than a massive hard drive. It consisted of three concentric hab rings and two major information and data centers constantly rotating along the rings and interlocking at random points in order to physically access some of the more secure deep core memories. In other words, the station had to physically configure itself in order to get at the more protected truths. This was thought to be an additional security feature.

The first trick, according to Doc—and there were two tricks to infiltrating Graveyard 13—was getting the station to give you clearance to land. That could be accomplished only during the weekly surfacing operation, when the station popped its broadcast array up from the ring for twenty minutes of reception. Dark Ops had planted a worm that would allow Rechs to put the station in a secure access mode, as opposed to the denial configuration it kept itself in most of the time.

The second trick was going to require G232.

"We used a repurposed THK we weren't supposed to have," Doc explained. "You got one of those, General?"

"I've got a service admin protocol bot," said Rechs without sarcasm or irony.

Doc chuckled before realizing his former general was serious. "Then I guess that'll have to do."

Now Rechs was flying the approach through the ring's dust storm. The *Crow* broadcast a signal that activated the worm the Dark Ops infiltration had left behind on one of its first visits. Essentially, the worm ran a maintenance failure hack that would require the station to allow outside access to attempt to fix the bogus malfunction. In this case, it created the appearance that the main gravometric compensators were falling within warning fatigue parameters, thus necessitating a system diagnostic and a repair team to make a call on the station. The AI that ran the station would assume that an automated repair report had been filed, and therefore any ship showing up broadcasting the correct credentials from Repub Navy Maintenance and Repair must be there to perform the necessary operations to restore the gravometric compensators to maximum operation.

G232 was not thrilled with his upcoming role in this. "Though I have indeed enjoyed your illegal exploits as an outlaw bounty hunter, master," the bot began hesitantly, while Rechs was busy trying not to hit the two large asteroids he'd decided to thread the gap between, "I am quite sure I am not suited to this type of operation."

"Rechs or Captain."

"Ah yes… *Captain*. Shall I restate my concerns again using your preferred title?"

The *Crow*, miniature compared to the two looming asteroids that seemed hell-bent on smashing into each other, shot through the rapidly closing window. The lumbering space rocks smashed into one another, exploding in an almost slow-motion spray across the yellowish dust field.

Rechs shook his head. That was a close one. An unnecessary risk? Was he too distracted with all these thoughts about the Dragon and Phoenix?

The small station appeared ahead, its deflector shield a protective bubble against the hostile field. Rechs reached up to his overhead console and signaled the station.

The Graveyard's AI responded immediately. "Freighter approaching Delta-309: abort course. This is a restricted access signal array station currently experiencing a Class Seven plague warning. Repeat, abort current course. Do not attempt to land at this time."

That was the standard warning the station AI used to keep away curious travelers or salvage pirates. Not even the space brigands who were looking to prey on any one of the hundreds of thousands of automated stations the galaxy kept along the star lanes were willing to risk exposure to a Class Seven plague. *That* was a death sentence.

"Three-oh-nine," replied Rechs, whose skills as an actor were non-existent, "this is a maintenance call. We understand you have some bad compensators. Repair code Blue Six. Sending our authorization to repair now."

There was a long pause as the *Crow* closed in on the deflector bubble, a normally invisible shield made crystal clear within the sea of floating dust.

"You are cleared to land," announced the AI. "Landing pad three. Warning! No biologics permitted beyond the designated landing zone. You may exit your ship only to effect necessary repairs and inspection. Please confine any biologics to the landing pad."

"Roger that," said Rechs, hoping he sounded as tired as he felt. He may not have been a good actor, but he knew how he *should* act. Like everything was routine and nothing was all that exciting. Bots and AIs liked normal typical biologic responses. Anything out of the ordinary might set off their sensors and get them asking questions or seeking permissions from predetermined authority firewalls. Sometimes that meant contacting another AI with different decision parameter matrices; sometimes it meant consulting with a living tech in some cube light years away.

Either way, Rechs didn't need that. He needed this to be in and out.

The AI gave a final instruction. "Have the maintenance bot ready to board the station once you touch down."

"That's where you come in," Rechs said to G232, never taking his eyes off the approach to the landing pad. The *Crow* flew in under one of the station's rings, currently in rotation as it moved a massive memory core to connect it to a new part of the rings. Ahead, pad three lit up, and the *Crow* flared, pivoted, and dropped her gears to touch down on the forbidden station.

From: ██████████
To: ██████████████
Cc: ████████

Subject: News on what's got ██████████ so sick.

Hey ████████,

Just a quick note to fill you in on what the docs said about all those guys from the project getting sick at once. Don't worry, it's not *that* bad. But it isn't good either.

Basically, the root cause of the problem, or at least this is what they're speculating, goes back to when the project docs were trying to replicate ████████ and they weren't able to get everything to copy perfectly. There were some gaps, and of course we knew about those when the AIs would run simulations based on the embryo's DNA pathing. So by splicing some ████████ into the ████████ they figured they'd get the same ████████ outcome that the Savages did with ████████. Pretty sure you know all this, I'm just telling you because I'd forgotten some of those details from early on and I wanted to refresh. So don't get pissy with me if I'm repeating what you already knew.

Anyway, until now it looked like it was working fine, for the most part. Specimens—especially ████████—were showing rapid healing and, obviously, weren't aging once we switched on the splice. It was a good thing ████████ pointed it out when they were going to activate the splice when the subjects were children. Can you imagine how ballistic ████████ would have gotten if they were stuck as kids? Haha!

But, here's the thing about them all getting sick. Because of the copying issue, it seems the treatments are kind of like a cancer. They work, but... over time it's caught up to them. By which I mean it's slowly killing them. The docs have addressed that by administering cellular regeneratives, which hurt like a bitch, in order to restart their systems. Then they'll be good to go until the next time. No telling how long. A year. A decade... a century? Nobody knows.

So, good news: ███████ will be back in the field after he goes through the treatment process. Bad news: this will happen again. Probably lots of times. But on the bright side, if he ever goes rogue, without the project docs he's gonna die eventually.

Oh, unrelated but are we playing a round this weekend? My calendar still says 0900 but I heard a rumor you and ███████ were going to be off planet?

███████

13

"Again?" asked G232 as it followed Rechs down the boarding ramp of the *Obsidian Crow*.

Rechs was jocked up in his Mark I armor and carrying at port arms a heavy automatic blaster cannon that was nearly three quarters his own height. It had a low cycle of fire but packed a powerful punch. He'd modified it to switch over to high cycle, but the barrel had a tendency to get too hot in that firing mode. Just in case, he had a backup barrel he could swap out if a firefight with station security erupted.

He was hoping that wouldn't happen. Hoping he could get G232 in and out without detection. The war machines that did sentry duty for the station were designed to stand up to boarding parties using overpowered weapons with reckless and violent abandon. A typical salvage pirate tactic.

"Right now seems to be a good time to review our plan, Three-Two."

"I understand, Captain," said G232. "However, the plan is yours alone. I have lodged my disapproval for the record. And I assure you that my memory banks are not faulty. I can recall your plan with perfect clarity."

Rechs grunted.

The pad was little more than a circle connected to one of the two main memory modules that were in constant motion across the rings. Gravity decking kept Rechs from flying away as the massive beam of the memory module traversed the station's three interconnecting rings. The constantly interlocking and shifting machinery created a weird and unstable sight line if one relied on it for visual reference. It was like being inside an alien clock.

A blast door hissed open, and out rolled two massive war machines—sentry variants on the old light mech tanks that had been developed by the Repub Marines for ground assault support. They were like large, squat, gleaming metal giants, each rolling on three titanium omni-balls. The mechs' optical sensors scanned the pad, panning back and forth as they approached Rechs and G232.

Rechs fought the urge to take a step back and assume a fighting stance. If anything, he should act a little frightened, a little uneasy right now. The arms of the mechs were mounted with linked N-50s, and with two of them coming out, it meant the station had sent a total of forty-eight heavy blasters to meet a simple maintenance crew.

When it came to protecting their secrets, the Republic wasn't messing around.

Rechs approached the machines all the same.

"Proceed no farther!" warned the war machine on the right. "Biologics are not permitted off the pad."

"Just making sure my repair unit makes it into the station. Been acting up lately," said Rechs in a soothing tone, as though he were not holding his own death machine in his hands.

The blaster cannon didn't go unnoticed by the bots.

"Why are you armed?"

Before Rechs could reply, the other machine said, "Your maintenance bot is a sub-performing unit for a critical repair order."

Rechs's bucket bobbed once as though he approved of both questions. He knew a few things about bot psychology, including that bots tended to react well to body language that reinforced the narrative one wanted to sell them. It was how they were programmed.

"Reports of salvage pirates," said Rechs, unsure if he sounded tersely bored, or just terse. "And this one is all we had. Code said urgent so we came right out."

"This one," said one of the war machines in a hollow electronic rumble tinged with disdain. "Indeed."

A one-legged circular bot bounced between the two war machines to arrive front and center. It barked something in Digita.

But G232 didn't translate for the little bot. "This is the station major-domo," G232 informed Rechs. "It is telling me that I should follow it to the repair station node, mas—"

Rechs held up his hand, cutting G232 off before he could finish saying the word "master." That would've tipped the mechs off to the fact that he was a private owner instead of an authorized member of the government.

"Be quick about it, Oh-Eight," growled Rechs. "I'm in a hurry."

G232 looked quizzically at Rechs, haltingly blinking its optical sensors and clearly not remembering that they'd had to forge a new identity for it for the operation.

So much for all G232's talk about perfect recall of the plan.

Rechs nodded once, hoping that the gesture would somehow jar something within G232's circuits and remind him that they were now supposed to be lying to the bots on the station. Rechs had had to refresh the bot on the concept of "lying" on the jump out. It had taken the better part of a day's ship time. And it had been a long day at that.

"Oh, yes," said G232. "That's right. I am FRO8. That is my correct and valid identifier. I repair... er... things."

Rechs moved his finger to the heavy blaster's trigger, hoping that the mechs wouldn't pick up on it and classify him as hostile.

"Gravometric compensators," said Rechs in one last attempt to keep the deception going before he had to start blasting.

"Correct!" announced G232, subtly shuttering one optical assembly to let Rechs know that it was now engaging in lying. "Take me to your gravometric compensators!"

The bot made the demand with a confidence and exuberance no bot had likely ever exhibited in setting off to repair such a system.

The circular major-domo bot jumped, pivoted to a new course in midair, and came down with a shock-absorbed hiss that made the whole ball bounce up and down. Various lights and diagnostics blinked angrily across its arcane control interfaces. Then it once again spoke to G232 in Digita.

"It repeats that I should follow," G232 translated.

As the station major-domo led away the admin bot, Rechs wondered how many minutes it would take for

G232 to completely derail the whole plan. Which was an outcome Rechs had incorporated into his plan all along, if he was being honest with himself. He was prepared to blast his way in, hard-hack the memory cores, and get the files he needed, leaving smoking holes everywhere, and in everything.

Rechs was a realist.

But maybe the bot would surprise him.

14

RECHS HUNG OUT NEAR THE PORTSIDE LANDING GEAR pretending to lock down a hydraulic line leak that didn't actually need fixing. At first he half expected the two mechs to suddenly spool up their N-50s and start shooting at any moment. But as time passed, he began almost to believe it wouldn't happen.

Until, after about twenty minutes of this, the mechs began to roll toward him.

As they crossed the slender bridge that connected the pad to the station, and their targeting lasers danced across Rechs's ship, seeking him specifically under the shadows of the gear and the open hatch in the belly of the *Crow*, the bounty hunter decided G232 had finally done something that had tipped off the station that they were *not* a licensed and bonded Republic Navy repair team after all.

He pretended not to notice the mechs' advance. "Lyra," he said softly into his bucket's comm.

"Here, Captain."

"Deploy the ALM-108 anti-personnel gun. Target the war machines and eliminate."

There was a pause as a small hidden hatch popped open and a mounted heavy blaster drone dropped away.

"Engaging," said Lyra dispassionately.

As Rechs reached for the heavy blaster he'd brought to the party, using the landing gear as cover, the ALM-108 targeted the leading mech and spat forth hot blaster fire like a stream of angry wasps.

Thirty-three blaster shots connected within seconds, smashing the war machine to pieces. Ceramic armor exploded in sudden sprays as internal components were shot through, lanced by gaping red holes of fused metal and circuits.

But still the thing stubbornly came on.

As Rechs steadied the barrel of his own weapon on the landing gear's main pylon bracket, Lyra instructed the drone gun to intensify fire, targeting critical systems. The drone blaster complied, tearing away the leading war machine's processor and optical units. And finally some kind of fatal error must have occurred within the thing's runtime. All the blasters on one arm went off as the thing flailed wildly and died, sending a hot stream of blaster fire off into the galaxy.

The other war machine had taken this time to activate its powerful defensive screens. Rechs couldn't help but think those should have already been up the moment the mechs' processors decided to roll up on the *Crow*. A flaw in their programming.

Rechs sent forth a burst from his powerful heavy blaster, managing to put shots center mass and climbing to the right of the advancing killer mech's torso. But every shot was deflected off into the nether by the defense screens.

Rechs pulled longer on the trigger with the next burst.

But now the bot was firing back. Bolts from all its heavy blasters smashed into the *Crow* in sudden sprays of sparks and electrical discharge explosions. Other bolts slammed into the deck of the landing pad and skipped off into space.

That could cause some real damage, thought Rechs. *Maybe I should have put shields up myself.*

Lyra retargeted the ship's anti-personnel blaster and acquired the bot. A blur of hot fire spat forth, easily overpowering the defensive screen before scoring fatal internals. The bot exploded, and its head left a trail of smoke as it disappeared over the side of the pad.

"Combat units terminated," Lyra said quietly—with just a small trace of pride in her voice.

"I'm going in," said Rechs. He hefted the weapon off its steadied position and ran forward toward the station, boots pounding on the deck.

Unfortunately, the blast doors wouldn't open. And the station's shielding and heavy armor would prevent Rechs from blasting his way in. He ran back to the ship.

"Omni-cannon!"

The little Nubarian bot waiting inside the gun cupola blew a massive hole in both doors. Molten slag flung itself all over the bay, causing damage control alarms to wail as emergency lighting took over. It had been an overpowered shot, with energy from the engines rerouted to the weapon's charging capacitors. The barrels of the omni-cannon smoked, sending vapor up into the atmospheric bubble.

It was a nice trick.

Rechs stepped gingerly through the hot gap in the doors, avoiding the still-molten metal at the edges. He was greeted by a surprised crew of variously configured damage control bots. He raked through their ranks, drawing a line of fire that cut each and every one of them down, flinging their spindly mechanical bodies in all directions across the pristinely maintained hangar.

"G232!" called Rechs over the comm.

He received no response.

"G232, come in!"

Two more war machines rolled into the bay from an access corridor that led deeper into the memory beam. The station's automated AI was announcing that the facility was under attack.

No doubt, thought Rechs.

"If it's a fight you want..." Rechs growled. He grabbed a pair of bot-poppers designed to stun and disable. The big mechs would require more than one.

The station AI announced, "Warning: self-destruct sequence initiated. Eight minutes to station self-destruct."

"Great." Rechs covered behind some kind of external maintenance vehicle and tossed the bot-poppers forward.

The war machines rolled over them just as they detonated. A soft crinkle sounded inside Rechs's bucket as his own armor was disabled by the explosion. It rebooted only a second later.

The mechs, on the other hand, were now defenseless and struggling to come back online. That usually took these models at least forty-five seconds. In the interim, Rechs filled each hulking torso with blaster fire. With no return fire, he was able to target critical systems and hardware with precision accuracy.

Both were dead before their reboot cycle could complete.

Rechs scanned the area and found what he was looking for. A control panel that ran docking operations. It wasn't everything, but it would give him access to the station's systems.

He found the data socket and depressed a small panel on the side of his bucket. A moment later he had a fiber-wire connection and was interfacing with the station.

He scanned the station's internal message files.

G232 was active and being taken to detention.

Rechs ran the map of the station and found where to intercept the security team escorting G232. Then he was running, heading deeper into the station.

"Warning: five minutes to station self-destruct."

Less than a minute later and approaching from the rear down a softly blue-lit ceramic white corridor, Rechs fired at the four armed bots escorting G232.

He dusted the first machine on surprise alone.

Number two pivoted to engage, arming its deflectors as it did so. The other two machines continued their progress toward the detention center with their charge.

The absurdity of the machines making sure G232 was incarcerated even though the station was set to explode in the next few minutes wasn't lost on Rechs. But the sizzling blaster bolts streaking by his head kept that thought in a recessed corner of his mind where it belonged.

Ducking into an alcove in the white ceramic wall, Rechs waited for a pause in the return fire. The second it came, he leaned out and opened up, flipping to full cycle. His blaster fire deflected off the bot's screens, but finally punched through once the available energy could no longer handle the barrage. Seeing direct hits being scored, Rechs yanked the barrel up onto the bot's processor housing and fired a nice short burst that tore the thing's head off.

Then he ran past its immobile body in pursuit of G232.

Both the other armed bots now turned to fire while still moving backward in a continued withdrawal. The docile G232 wasn't resisting them in the slightest.

"Warning: one minute to station self-destruct," announced the automated AI calmly.

"Lyra, lift off."

Rechs had eyes on G232. He connected via comm laser.

"G232, did you get the file?"

"Oh, yes, master. I did. But I'm afraid that in getting it I alerted them to the fact that you are my master. That seemed to make them suspicious. They threatened to end my runtime. So in an effort to avoid such a fate, I told them everything. I have failed you, master, and I am deeply sorry that your illustrious career is about to be blown to smithereens across this forsaken dust ring."

Rechs fired hot short bursts into the retreating escort bots. His heavy blaster's barrel was glowing red. It would be dangerous to fire much more with it.

"Three-Two," began Rechs as he ducked into another data access alcove, closer now.

"Yes... Captain? I did get it right that time. For what remains of our runtime, I will never again make the same mistake."

"Is there an escape pod near your location?" Rechs cast his weapon's old barrel aside and slotted in the new one. The two bots were dispensing a storm of blaster fire across the corridor, centered on the walls surrounding the alcove. Massive glowing red smoking holes were chewed into every surface of the once-pristine corridor.

There was a slight pause before G232 replied. "Yes, master. Right across the corridor."

"Good. Enter it now."

"But master, I'm being *escorted* to prison!"

"They're too busy to stop you!" Rechs screamed, unloosing another burst at the bots.

"Captain." It was Lyra. "I'm detecting a surge in power to the station's reactor. This is dangerous and will cause—"

"Lift *off*, Lyra! We're ejecting in an escape pod. Get clear now or my ship is going to go up along with the station."

Rechs slapped in a new charge pack, tapped it, and left the heavy blaster on over-cycle. He corner-peeked to make sure G232 had gotten to the escape pod. The bot had, and was waiting patiently inside for Rechs to join it.

"Warning: thirty seconds to station self-destruct," announced the station AI calmly. "Please make sure to defragment and upload your last work to the station's final packet transmission. It has been an honor serving with you all."

Rechs popped out of the alcove—only to take a shot right in the chest plate. It felt like someone had swung a sledgehammer into his chest, and he was fairly sure his sternum was broken. His mind screamed in a primal fear—the fear that he couldn't get air. But he knew better. His rational mind—and his many experiences of having been shot before—told him that he was, in fact, breathing.

It just didn't feel like it.

He snapped off the mind-killing fear and engaged the bots, stumbling toward them as he unloaded with the cannon. Then he activated the armor's personal shield, dropped his blaster to move more quickly, and ran.

The bots poured hot blue fire into the shield as he ran past them. Stumbled past them, really.

The station AI began to croon a somber countdown. "Ten… Nine…"

Rechs reached the escape pod and pulled himself into the tight compartment, joining G232 inside. He prayed that Lyra had lifted off as he killed his defensive shield and slammed the hatch control.

When the door sealed, the sound of war machine blaster fire was silenced. And just as the station AI reached "three" in its diligent countdown to its own destruction, its doleful voice coming through the linked speaker system, Rechs reached up and pulled the ejection bar.

He wasn't strapped in as the pod exploded way from the doomed station. There had been no time. As the fleeing lifeboat rocketed away, Rechs crashed hard against the pod's interior.

"Zero," the AI intoned.

Rechs felt rather than heard the explosion as the station's main reactor triggered the Romula nuclear space mine housed inside Graveyard 13. The shockwave engulfed the escape pod in a sudden typhoon of violently released energy. Rechs's body, already screaming from the acceleration trauma, now roared blue murder.

With only the strength of his arms, his mind wracked with pain, Rechs held on as the pod was flung away from the doomed station. Flung off into the vast interstellar darkness that surrounded the swollen gas giant.

***

The pod had only just barely escaped the expanding debris wave of the station's detonation. Tyrus Rechs and G232 had survived the blast. But that was only the first hurdle. The second came moments later when the pod aimed itself directly at the crushing gravity well of the super gas giant, a violent spinning iridescent green planet tormented by intense storms. Its mass was so significant that instant death below a certain altitude was assured.

Lyra, running the *Obsidian Crow,* came in fast. But the new AI had little confidence in her ability to pilot the freighter. She made three attempts to connect with the escape pod and reel it in, missing each time. As the pod plummeted deeper and deeper into the atmosphere, Lyra grew more and more annoyed with herself with each missed opportunity.

"Clearly this unfortunate situation is not your fault, miss," soothed G232 as the pod began to enter the atmosphere's outer reaches. The violent shaking even at this height was incredible. Within minutes the powerful gravitational forces of the massive giant would crush the pod like an old nutrition pack. "Someone failed to set the pod's escape parameters in a sufficiently safe direction. It is almost as though they deliberately aimed us directly at the one place in the system that would kill us the fastest. The nerve of such shoddy programming! Further problematic still is how the pod allowed Master Rechs to activate the escape controls *before* having strapped in."

Rechs fought to catch his breath. His ribs, already tender from the events at Minaron, were now certainly broken. The violence of the unintended atmospheric reentry, short-lived as it would be, wasn't helping.

"Tyrus," exclaimed Lyra over the pod's internal comm, "I can't do this!" Frustration and despair were evident in her voice pattern.

Rechs didn't trust his ability to remain conscious after the battering he'd just endured. The front of his chest plate was heavily damaged where he'd been shot.

"Must…" croaked Rechs, feeling as though all the seas on all the planets were resting on his chest. As though some merciless giant were squeezing the life out of him. Tranqs and painkillers were not an option. Anything strong enough to deal with the pain would remove him from consciousness. And who knew how much of him might be needed to avoid being crushed in the unforgiving gravity well of one of the biggest giants he'd ever seen.

Lyra sighed. "Coming in for an additional pass."

There was silence over the comm as the AI tried once more to rescue Rechs and G232. The escape pod continued to rattle violently through the poisonous atmosphere.

"You can do it, Miss Lyra," cheered G232. The bot then turned to face Rechs in an aside. "Or at least I certainly hope so for our sakes, master. I mean, Captain."

Rechs nodded, just for something to do. He felt as helpless as he'd ever had in his life. It was a feeling he'd not felt since… since slavery.

"Because we'll be crushed to death in less than a minute," the bot needlessly explained.

A moment later the pod's shaking was punctuated by a large jolt.

"I may have miscalculated," murmured G232. "We seem doomed *now*."

"No," grunted Rechs, the very word torture. "Docking... tractor. She's... got us."

As he slipped into unconsciousness, Rechs wasn't quite sure if he'd said that last part out loud. But he had managed to close a gauntleted fist to activate his tranq controls, flooding his system with a full suite of painkillers. Because escaping the pain was all that mattered right now.

Gone from the pod, he dreamed of ravens who handed him a ball. Squawking one word at him.

"Ball."

The lost raven child from long ago, a boy playing in a rainy forest, had said that one word to the stranger he discovered watching them from the woods.

"Ball."

Rechs had forgotten that. Or maybe it was just the dream. Maybe it hadn't happened.

But then, from the hollows of the forest, came an echoing word that Rechs hadn't heard or used in centuries... and the darkness of all those lost places took hold of him, and he could not remember what lost wonders they showed him from their hidden treasuries.

To: ███████
From: ███████
Re: Psych Eval, Operator 901

After a final medical assessment completed during Operator 901's last deployment into the Reach, specifically ███████, to work with the disenfranchised factions of ███████ in their struggle against the Mid-Core Separatists, the subject showed signs of stress regarding a variety of issues. As this subject has been flagged for special analysis under a program of which I am not familiar, I have been required to submit this report—though there is little to note beyond what I have already stated.

That he is Sinasian, or half-Sinasian, is clear in his features, though his medical records are unavailable to me. I only bring up the subject of his race and genetic origin due to the strong family and cultural ties most Sinasians exhibit. Yet the subject seems to have no familial connections or distractions, which may contribute to his low psych eval performance indicators. More generally, the subject never relates anything of his personal history during our sessions.

When probed about this, the subject withdraws.

I was specifically asked to address and report on whether the subject seemed hostile to the Galactic Republic. I do not find in the subject any great level of dissatisfaction with the government. No more than the average legionnaire.

I can find nothing else that may be of importance, and I myself am unsure of the importance of the above observations, such as they are.

I recommend that the subject be mentored by a senior career officer. This might alleviate some of the stressors and provide a father figure to which the subject can confide.

15

Taijing was the gateway to the Sinasian worlds. It was the only world within that stellar cluster that had been directly settled by colonies from what was once known as Asia. A lost and mythical place the stellar charts couldn't find anymore. And it was the Republic's only port of call within Sinasia, the spread of worlds now designated a protectorate.

In the worst days of the Savage Wars, when the struggling Galactic Republic needed every ally it could muster, the Sinasian worlds had elected not to be among those allies. Under the sway of a powerful khan known as Gatsu the Merciless, the Sinasians, a closed and secretive society that brooded no outside interference and was known to shoot down a trade ship just as soon as allow it to land, threw in with the Savages instead.

There was no shortage of speculative historians explaining the reason for this. Most believed they'd simply sensed their opportunity to be finally and fully free of the society that had spread across the galaxy with the discovery of faster-than-light travel. But others postulated darker reasons. Blackmail. Treachery. Even a Savage-created mind control parasite.

Whatever the reason, their technologically advanced forces had come to bear against the young and desperate Republic. And against the Legion. All at the most critical of times.

The Sinasian Conflict was Casper's war, remembered Rechs.

He eased himself behind the controls of the *Crow*. During the week's flight time required to reach Sinasia, he had begun to recover from the injuries he'd sustained at Graveyard 13. Now he studied the approach to Taijing.

Rechs had been at the front lines of the war against the Savages from practically bell to bell. That included the battle on the wild desert world Kangok.

The battle that brought an end to the Sinasian Conflict.

And almost destroyed the Republic at its most vulnerable moment.

Rechs throttled forward. Over Taijing's main port of entry hung a Republic super-destroyer—what they'd once called a "pocket battleship" back during the Savage Wars. The destroyer's traffic control was handling landing clearances.

"Freighter Alpha Seven Niner One Zero," the traffic controller said. "Provide clearance or wave off. You're approaching a restricted planet."

Rechs waited a second, as though he were busy with something else. Then he flicked the switch for the comm and guided the *Crow* straight in toward the group of ships. "This is freighter *Balcytron* out of Sturgis Wells. Regular run. You'll find my previous idents from every week for the last fifty-eight. Transmitting codes now."

There was a pause.

"You're in order, *Balcytron*. You're advised to get your load and get clear if you know what's good for you."

Because such a vague and ominous comm required a question if the role of average lonely freighter captain were to be believed, Rechs asked it.

"Something going on down there?"

Pause.

"State business."

And that was all. Which in its own way said a lot. There was an unspoken rule between comm operators—even military, so long as their CO wasn't standing over their shoulders—that information, gossip, and general scuttlebutt got distributed.

The space lanes were a lonely place. Information was gold. Information meant connections. So for this Repub comm operator, who likely was as bored as he imagined the freighter jockey on the other end was, to be so sparse with the gossip spoke volumes.

People were watching. Nothing was left to chance.

And Rechs knew why.

The Dragon.

For whatever reason, they wanted him dead.

Rechs was patched through to someone on the ground who assigned landing pads. And then the *Crow* was diving through the outer atmosphere of the jungle world, falling through a soup of yellow haze and seeing glimpses of the river systems and volcanic mountains below.

Ionic interference that affected local comm, which was no doubt being listened in on, made the approach a perfect time to open a channel to Gabriella. When she answered, her voice sounded as though she'd been sleeping.

"Rechs?" she whispered into the ether of wherever she was, whoever she was with.

"I'm taking the Dragon," Rechs said. "Tell everyone in the guild to stay out of my way."

Gabriella knew that wasn't a threat. It was a warning. A courtesy. Specially offered for those who wanted to go on living. But most of her contractors, type-A testosterone junkies and flat-out sociopathic troublemakers, weren't used to heeding warnings.

"I'll pass on the message," she said softly. "But Rechs… I don't think they'll listen. There's just too many credits. And the House is supposedly adding more benefits. No tax on the prize. Full pardons for any outstanding crimes. Half of them would be stupid not to take the offer."

"I know."

They were stupid either way.

Rechs spotted the big ramshackle wood city just off the southern shores of a large equatorial mass. It was essentially a floating island built on top of ten thousand manmade mats, each the size of a city block. The mats were composed of high-tech materials that could sense and adjust for currents and temperature. Well, some of them were. Others they were made of nothing more than bamboo.

The floating city lorded over the shallow waters of a vast aquamarine lagoon. Up in the highlands, along the slopes of the coastal mountain range, duracrete abutments had been molded and leveled like ancient terraces. And it was here that the local ground control directed Rechs to land the *Crow*.

Pad N8873.

Rechs cut the thrusters to one quarter and threw out the landing gear. Throughout the ramshackle city, giant floating neon spam boards offering everything from the lurid to the enigmatic competed to distract him. But he dropped the *Crow* down with a low hum onto an ancient gray pad, where she settled onto her absorbers. Rechs was snapping off power and other systems when he realized he was still in a conversation with Gabriella.

She'd been sitting there, waiting for him to speak. It was the middle of the night where she was, and she was waiting for him to say something.

"Where are you?" she finally asked, sounding like a family member he hadn't talked to in months. Asking him what new and exotic part of the world he'd traveled to so he could kill more people.

Not the world. It's the galaxy now, thought Rechs. He went to new and exotic places in the *galaxy* to kill people.

He'd left the world long ago.

But the question brought about a feeling Rechs had not experienced in a long time. Someone wanting to know where he was, but not so that they could kill him. Or arrange for him to be killed by someone else. Just... to know.

It brought forth a vague memory from long ago. Standing on some desert base, back on Earth. Using a... phone... and telling someone—he could no longer remember who—that he was okay. But that he couldn't say where he was. Or where he had been. Or where he was going.

And he remembered in that long-ago time feeling not so alone and dead simply because *someone* had cared enough to ask where he was calling from. Even though he couldn't tell them.

Gabriella in the night was like the second coming of that long-lost memory. And before he could wonder if he really should trust her as much as he did—which was considerably more than he trusted anyone else in this rotten backstabbing galaxy where anyone would sell you out as fast as they could for a few credits more—he told her.

"Taijing."

"Why there?"

"It's where I think he's gone."

"All our intel and reports say Tyran or Sussa. What makes you think he went to Taijing?"

Rechs paused. There was trust… and then there was *trust*.

He didn't trust her *that* much. Not with everything.

Not yet. Probably not ever.

"Some intel."

"Okaaay," she said slowly.

"Clear everyone off. I don't want anyone getting hurt. This is a courtesy call, Gabriella."

"I know that, Tyrus. But again, I don't think they'll listen. And… nobody is looking at Taijing."

"I know," said Rechs. "Not yet."

And then the comm was dead, likely leaving Gabriella to lie there in the night, guarding all the secrets she knew, and thinking about Rechs.

Because no one else ever really did. Not the way she did.

███████

[Fumbling sounds of recording device being turned on]

████████: … Operator 901 didn't do anything other than what the rest of us do. ████████ Team watched him for six straight days. He drank, spent time and probably money on various local ladies. All of the Sinasian race. Gambled on Green Dragon Street. Ate a lot of food off the street. He also took a couple of tours of the various historical sites on Taijing, including one temple.

Most of these were off limits because ████████. Distance observation and audio tracking compensated adequately except for some signal drop at two sites. Drone recon was used to track the visit to Museum of Sinasian History and some little temple called Temple of the Giant in the local dialect. It was located in a neighborhood district known as ████████.

[Untranslatable audio from other end of comm]

████████ No. Nothing detected was anything other than the expected. But it should be noted that the subject's skill set, from what ████████ Team has been allowed access to, would be consistent with conducting operations under direct observation. Keeping that in mind, we…

[End of recording]

16

Rechs was in his armor and ready to go within thirty minutes of landing. He left G232 and Lyra to watch the ship, exiting via the boarding ramp and sealing the hatch with his personal ident.

Taijing docking berths were a massive engineering feat that acted like a giant elevator carrying mass quantities of shipped products from the Sinasian worlds. Everything in Sinasia flowed through Taijing before being allowed out of the protectorate, and the berths subsequently needed to be intricate, industrial, and powerful. Untold amounts of cargo passed through or was stored in a massive deep warehouse complex built inside the mountain. The warehouse was said to be so wide that freighters larger than the *Crow* could fly side by side through the long corridors, like two people passing in a hallway.

Between the stadium-sized cargo platforms ran tram cars that seemed wild and out of control as they switched lines to avoid the constant stoppages caused by lift platforms halting to load or unload their cargo. The tram cars were covered in graffiti in a hybrid of Standard and Sinasian—the latter of which was an amalgam of the ancient languages said to have come from that mythical land of Asia.

Most of what was written was anti-Republic. The war, long ago as it was, still left a bitter taste.

At the base of the mountain, the trams entered the central station—a shining piece of architecture thirty years out of date, built during the days when the Republic promised wealth and prosperity, even inclusion, for Sinasia.

Rechs stepped out of the tram car into the city proper, ignoring the beggars and gangs who watched for easy prey. Seeing as he was carrying a hand cannon, a medium blaster with a scope, and the carbon-forged machete strapped to his back, along with a few fraggers, he was clearly the opposite of "easy prey."

Rechs knew enough about Taijing to figure out what temple was spoken about in the reports. It had no grand spire of opulence or beaten gold-fronted minaret offering salvation through the donation of wealth. Rechs had seen many of that sort of holy site serving the hundreds of other faiths that wandered the galaxy, promising much, and taking much more.

But this temple was an old, squat pagoda. Dark and shadowy on the inside.

An old woman, brown wrinkled skin and flashing green eyes, smiled at Rechs as he approached the temple's entrance. The street outside was quiet. Crowds and music could be heard from distant blocks, but in the temple's residential neighborhood there was little noise beyond the old man sweeping the temple steps.

The top of the steps revealed a wide, empty dura-crete floor, clean and smooth from lifetimes of constant sweeping. Across that floor, in the back, stood an old man lighting joss sticks before a hulking statue.

Rechs crossed the sharp line that divided light from shadow. Passing from the wan, yellowish daylight into the inner darkness. He felt the chill through his armor. His footsteps echoed through the empty temple. Each resounding step a sort of sacrilege in this quiet inner sanctum.

He arrived at the statue. An idol, some might say. But Rechs knew the statue for what it once was. It was real. Not some likeness. But a thing that was real. And, a long time ago, deadly. Something that laid waste to legionnaires by the score.

"You come seeking wisdom?" asked the man, small and spritely, lighting the joss sticks before the statue.

Rechs answered through his bucket, his voice made ghostly and even more gravel-laden by the bucket's external comm. The sound matched the mood and the darkness of the place. But the tech itself was out of place in the simple temple. And especially at odds with its idol.

"I've come for the Dragon."

The old man, bent and small, laughed like a maniacal little demon who knew all secrets. Held all the cards.

"Then you do not come for wisdom. Because only a great fool thinks he comes for the Dragon. The Dragon comes for you."

Rechs remained silent. Listening for something he wasn't quite sure of.

"Everyone comes for the Dragon now," the old man mused. "The price is very high. His head is worth much. But his soul... *it* is worth more. So much more to people yearning to be free."

The old man pronounced the word "soul" like it had more syllables than it should. Like it was a whine instead of a word. Or a song instead of a thing.

"I've come to save him," said Rechs.

The old man laughed in the off-pitch, singsong way those who don't speak Standard as a first language think that laughing must sound. Only he genuinely seemed to be laughing.

"That is very funny. *You* save the Dragon." The old man's face turned to stone. "*You* are just a man. *He* has killed thousands of men. What makes you think he needs to be saved?"

Rechs didn't answer.

The old man continued. "Maybe he has gathered all of his enemies in one place," the old man poked a finger against the flat of his hand, "so that they might die together. Is that not merciful, fool who seeks the Dragon?"

"Maybe."

"To die alone is the way of the galaxy. A noble heart would never wish such on one's enemies."

"I'm not an enemy," insisted Rechs.

"*Saying* so much is easy. Living as a friend… is very hard."

The old man waddled close to Rechs, and it became apparent that he was blind. His aged face was badly scarred from some ancient horror. "This temple… is illegal."

"I know."

"You could call the Republic about us. Tell them we are worshipping our ancient tech in this place. That we are a cult. Then I would talk."

Rechs waited. There was something happening.

"I flew her once. The VF-71 Samurai."

The old man was close enough to touch Rechs's armor, and so he did.

"Ah! Iron. I wore such once. Iron sharpens iron."

Still, Rechs said nothing.

The old man, his ruined eyes looking off toward the ground, rested his hand on the old Mark I armor. "When men wore iron, they were men. Now… Now…"

He sighed.

"Now everything is different," finished Rechs.

"You know the Confession of Hiro?"

"I do."

"Those days are long gone, when once we flew into battle like demons against you legionnaires. Great days. Great battles. Great foes were the Legion."

Rechs waited, but the old man said nothing further, his scarred eyes roving as if he could still see all the carnage and destruction of that last battle.

"I was there," said Rechs.

"Nooooo," exclaimed the old man in a long sigh of disbelief.

Rechs searched his mind to find the memory he sought. "The base. When it came down, in pieces, smashing into the sea… I jumped at seventy-five-thousand feet and listened to the Confession of Hiro over broadcast until impact. He never finished the last line. The history books just add that part about knowing the end all along."

The old man's blind face was a mask of amazement. "You were young then and so as old as I am now?"

"Older," replied Rechs.

"How?"

Rechs answered by changing the subject. "The Dragon will die here if he doesn't have a friend."

The old man nodded once. As though the ice of his disbelief was now beginning to melt.

"I can help him," continued Rechs. "I can take him away. All that waits for him here is death."

"Everyone dies sometime."

"Not him. Not yet. He's is young and he's never lived."

"Who ever truly does?"

Rechs said nothing.

The old man's gnarled hands fretted with his robe. "We trusted in our mecha. Thought we could beat you. Fell for the lies of the Savages. We were... wrong."

"Time is running out. They're searching the city for him."

Rechs waited for a long time as the man considered his words. A wait that felt interminable given the need for haste in finding the Dragon.

"Yes. They are," agreed the old man after an eternity. "But they will not find him after the sun falls. By then he will be gone. Upriver to Shangri-La. He will unite the clans. We will be great again. Strong again. *Free* again."

"They'll kill him." Rechs didn't bother explaining why. He knew why. What the Dragon had planned was something the House of Reason could never allow to happen. "Where can I find him?"

"You are... a *friend* of the Dragon?"

"I am," said Rechs, thinking of that raven-eyed boy in the forest.

Ball.

"Ball," Rechs had answered as he handed it over to the child in the forest. He watched the lad run back into the field where the other little ravens played. Watched the boy tell them in their code language of the strange man in the forest.

They'd come looking because they weren't afraid. They weren't bred or built for fear. They'd been made for other doomsdays.

They were made to fight. And to explore. And to conquer. And to never give up. And to fight. Always fighting.

"Dan Dan Plaza. Up the Street of the Blue Lotus on the island. Chung's Pit. You will find him there this afternoon. It will be your last chance."

Rechs turned, running from the Temple of the Giant. He hustled down the steps, tapping into the city maps. Trying to get a handle on where Chung's Pit and the Street of the Blue Lotus were. Because time…

Time was running out.

In the galaxy, time was not a luxury.

Even for Tyrus Rechs.

The old man knew that Rechs had left. He begins his shuffling walk back to the idol in the darkness. Back to burn the joss sticks. To the idol where the candles had been lit for all these years. Dripping their wax down onto the silent frame of the ancient war machine. Making it seem like some iron giant, resting in the darkness. Its blasters long gone silent. Its missile pods and racks long empty. Its markings a thing of the past.

Its glory hidden in the shadows.

17

Rechs was running fast into dark territory. And that was something no bounty hunter should ever do. On a good day, the odds were stacked against him. And that required preparation. Surveillance. Planning. Execution. Doing those might not even the odds, but they made them a whole lot better. Enough to get the job done.

But running in blind? Maybe the old man had been right about Rechs being a fool. Or at least having foolish tendencies. But this was what needed to happen.

And this was no bounty hunt. It was different, so much so that it was setting off a fire inside Rechs. He felt a deep urgency as he ran down dirty alleys. Navigating crooked and maze-like streets no city planner would ever approve. He crossed rickety bamboo bridges that connected the main city flotilla to expanding islands beyond the docks and water's edge.

There was no direct route he could take off the island to reach Chung's Pit, which lay in a place where visitors to Taijing were warned never to visit. To ignore that warning was to take your life into your own hands.

"Bounty hunter!" shrieked a young man in threadbare clothing, his gold tooth gleaming as Rechs moved along a filthy dock.

"What?" Rechs slowed, unnerved that the spindly man would call him that.

"Yeah, don't play dumb. You bounty hunter for sure." The young man looked from left to right. "Lotsa bounty hunters coming through the lilies now."

"The lilies?"

"All these islands. We call them lilies. You bounty hunters be careful. Don't run into each other and start shooting."

"What're you talking about?" Rechs felt a rising sense of concern. Gabriella had said that the hunters were all on a different trail. So why was this kid saying otherwise? Had she flipped? Sold Rechs's courtesy as information?

"No one want to share the Dragon."

Rechs stared at the young man. When no further words came forth, Rechs started moving again toward the next island—the next lily.

"You pay me money," said the kid, following Rechs. "I show you way in Chung's no other bounty hunter know about."

Rechs stopped again to better study the young man. In lieu of carefully farmed intel, the local stuff would have to do. And if nothing else, this word on the street confirmed what the old man at the temple had said—that something was going down at Chung's Pit.

But whether that something was a trap, or something else…

"All right," Rechs agreed. "Lead on. You get paid when we get in."

"Half now. Half in Chung's when you see Dragon."

"Fine. Show me your card," Rechs ordered.

The kid erupted into a happy grin. He produced his card from some secreted fold within his faded yellow shirt like a street magician, and proudly held it out for Rechs.

"How much?" asked the bounty hunter.

"Twenty too much?"

"Okay."

And the transaction was complete. The kid checked the numbers on the card's face, smiled, and with another sleight of hand made the card disappear. He took off at once, sandals slapping on the wet walkways that occasionally dipped into the water, leading Rechs along.

"Avoid the bridges," the kid said. "Gangs control those. They would've shook you down at Sen's."

"Not worried about the gangs."

"Worry that they slow you down, though?"

"Yeah."

"I know better way that avoid all these problems."

Some of the islands—the lilies—were so close together that you could leap from one to the next, leaving one junk-made island world for another. Rechs could have made some of the larger jumps easily by using his jump jets, but with the Legion and Nether Ops running constant scans in search of the Dragon, his jump jet signature was sure to show up somewhere. Which would introduce complications. For as long as possible, Rechs wanted to remain just another armored treasure hunter, looking to collect on the target everyone wanted dead. A kind of ally to the Republic so long as no one bothered to look too closely. They were all too focused on their primary target.

Which for once, wasn't him.

But he'd gotten mixed up in it all the same.

Leaving the last lily, Rechs followed his guide into a tunnel that led into the main floating platform. Rechs recognized the tunnel as belonging to an old astrodrome from the early days of space flight. They'd been common on worlds that didn't have a lot of wide open spaces. A sea-based starship support facility.

Of course, as mobility and rugged improvements in private starships increased enough that they became capable of landing almost anywhere, such places had fallen into disuse. The Sinasians had built a city around theirs.

Rechs didn't spend much time wondering how many of them even knew what it had once been. He'd long ago tired of such mental games. Games in which he counted what he knew, or recognized, or caught a glimpse of in the old architecture of some now ancient place, and how few observers in the rest of the galaxy actually knew the same.

Tyrus Rechs could have been the galaxy's foremost historian and archaeologist.

Instead he killed people for a living.

The tunnel was one of the old fuel resupply connectors meant for the ships that would come alongside the astrodrome for refueling. Now it was a twilight bazaar of lotus dens. The smell of the fuel had probably hung around for centuries though. Rechs imagined that he could still smell it now.

Dead-eyed men inhaled from long pipes at their kiosks—small desks and bars that guarded dens and warrens farther in and beyond. Places where the smoke drifted before paper lanterns to make strange shapes and shadows along the walls. Music, simple and ethereal, drifted from the depths of such places. Gongs and wooden wind chimes. Bowls that sang like aliens most of the galaxy had never heard.

Sleepy-eyed beauties—all of them Sinasian, no foreigners—watched them pass with a kind of quiet contempt. They were barely clad, and beautifully tattooed with dragons and stars. Each marking a work of mastery of the art, competing for space on the ample delights of flesh. But Rechs could see in the girls' eyes that there was nothing but the lotus. The need for more of it was there. The hopelessness of it all was there too.

"Dragon change all this," said the young man as he led Rechs off the beaten path. He whispered, "Slaves to lotus. Dragon going to kick the Republic out and make us free. He become great khan and samurais will fly once again. We ready. Time is now."

And that's when Rechs decided he wasn't being led to Chung's Pit, or wherever else the Dragon was. He was being led into an ambush. And he'd even paid this kid to do it.

The Sinasians, they believed in the Dragon. Because that's what Dark Ops had *taught* the Dragon to do: make true believers for the war effort. Only now the Dragon had come home to do it in a place where the Republic had no desire for such things.

Now the war would be with the Republic.

There was an old saying Rechs should have remembered. About Sinasia and the worth of a promise there.

But he couldn't, because he was diving for the floor the moment what few lights there were in this section of the tunnel went out. Going down just before the blaster fire started.

They were on the verge of entering an old chamber. A well of sorts. High up were the yellowish skies of

Taijing. But down here, along the walls, were a dozen kids sporting blasters. Sinasian gang members. And all were pulling and firing. Because freedom was at hand.

Rechs reached up and grabbed the kid who'd led him into the trap by the hem of his shorts. He flung him through the opening, right into the center of the chamber. The fire came at him from every direction, and the kid was riddled with blaster bolts.

Someone barked in a language or dialect that Rechs didn't know. Probably to say that they were shooting one of their own, because the firing stopped.

Fang was the dead kid's name. Someone was screaming and saying that name over and over.

It was too bad. Rechs held no ill will for the kid.

What came next was also too bad.

Rechs took advantage of the lull, firing slugs from his archaic sidearm. He first dropped the gang leader, the one who was shouting that they'd killed Fang. Twice in the chest. The kid went down, his face snarling and twisted with pain as the two fifty-caliber bullets tore his body to shreds and sent him spinning.

The others returned fire, but only as they ran. Like jackals with no heart. In the end it was as though they'd never been there. Only the sound of their sandals slapping ancient metal in distant tunnels could be heard.

Rechs got to his feet, still feeling the broken ribs that had only just begun to heal thanks to the voodoo the Savages had done to him long ago. Technological wonders the galaxy's finest scientists had only begun to discover.

The same dark magic that had made him outlive everyone. Whether he wanted to or not.

That's not entirely true, is it? If you wanted to die…

Rechs pushed the dark thought from his mind.

The process of this advanced healing and longevity was a miracle. But it still took time. As some miracles do.

The bounty hunter stood in the darkness with two corpses. There was no easy answer to this. No wins. No battles where the last redoubts were stormed. No explosions of some formidable dreadnought brought to bear in the crucial tide-turning moment. No breaking of the enemy's will.

This would end with a lot more dead people face down in the worst kinds of violence the galaxy had to offer.

The Sinasians wanted the Dragon because he might be a messiah.

The Republic wanted him dead for the same reason.

And Rechs...

Well, everyone should have a chance at life. Even if they never knew it.

He continued along the tunnels. In time he found his way out by following the roar of a crowd. Something big was happening.

The Dragon was happening.

18

CHUNG'S PIT WAS A HIDDEN FORTRESS AT THE CENTER
of the old astrodrome. A walled citadel made like a piece
of art from some lost age the galaxy hadn't known for a
thousand years. A time when mythical monsters curled
about wizard's towers and heroes were needed to slay
them. With the sorcerer inside, always watching.

Even with the scarcity of room in the astrodrome,
Chung's Pit had a nice wide avenue between it and the
other recycled buildings in the area. But what most people would have called a street, Tyrus Rechs called a kill
zone.

Groups of men armed with blasters, illegal for the
disarmed Sinasians, smoked lotus as they stood gathered
at measured intervals all along the walls. Rechs studied
them from the darkness of an alley. And somewhere
beyond the guarded walls, adorned with ancient symbols,
beyond the long, curling, thin-bodied dragons topped by
statues of tongue-lolling dogs reminiscent of Sumorian
war hounds… beyond all this, an unseen crowd roared
in waves. As if there were a championship match taking
place inside.

Rechs's options for entering the citadel were limited. Strolling into the fortress from the street like just another Sinasian was a non-starter. He still wasn't willing to use his jets to fly over the wall. And storming the place meant fighting everyone all at once.

For now, he decided to work his way along the back alleys toward the entrance of Chung's Pit. He passed old women cooking multi-tentacled lobster-like creatures in big woks filled with boiling oils over gas fires. They refused to see the bounty hunter traversing the maze, entering their world and disappearing like an unclean and lost ghost not of their people.

They didn't want any trouble. Just to keep on living. Surviving.

An old bot sat in the darkness of a massive, looming apartment house with a bridge cut through its center. The bot's outer covering had been stripped off, but one working optical assembly followed Rechs as he moved through an alley that had been transformed into a sort of shop full of bizarre curiosities. Wind chimes made of the indeterminate bones and the shells of those flash-fried crustaceans hung in the breezeway, causing Rechs to duck to avoid their hollow songs.

"Oobabi tu watangu oso?" asked the bot. Its vocal modulator hadn't had a tune-up in years. It spoke in a slow and ponderous voice.

But Rechs recognized the old dialect. It was a bot-mummra pidgin from out near Cestus. Rechs had overseen a Legion campaign against the Savages who'd traveled to that world. The mummra were the natives who had almost entirely been turned into living nightmares by the Savages. Rechs had fought alongside the survivors to liberate them.

"No, I don't need a wind chime."

"Oosaba booo," said the old one-eyed bot sadly. *"Meto saadz."*

Rechs stopped. Old bots turned invisible in most societies. Often degrading down into a sort of senile run-time until one day they just stopped working—either from the sands of time or the hands of scrappers—and were scavenged. Locals in some cultures were superstitious of stripping them down until their last bit of power had faded.

"What's going on in there?" asked Rechs, tilting his head in the direction of Chung's. The crowd within had erupted in shouting, the sound one of shock and disbelief. As though they were witnessing the unbelievable, and finding it to be all too real.

"Dragaroom untato all Sinasia. Makastapa tada... tada..." The bot searched for the right word.

In Mummrasi there wasn't really a good substitute for the word the bot needed. But Rechs knew the answer from context, and he supplied it in Standard. "One."

"Tada one," the old bot agreed.

That was the word. One. In Mummrasi there was no word meaning *one.* Or *individual.* They were a truly symbiotic species. The large, bat-like creatures had on average more than five other sentient beings either physically attached or mentally linked to themselves. Each mummra, so to speak, viewed itself as all of these. They were always *we* or *us.* Never *one.* At least, not until the Savages came and starting to carve them up...

"The Dragon is uniting the Sinasians into one," Rechs repeated.

The sad old bot nodded slowly at him in the dark beneath the bridge, and its lone unblinking optical assembly brightened in confirmation.

The machine clearly didn't have much left to its run-time. The light in its optical sensor was flickering a slow march to nothingness. Soon. Not now, but soon.

Rechs selected a chime and took it down from where it hung.

"I'll take this one."

The bot's lone eye flickered happily.

No credits were exchanged. The change of ownership for the thing the bot had made, another machine of sorts, was simply enough. It had passed itself on to the galaxy.

Rechs moved on. He stopped beside an old abandoned building, crumbling and condemned by whatever local government ran things on Taijing. Warning sensors and hazard flags clearly marked the building as off-limits. It climbed high up, several stories. Almost reaching the rim of Chung's Pit across the street.

It would do nicely.

He entered the building, finding sleeping lotus users spread out in the darkness. One of them shifted and rolled over, disturbed by the noise of the wind chime that hung from the bounty hunter's carbon-forged machete.

Rechs followed a central stairwell leading up into the heights, its railings missing. The steps creaked and groaned, threatening to finally quit as Rechs ascended, passing doors on each landing that lay open like gaping mouths shocked at the destruction of the long-abandoned living spaces that had once housed happy families.

The stairs led all the way to the roof, a wide and open space, hot and burnt by the last of the fading sun. Rechs took the wind chime and hung it on an old bent nail sticking out of the roof access shelter.

The light in the sky had turned everything a bloody red, causing even the yellow haze that had lain over the world to halo and bleed as Rechs studied the street below. The clusters of gang members stationed along it looked to their left and to their right. But not above.

They never looked up.

Elaborate sectional dragons made from nylon were strung on taut cords that spanned the width of the street, undulating in the wind. It was for these cords that Rechs had made the climb to the top of the condemned building. They were anchored to the edge of the condemned building's roof by heavy-duty tension bolts, and on the other side of the street, they connected to the outer wall of Chung's Pit.

Rechs walked by each decorative line, testing them with a hard pull as he went. When he settled on just the right one, he swung his feet out over the rooftop ledge and wrapped his arm around the cable, hanging upside down like a Leegan spire sloth. With arms and legs wrapped around the wire, he pulled himself out over the street. He crossed quickly and unnoticed, the sentries below too busy talking and smoking, or gambling and smoking, or merely smoking. Looking to the left and right.

But not above.

Reaching out with his lead hand, Rechs grabbed the uppermost ledge of the fortress known as Chung's Pit, his legs still wrapped around the cable. Ten feet above lay a series of wide, almost transom-like windows beneath the curved roof of the fortress. It was through these that the thunder and roar of crowd noise escaped to sweep out across the district in triumphant ululations or angry groans of despair.

Working slowly, Rechs retrieved a grappling needle from his cargo pocket and raised his other gauntleted arm above his bucket, willing his body to become one with the wall. Blindly, he fitted the grappling needle into the left bracer of his armor and waited for the pneumatic hiss that meant it had locked into place.

He picked out his target. Guarding two of the transoms was an old, hand-carved lion—or maybe it was a dog—just like the ones along the roof.

Some form of Sinasian gargoyle, thought Rechs as he aimed for the thing's chin and sent the bolt straight through its stone head. The grapples deployed out the other side of the snout. The hold was good.

Rechs didn't trust the old stone not to crumble, so he resisted the temptation to let the armor simply winch him up into position. Instead he free-climbed, using the nano-cable to bear some of the weight. Upon reaching the window he released the cable, leaving the grappling bolt in the gargoyle. He had two spares and no time if what he saw below, inside Chung's Pit, was to be believed.

Dragon Identified read a display on Rechs's HUD.

Rechs had downloaded the non-guild termination contract, of course. That had been virtually step one in his research. Now, it seemed that the program had encrypted some sophisticated bio-scan data purposed with telling any hunter or assassin on the trail that they had the right target. He should have put in the time to decrypt it, but it was obviously a tough nut to crack.

But there it was, plain to see.

Dragon Identified.

And if that wasn't a mistake, then the Dragon was in a lot of trouble.

Rechs slithered through the transom onto some kind of maintenance catwalk above the crowd. He moved quickly behind a sculpted support pillar curling with serpentine dragons, the gold leaf flaking from their snarling jaws.

Row upon row of Sinasian men, shouting and angry, sweaty and desperate, roared in the small arena below. A pall of cigarette smoke hung in the room like a storm front as vendors moved through the crowd taking bets or selling steaming bowls of fried rice.

On the floor of the arena lay several men. Some clearly had had their necks broken. Others lay with busted arms. Some had been gutted by blade. Exotic weapons lay around them, sometimes within reach of the twisted and forever broken bodies. As though in their last moments the dead's last hopes had been just tantalizingly out of reach.

Four men were alive. Three wearing red headscarves and black pajamas, each carrying a melee weapon, circled the one identified as the Dragon. He was shirtless, with deep brown skin.

And he was unarmed.

One of the men whirled a ball and chain. He launched the weapon from its deadly orbit above his head, straight at the Dragon.

The Dragon dodged, bending like a cobra rearing to strike in order to avoid the weighted ball. He reached up and grabbed the trailing chain as it passed by.

Even to Rechs, who was rightly rumored to have some of the fastest reflexes in the galaxy, the Dragon's agility was incredible. He pulled the chain from the man's hand with a mere yank, then raced forward at him, knotting chain lengths around both fists.

The attacker seemed stunned into immobility, as if nothing in his mind had ever prepared him for this turn of events. Who could have imagined such an unforeseen and rapid counterattack?

The other two men, one holding a short tanto-style sword with a red cord and feather, and the other a gleaming, wickedly curved tomahawk, seemed just as stunned. They stood dumbfounded as the Dragon passed the chain over the first attacker's neck, executed a cartwheel, and snapped the man's neck.

The chain was dropped from the Dragon's hands before the dead man's body hit the arena floor. Resuming a fighting stance, the Dragon thumbed his nose and bounced slightly up and down on the balls of his bare feet.

The crowd erupted in cheers.

Regaining themselves, the two remaining attackers came at the Dragon with swift, economical cuts. They clearly weren't amateurs when it came to blade fighting. Working as a team, they kept the Dragon shifting at the waist to avoid blows. With each cut through the air, the Dragon gave ground in short, staccato steps.

And then, almost unbelievably, the Dragon threw a blindingly swift jab into the windpipe of the tomahawk-wielder. Rechs thought he could hear the crunch of the busted airway.

Instantly the man went from attacking to struggling simply to breathe. The panic Rechs knew all too well showed in his eyes.

The Dragon turned away from the flailing man, content to let him die fighting for one last breath.

The remaining swordsman flowed into a series of twirling cuts, never allowing the blade to stop threatening its target with sudden jabs and thrusts. His body stayed in motion from a seemingly limitless supply of energy.

Again the Dragon gave ground. And then he simply reached out and grabbed the swordsman's forearm mid-stroke. Rechs could see from the way the shirtless man's muscles moved that he was not fighting the blow, not trying to break the arm. He wasn't forcing anything. Instead the Dragon simply redirected the blade's next pass into the lower abdomen of its wielder.

All in the blink of an eye.

The force of the twirling body drove itself down onto the sharp tip. The man was still standing, run through by his own weapon as the Dragon walked away, rolling his sweaty shoulders and shaking out his fists.

As the swordsman fell over to die, the crowd erupted once more in a gleefully ecstatic wave. Any groans of dissatisfaction were all but absent now, save from those few who took the wrong bet.

Rechs had thought the Dragon was in trouble. He was wrong. The Dragon was the killer. Like a wolf among lambs who thought they were lions and discovered only too late that he was impossible to kill. Because he wasn't just a wolf... he was a Dragon. A thing that surpassed understanding.

The Sinasians had no idea what Project Phoenix had done to the Dragon. What it had made him into.

But Rechs did. He knew what the plan had been all along. He'd just forgotten it. Because he'd had to. Because he'd wanted to.

He'd *allowed* it to happen. Even saw it once. But to interact… would have ruined it. At least according to the researchers.

Still… there had been that day in the forest. In the rain.

Ball.

They had wanted to make their own Rechs.

Now, thought Rechs, forgetting all those mad scientists and their plans, the rightful heirs of the Savages, *how to get the kid out of here?*

Who?

Ball.

The kid.

How to get the kid out of here?

He scanned the crowd looking for the catalyst of it all. The colonel who showed up as "redacted" on all those secret memos and files. Ajax. The one who had seen the potential and whispered what *really* needed to happen.

Ajax. Another piece of Rechs's memory fell into place.

If Rechs was right… if the Dragon really was leading a new Sinasian revolt… then Colonel Ajax would be here.

But so far there was no sign of the legendary Dark Ops commander. Everyone Rechs could see was Sinasian. Almond eyes, dark hair, skin tones that ran from ashen gray to an almost glowing brown. Long ago they'd been a dozen different races throwing in together to get off the nightmare that Earth had become. Now, two millennia later, they'd all tell you they were simply Sinasian.

No gaijin, thought Rechs, wondered how he'd first learned that old word that meant "outsider" in its less polite form.

Another tale from another time.

And then he spotted her. An unexpected player. A blonde. Ponytail sticking out from under a ball cap. Tac vest. Cargo pants and boots. Mirrored shades. In the back. Under the shadows of the upper levels. She was watching too.

Bounty hunter?

Not one of the bounty hunters Rechs knew. No armor. Not carrying every weapon in the world. Maybe she was strapped on her thigh, but Rechs couldn't see her that far down. Her body was below the crowd, shielded by a sea of faces. But she still stood out, despite the hat and sunglasses.

Dark Ops?

Maybe. Nether Ops, more likely.

Rechs was turning over the question of how to get the kid out of here, off Taijing, and to a place where the House of Reason couldn't have him killed, when four more contestants—this time wearing royal blue and carrying staves—entered the arena.

In short order, even as teams of men were still dragging the bodies of the recently deceased away from the center of the corpse-littered floor, the Dragon set to work on the newcomers.

Because Rechs knew that's all it was to the Dragon: *work.* Even though others might have called it art. To the ones charging it was a fight to the death—for love or glory or money. For any of the reasons men think up to justify a death match. But to the Dragon it was work.

In no time he was breaking bones with powerful kicks, shattering the whirling wooden bo staffs of his opponents and dodging gut-busting thrusts that passed harmlessly into the thin air the Dragon once occupied.

A succession of three twirling roundhouse kicks shattered three jaws, sending blood spraying and teeth flying. The closest any of the new attackers got to harming the Dragon was when one landed a bell-ringer upside the Dragon's head. That blow would have stunned most men, or at least made them sit down and see double for a few minutes.

But not so with the Dragon. He threw a series of punches, badly aimed but enough to drive his foe back, until he regained his focus and landed a flurry of whirlwind haymakers against his lone remaining target.

The reward for striking the Dragon was to bear the brunt of an assault that was neither furious nor recklessly driven by pain. It might have looked that way to virtually everyone else in the arena… but not Rechs. The bounty hunter, observing from above, saw a man calibrating an offensive system in light of new data. Staff upside the head and seeing double? Switch to a rush of blows designed to move your opponent to the defensive. Make them withdraw. And if they don't move, make them protect as they hold position.

Which is perfect when you can't see straight. Stand still so I can know where to hit you.

Which was how it turned out.

Savagely so.

The last fighter went down hard, breathing heavily. For a moment it looked like the Dragon was going to let him lie there like a sack of forgotten laundry. Then, like a jackhammer, he raised one bare heel to just the height needed, and rammed it down onto the man's exposed neck.

Payback.

Don't hit the Dragon. That's a free lesson. The dead guy paid with his life for it.

Which was also part of a system. A plan. Did they hurt you? Never let your enemies know how badly. Teach them that hurting you makes them suffer more. The next bunch would remember that lesson for sure. Swings and attacks would come with the memory of a neck breaking with such a loud crack that Rechs heard it high above.

Already a new batch with new colors and a new variety of weapons were coming out.

Tyrus Rechs didn't have all day to watch the spectacle.

And evidently, neither did another team of bounty hunters. Newcomers.

Bounty hunters generally worked alone. Teams were rare. And when well coordinated, they were incredible to behold. These arrived with shock and awe, going all out. A small section of the roof was blown open, sending teak shards raining down into the crowd. Immediately two massive repeating blasters opened up from the upper gallery. Support fire for the snatch team moving in. But where were they?

Rechs covered himself behind a pillar-like cross-section of the catwalk, scanning the panicked and fleeing crowd through his blaster's scope. He switched the optics from CQB to ranged.

The hunter team's heavy high-cycle blaster fire raked the crowd indiscriminately, doing horrible things to the Sinasians who were trampling each other as they ran for cover. Some remained in their seats, bewildered. Each heavy blaster worked a different side of the vast chamber.

Eyes on the Dragon, Rechs reminded himself, and looked at his objective. The kid was running for an opening that must lead into locker rooms or a waiting area for the contestants beneath the pit of the arena.

That was when the Dragon got nailed by a sniper with serious skills.

It was a low-power shot that took him right in the leg. Professionally executed to stop him from moving.

Mission accomplished. The Dragon tumbled end over end across the floor of the arena.

Rechs spotted the sniper working from behind a grand and opulent coupling of intertwined golden dragons that was the centerpiece of the room, just below the roof and just above the highest tiers of seating. Rechs lined up a shot that knocked the man back into the shadows, then he squeezed off three more rounds where his HUD told him the man might be lying. Just for good measure. No sense in having a sniper with room to choose.

One of the heavy gunners swiveled his weapon on its tripod, seeking to eliminate this new threat. The incoming blaster fire was overwhelming. Stone exploded, teak splintered, and the metal catwalk clanged and dented as blaster bolts rammed home. But Rechs was already moving. Shifting positions to get to the Dragon who lay wounded on the floor of the arena.

Rechs heard the howl of reverse thrusters as a dropship came in close to the hole in the roof. It was a little too soon for a Legion QRF to already be responding to a shooting in this district. That meant it had to be the bounty hunters' snatch team coming in for the grab. They didn't want a kill. They wanted to see if they could get paid a little more for a *live* Dragon. Or perhaps they were hoping to bargain, threaten to let him go unless their price was met. *Then* they'd kill him.

Three rappel lines uncurled and hit the floor with length to spare. A trio of armored players then fast-roped into the arena, two with blaster rifles slung over their shoulders and one with a stun pistol at the ready.

Hidden among the gargoyles surrounding and obscuring the catwalk, Rechs fired at the ones with the more lethal weapons first, hitting one of the men and knocking him off the rope halfway through his descent. The fast-roping bounty hunter flailed in the air before landing face-first with a sickening thump on the arena floor, his corpse finding a home among those the Dragon had killed.

The other two reached the bottom seconds later. Rechs took a second shot, going again for a hunter with a blaster rifle. He knocked the man to his back. He was down, and the smoking hole in his armor said he was hurt, but he still fired wildly back at Rechs while his partner moved toward the Dragon, who was still lying prone.

Having revealed himself again, Rechs had to move once more as both heavy gunners swiveled their weapons and opened up. Rechs abandoned the catwalk, using his jets to hop down to the arena's top seating tiers. Then he ran down the concrete steps, seeking the cover of the next gallery.

The heavy blaster fire was leading him, sending explosive plumes of seating, concessions, and concrete flooring up in the air mere feet in front of him. He dove over a railing and landed out of the gunners' line of sight in an access tunnel. Though he was still on the upper level, from here he could see the Dragon, and the gunners couldn't see Rechs.

The Dragon slithered on the ground like a snake, like you'd expect someone who'd been shot through the leg to do. The man with the stunner approached—almost arrogantly so. The conquering victor arriving to claim his prize.

So much for this… *Dragon.*

In a blur of motion, the Dragon whipped his legs into a scissor kick, sweeping the guy with the stunner off his feet and causing him to land unceremoniously on his back. The stun pistol clattered across the floor.

All eyes were again on the arena, as though the bounty hunters who'd come to take the Dragon were now content to watch just what the man could do.

Rechs decided to let the Dragon deal with the man in the arena. He seemed more than capable. Now was the best time for Rechs to take care of the mounted heavy gunners.

The ancient bounty hunter ran for the next set of tiered seating and leapt, firing his jump jets to fly out above the arena. He moved quickly toward the gunners through the air. They opened up, jamming the butterfly triggers with their thumbs even as they tried to drag their heavy weapons and targeting reticules onto a flying, moving, closing target. The old blaster cannons, great for suppression and open warfare, were not ideal at close range.

Rechs maintained altitude just long enough to fill both blaster gunners with at least three blaster bolts apiece. The gunners' armor might have saved their lives—or it might not have—but either way, they were certainly wounded to the point where fighting was no longer an option.

Rechs continued downward in a slow arc to the arena floor. Cutting the jets, he landed with a fury of grit among the corpses littering the arena. He was no more than twenty meters from the Dragon, who'd taken a blaster off one of the dead.

The Dragon brought the blaster to bear faster than Rechs thought possible, aiming it him just as Rechs was about to say something... though he wasn't sure what.

Hold!

Don't fire!

I'm here to rescue you!

Something.

The kid fired on full auto. Blaster fire slammed into Rechs's armor and smashed into his medium blaster, knocking it from his hand. Each shot was like a jack-hammer, driving Rechs to his knees. His HUD flared with emergency damage information and armor integrity warnings. And something had gotten through. He felt the hot sear of a bolt that had grazed his arm as he tried to cover himself.

On his knees and panting, his forearm on fire, Rechs watched as the kid turned and ran for a tunnel. More dropships were coming in overhead.

Rechs picked himself up, shaking all over and breaking out into a cold sweat. Adrenaline pumped his body full of fight over flight. Getting shot that quickly with bolts on target had been no small thing. Even Tyrus Rechs wasn't sure he could have made it look that easy.

He looked down. His medium blaster was smashed and smoking from a shot through the energizing chamber. It was useless. And Rechs was lucky he hadn't lost any fingers.

He pulled his hand cannon and checked the load. He hadn't wanted to use the slug thrower, because there was no way to dial a bullet down if he needed to, but now he would need it. It was fully loaded. Something he already knew. That was standard operating procedure before any op and every time he put on the armor. But his mind was trying to reboot. If the kid had kept firing instead of leaving to escape... Tyrus Rechs would be dead.

"No time to think about that," Rechs growled, sounding angry at himself. Which was how he'd dealt with all the other times he'd come within a razor's edge of death. By yelling at himself to move or die. He'd learned a long time ago that to think too much about those times of near death was to go mad.

And going mad wasn't an option. Not for Rechs. Not with his mission to wait out along galaxy's edge for...

... *for what?*

His mind asked such questions at the most random of times.

For what?

No time, he told himself. *Move. Or don't ever move again.*

Hand cannon out, he raced across the arena and into the darkness of the tunnel that had swallowed the Dragon. He was unsure whether his mission was still to save the kid, or if he was going to have to kill him.

Save the Dragon...

Kill the Dragon...

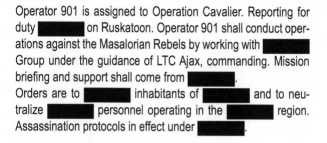

Operator 901 is assigned to Operation Cavalier. Reporting for duty ███████ on Ruskatoon. Operator 901 shall conduct operations against the Masalorian Rebels by working with ███████ Group under the guidance of LTC Ajax, commanding. Mission briefing and support shall come from ███████.
Orders are to ███████ inhabitants of ███████ and to neutralize ███████ personnel operating in the ███████ region. Assassination protocols in effect under ███████.

Legion Personnel Assignment

19

THE CAVERNS BELOW CHUNG'S PIT WERE DARK AND full of support pillars and wide-open spaces. Many of the combatants the Dragon had killed had been brought down here and left for someone else to clean up. Rechs switched to low light. He could see tunnels leading off in several directions. Some out of the building, no doubt. Others down into the superstructure of the old astrodrome.

He heard boots coming down the ramp behind him. He spun, hand cannon at the ready as a woman shouted, "Tyrus Rechs!"

It was the blonde. She had a heavy Python blaster out, and she followed the sights as she moved forward. In the darkness she switched on an ultra-beam.

Rechs slipped behind a pillar as she came down into the darkness, calling his name.

If she was Nether Ops, or even one of the new ones from Dark Ops who hadn't been smartened up by the old vets, then she'd know how much the House of Reason wanted him dead. And executing that termination order, as it was called in certain government circles, meant that a whole new world would open up for her.

"Rechs, I know that was you! I need you to come out so we can talk."

Still Rechs waited, hand cannon up and near his bucket. His finger moved the selector switch to single fire without even thinking. She wasn't wearing any armor. One round would do the job if that's what it came to.

But, if he was being honest with himself, Rechs wasn't exactly sure if what he was doing at that moment was the right thing. The Dragon's blaster bolts, all on target, had rattled him—to say the least. Was the girl really the one he should be thinking about putting down?

Was she here for the Dragon but willing to take Rechs as a consolation prize?

And in either case, who was she with? The bounty hunters? A spotter?

Someone had to have been inside before the hit team made their play. Someone had to have confirmed that the Dragon was in the building.

Was...

"Rechs, I'm here to *save* the Dragon!" she said breathlessly. "Just like you... General."

Her voice sounded lost and forlorn down in the caverns beneath Chung's Pit. But how could any sound be anything but lost and forlorn in the miasma of the underfloor beneath an arena of death? The misery of this place was a palpable thing.

"Or at least," she continued, walking right past him, invisible in the dark, sounding almost as if talking to herself. "I *think* you're trying to save him."

Rechs stepped out from behind her, his massive hand cannon pointing at her head.

"Who are you?"

The woman took a deep breath and lowered the snub-nosed Python she held with both hands.

"Captain Wendy Jacobson. Republic Marines, discharged. Nether Ops."

Rechs raised his weapon to shoot.

"It's not like that!" she shouted in a last bid effort at self-preservation. "I'm Section Six."

Rechs pulled his finger off of the trigger, if only for a moment. "What's a Section Six? Wasn't a thing back in my day."

"No. It wasn't. We're black book funded. Private. Relatively new. About five years. Our purpose is to keep the Republic from hurting itself despite orders from the House of Reason. Not every corner of Nether Ops is corrupt. Not all of the House of Reason serves itself."

"Hmmmm…" hummed Rechs. What she was describing was technically treason. But it was the sort of treason that needed doing to keep the Republic from consuming itself.

"General… you could have killed him, but you didn't. I watched the whole firefight go down. You were trying to save him. We are too."

"We?"

"Me. Really. Everyone else thinks he went out to the edge. Tusca was the last spot they were all focusing on. I went through his file and made a guess that he would… come home."

"Good guess. What was going on? Before they showed up?"

By "they," Rechs meant the bounty hunter hit team.

"He was uniting the clans," Jacobson said. "They're all Sinasian, and that's all they ever claim to be. But when you dig deep down, there are ancient clan loyalties—probably carried over from Asia, if that was a real place."

"It was."

Jacobson paused, as if considering whether she should ask how Rechs knew that. "Well, whatever the origin, these ancient tribal loyalties are strong, even if none of them know why."

"Why does that require a series of death fights?" Rechs asked. He was still so rattled that he couldn't see how the pieces fit together.

"In order to lead the tribes—there are over eight of them—you have to beat their best warriors. It's the same thing Gatsu did back during the Savage Wars, when he brought all of Sinasia to the Savages."

"Okay. But he was fighting three and four men at a time."

"Yeah." Jacobson smiled and looked down, as though taken with the Dragon's otherworldly abilities. "He, uh, told them to bring their first, second... up to fifth best."

"And now the tribes are all behind him? Or has that not happened yet because those hunters interrupted the ceremony?"

She made a face and holstered her weapon, slowing down when Rechs straightened his shooting arm. "Most of it already happened officially prior to today. He beat the vast majority of those who challenged his authority as khan. And even if he didn't kill them all, I'm sure that the others are giving prayers of thanks that they didn't have to go up against him. So my guess is... *yeah*. He's the one. They'll go for it with him in charge. All the worlds of Sinasia will rebel."

Rechs gave an imperceptible moan. "And the Legion will be sent in to kill everybody."

Jacobson nodded. "All the Sinasians need are military-grade arms. And the thing about that is—"

An ominous howl filled the tunnels, like a jet engine suddenly humming to life, throbbing and pulsing, its energy levels rising.

Rechs turned toward the noise. "That sounds like the engine system of a..."

"Samurai," Captain Jacobson finished while Rechs's memory was still diving into the deep corners of his mind to find the word.

A Samurai. He'd once faced them in a battle where, at its worst point, thousands died every second.

"Word on the street is that they've resurrected their old tech." Jacobson shook her head as she spoke. "But they've updated it. New components... materials... all new design."

"Who's paying for that?"

"We think it's the Mid-Core Rebellion. They have... deep pockets. From somewhere. And they desperately want to make a name for themselves in the galaxy."

For all their bluster, the Mid-Core Rebellion wasn't considered much of a threat. A nuisance to local planetary militias and police forces, sure. Good for an ambush that might drop a leej or two in exchange for thirty of their own. But if they managed to instigate the second coming of the Sinasian Conflict... that would raise their reputation in a heartbeat.

Rechs was skeptical about what he was hearing. "There are monitors orbiting every planet. Advanced tech is forbidden. They can't even have blasters."

"How many blasters have you seen them with today? Can't and don't are entirely different things on Sinasia, General."

A second hum entered the soundscape.

"Twin engines," muttered Rechs. "Just like the old Samurais. Guess some things don't change."

But he was growing more and more sure about one thing: the kill order on the kid had been a good idea. The Dragon was on the verge of starting a major war inside the Republic. Sinasians would die. Legionnaires would die. And the House of Reason would find some way to line their pockets.

Maybe…

"We think we can get him out of this, Rechs."

"How?"

"Because it's not him. It's Lieutenant Colonel Ajax. The Dragon is under his spell."

That seemed plausible. Ajax wrote the book on psychological warfare. He was the galaxy's foremost expert on creating and then recruiting factions to fight for a cause.

"With what we've been able to get our hands on in Section Six, our take on this situation is that the Dragon can be brought in, that his mind can be cleaned."

"And then he can become an unstoppable hit man for your department."

"No. And then he'll be *thanked* for his service and hidden somewhere so he can live to a nice old age. We're the good guys, General. We don't want to kill him. He's saved the Republic and countless soldiers several times over."

Rechs studied her. Tried to find some fracture or lie in her that would allow him to pull the trigger and clear her from his back trail so he could concentrate on following the Dragon. What seemed like an eternity—probably to both of them—passed as Rechs, unmoving, weighed his options.

"Follow me," he finally said, heading into the tunnel from which the evil sound of the twin engines was coming. It was like a war cry one never stopped hearing even though the battle was long over.

20

THEY RAN FOR THE END OF THE TUNNEL, PASSING through the darkness. Rechs didn't slow his pace, trusting that Captain Jacobson could find her way without imaging assist gear.

Halfway down the tunnel they heard massive hydraulics engaging. Some ancient low creaking sound like a gate being winched open. Locks slipped out of place with ominous booms. And then the unmistakable hushed roar of water rushing in.

"The lagoon!" shouted Captain Jacobson. "Someone's opened one of the old submersible locks!"

Water rushed toward them from the tunnel ahead. Rechs spotted a rung system built inside the tunnel leading to an upper level.

He pointed. "This way!" he shouted above the boom of the water hitting the walls.

Captain Jacobson didn't hesitate to take the rungs. The water was rising fast. Without low-light imaging or breathing equipment, she would drown in the dark. She made it up several rungs and looked down. The water was now a stream around Rechs's legs. He had ample room to climb up after her, but he just stood there.

"General! What are you doing?"

Rechs waded into the crashing waves, the weight and power of the suit keeping him from being swept away by the foamy iridescent green water now rising above his chest. "I'm going after him!"

And then he dove beneath the water.

His HUD confirmed breathing integrity and switched automatically to best imaging for underwater operations, which involved a combination of low light and the suit's active lidar imaging the dark tunnel ahead.

It took some hard kicking, even with the suit assist, for him to reach his destination: an ancient submersible diving hatch. He got there just in time see the head and shoulders of the old Samurai mech made new as it dropped through the hatch and into the waters beneath the floating city.

The water pressure had eased off; it was easier to move now. Rechs swam through the hatch, and it was like traveling through a window into another world.

Down below the lily pad city on top of the lagoon lay the sandy bed of a strange ocean. Despite having a floating city above it, blocking out much of the sun, it teemed with strange serpent-like fish that glowed in the bare light of the now-risen cracked moon, which cut through the gaps in the pads as through breaks in clouds.

Rechs spotted the Samurai weapon system—a humanoid-shaped mech—pulling itself hand over hand along the bottom of the launch platform. And then it was pulling itself up into the city between two lilies.

He's going for it, thought Rechs. *He's beaten the best his people have to offer, and now he's going to show them that the Legion can't stand up to him either.*

Especially if he got to bring a Samurai into the fight.

The war machine moved fast, swifter due to its size than Rechs could hope to keep up with. In seconds it was totally out of the water and on the surface streets of the floating city.

Rechs grabbed the underside of a platform to pull himself toward an opening out of the lagoon. Tidal currents pulled at him; the water seemed to want to fling him off and out into the open ocean. He fought hard to hold on, and eventually reached a gap in this strange landscape where the sky was the bottom of a city and the ground far below was a sunken aquamarine desert.

Before Rechs could surface, a dropship plunged into the water, smashing right through a nearby lily pad. It sank rapidly to the bottom of the lagoon, trailing bubbles along with the debris from the tiny island neighborhood it had just destroyed. The pilot, still inside the cockpit, head down against the controls, did nothing to rescue himself from the watery descent.

Other people now entered the lagoon as well, jumping into various rifts in the floating city of ten thousand lily pads, apparently attempting to escape whatever mayhem was going on above the surface.

Rechs pulled himself from the lagoon. Water streamed off his armor as he rose to his feet on a dock that ran alongside a two-story apartment. Singsong violin music warbled out of a bot who seemed oblivious to the recent abandoning of a waterfront bar. Drinks were left next to still-smoldering cards and ivory tiles on round tables, the chairs all kicked over from a mad dash to get away.

Rechs moved quickly around the bar to a broader route through the city. In the distance, over the rooftops, he saw the four-story gargantuan Samurai mech moving away, leaving destruction in its wake.

He had faced these beasts back at the Battle of Ono. They had been the Sinasians' elite armored fighting system. Paired with infantry, they'd almost been impossible to take out. Artillery strikes couldn't pin them, and their anti-air capability had been state-of-the-art. Shooting their legs out from under them had been the only option. And that hadn't been all that easy.

Republic R&D created the HK-PP model specifically to deal with this threat. Rechs wondered if any were stationed here on Taijing—though it would take more than one to take down the hulking Samurai.

A memory from the war came to Rechs then. Some forward legionnaire calling out over the comm, "Samurai inbound!"

And panic swept through the trenches.

Now the mech had returned.

Tracking the Samurai through the floating city required no skill; Rechs simply followed the wake of destruction. Whole blocks of housing were flattened or reduced to splinters. Fires were everywhere. The occasional Sinasian stared in horrified disbelief at what had become of their homes, their neighborhoods.

In the distance dropships were lifting off, their searchlights scanning the waters and area around the Repub base that watched over this area of the protectorate.

The Legion was inbound for a response.

But the first Legion dropship to get close had never engaged a Samurai mech during the Savage Wars. How could they have? That had happened years before any of these kids had been born. Rechs looked up as a pack of missiles, like a nest of smoking snakes, streaked out and slammed into the slow-moving dropship approaching on a direct intercept.

The other two dropships broke off their attack. Missiles streaked at them as well, but this time they didn't find their target. Legion tech had definitely upped its ECM game since the days of the Conflict, and the confused missiles veered away. In the Savage Wars, those missiles wouldn't have been fooled.

Rechs moved forward, aware that at any moment the Dragon might check his back trail and send a slew of missiles straight at him. His armor was already badly damaged. If he couldn't get the system's personal defense shield up, an unreliable thing at best, Rechs would be cooked for sure.

Legion dropships were descending below building level now, dropping squads of legionnaires so they could deploy their anti-armor weaponry. And near the main bridge over the city a furious firefight was underway. The giant mech was using both of its wrist-mounted mini-blaster cannons, cycling them like ancient Gatling guns on some unseen target. A swath of fiery destruction erupted over that portion of the city.

Rechs was about to see if he could get ears on the general L-comm to find out how bad it was going for the leejes when he heard someone call his name.

Not Captain Jacobson. Someone with a voice gruff and harsh. Like a monster growling through a mouthful of bloody meat.

"Tyrrrusss Rrrechsss!"

The bounty hunter turned.

It was Harsk.

Harsk wasn't a famous bounty hunter, more like… infamous. He took bounties indiscriminately, but preferred terminations. And he kept himself out of every other bounty hunter's good graces by repeatedly violating a cardinal rule: Don't collect on other hunters' contracts.

Everything was fair game for Harsk.

The guild had suspended him a number of times. Rechs had no idea what his current status was.

Harsk was a Boson from that violent, almost prehistoric world of the same name. He looked like he was half Wolfman, half saber-toothed tiger. He didn't wear armor, preferring a jumpsuit and a utility belt to better allow the use of his natural agility and speed. His clawed hands were ungloved, and he had a wicked double-barreled blaster strapped to his thigh.

Rechs had holstered his hand cannon, and was regretting that right about now.

"Maybe no collect bounty on Arrdragggonssss…"

Rechs kept a close eye on Harsk's hands as the beast-man crossed the rubble-strewn street that lay between them. In the distance, doomsday sirens resounded across the city. A hiss of more missiles was followed by a string of explosions.

"Maybe collect on Tyrrrrusssss Rrrreechhhssss."

Harsk stopped a short way from Rechs, and the two bounty hunters stared each other down. Each watching the other like gunfighters on some ancient Earth street come out to settle grievances.

Rechs spoke calmly. "You can try, Harsk."

A distant fireball lit up Harsk's crimson fur and danced in his soulless, coal-black eyes. His fangs worked back and forth for a moment and then, with the speed his species was renowned for, he pulled the double-barreled blaster from his thigh.

Except he was already dead.

The pull hadn't even cleared leather. It just hung there halfway out of the big holster. Harsk opened his mouth in disbelief to roar, or rage... *something*. But nothing came out. Rechs had shot him twice in the chest. Drawing lightning quick in the moment he'd seen the first muscles of the beast began to yank the weapon up hard to fire at Rechs.

That fast.

Rechs engaged the Mark I armor's jump jets and bumped himself up to a nearby rooftop as Harsk dropped to his knees, blood now matting down the fur around his mouth.

The beast-man already put out of his mind, Rechs looked once more toward the action. The Samurai was now engaging a group of fighters firing from one bridge to another. Bounty hunters, by the looks of them.

The mech's mini-blasters raked the bridge they were fighting from, chewing it to shreds. A micro-missile lanced out from one of the bounty hunters and slammed into the war machine, blossoming into an orange fire flower of an explosion—but the Samurai mech was unfazed. It unleashed a full suite of missiles, and a series of explosions erupted in apocalyptic red along the bounty hunters' bridge.

Using his jump juice judiciously, Rechs hopped and bounced like a grasshopper from building to building, getting closer to the Samurai. Hoping to find a way to get the driver's attention. Hoping for a way to end this without the loss of millions of lives.

Then he remembered the laser comm.

He took a knee, switched over systems, and lased the mech. If it had standard comms, the operator would get a message request.

The response was immediate.

MESSAGE DENIED.

Rechs sent another.

I know who you are. I'm here to help.

MESSAGE DENIED.

This is General Rex. I'm here to help you.

MESSAGE DENIED.

The mech shot down a dropship like a hunter bagging a waterfowl. The ship exploded in midair, no chance of survivors as its fireball expanded across the sky, drowning out the bone-white moonlight that revealed the mech in its updated form.

Gone was the old Sinasian grayscale and white. Gone were the enigmatic markings and the raging red war flag of the old Sinasian military. Instead, this mech was skinned in nano-graphene carbon. It was like looking at a moving shadow. Or a giant nightmare. Missile pods cycled and reloaded. Both of its mini-blaster cannons were smoking from overuse. Wisps drifted up in the moonlight.

Thicker smoke trails abruptly blossomed away from its massive shoulders, right beneath the pilot's cockpit, and star shells streaked up into the night. All of this, Rechs knew, was part of its defensive package. Storm fronts of smoke and signal-jamming lighting.

Republic Lancer interceptors streaked over the battlefield, firing their blaster cannons.

The Samurai emerged from the cloud and strafed a retreating interceptor with deadly accuracy. The starfighter broke apart, its engines becoming vehicles of their own destiny as the main canopy exploded.

Then the mech moved back under its cloud of smoke and sent up more star shells like dying comets.

A second flight of Lancers swarmed in toward the mech. Catching glimpses of it through the billowing storm front it had shrouded itself in, the pilots released their ordnance. Old-school guided explosive munitions. Seconds of hang time were rewarded with a series of crescendoing explosions that ripped through that half of the city.

Squads of legionnaires moved into the mass of smoke, those with anti-armor launchers holding them ready on their shoulders. The dying infrared distracting flares the mech had fired were now falling onto the city, leaving defeated smoke trails in their wake. Starting fires at their landing.

Rechs had halted on a rooftop to watch all of this unfold.

The Legion, as always, had put together a sound battle plan. The noose around the Dragon was tightening, even if the kid was making the Republic pay a heavy price for it. And whether Rechs wanted to save the kid or not was about to become a moot point. Though the Legion had lost men and dropships, and the city it was charged with protecting was on fire, whole blocks having been destroyed, the mech couldn't stand up to the combination of overwhelming firepower from the air and infantry with anti-armor capabilities on the ground.

The Samurai emerged from the smoke, moving swiftly now, mini-blaster cannons roaring in every direction, sending hot blurs of bolts across whole sections of the city from which the Legion troops emerged. Wooden buildings and even the occasional impervisteel structure came to pieces as though they were nothing more than back-country postal boxes being shotgunned at close range.

The mech moved fast toward the Legion base just off the main bridge. Too fast, in fact. And there was something Rechs was seeing that his mind told him didn't add up.

Something that said this was a misdirection of some sort.

He wouldn't see it until later when he ran his bucket's playback over and over, again and again. But the recording was the truth: the Samurai pilot's canopy had blown, and the Dragon had ejected. But in that moment, as the metal monster stomped through the city, tearing through structures that stood in its way and blasting everything else to shreds, the spectacle was too jaw-dropping to take your eyes off of. Even for Tyrus Rechs.

And just shy of the gates to the Legion base, where dutiful legionnaires sent anti-armor missiles and a relentless barrage of fire from crew-served N-50s… the mech detonated.

The bright flash lit up the night. And then came the expanding debris wave. The base spared only because of its modern materials and designs. The bridges and the stews and all the other nearby structures either collapsed or were blown away.

And then the uncountable massive chunks of those buildings and stews and bridges slammed into the rest of the city, creating even more damage and destruction.

For someone seeking to save the Sinasians, the Dragon sure was putting a hurting on its residents.

Rechs threw himself down on the roof of the building from which he watched all this, expecting it to topple as the blast wave reached him. But he was still far enough away that the building miraculously held on and remained upright, though it swayed like a drunken point arriving to inspect PT.

And when the bounty hunter got back to his feet, a thousand fires were spreading their way across what remained of the city within the blast radius. Everything was charred black. And the structures of the few buildings that remained looked like the skeletal hands of a corpse sticking out from the grave.

After-Action Review
Operation Cavalier, Engagement at Howda Wells

On ██████ an enemy force estimated to be well above brigade strength came out of the Suma Desert east of Fardur. Intel from Operator 901, embedded with loyal tribesmen of the Suntee faction, stated that this was indeed the force of the Grand Pashwanda of Sulitgo that we have been attempting to engage in battle.

The decision to commit our few on-planet forces to the battle was reached after conferring with Dark Ops Command and authorized by General ██████. It was further directed that the House of Reason is still not to be informed of our operations in this sector.

As we moved our main force out from the green zone via armored sleds, battlefield recon and planning was left to Operator 901.

The engagement took place on ██████ at ██████ as designated by Operator 901. Due to superior positions on the field, the ambush that destroyed enemy forces resulted in few casualties. Most of the fighting was done by the locals under the direction of Operator 901.

Of note: Operator 901 has so captured the hearts and minds of our allies that the local war leaders allowed him the first drink of the dead Pashwanda's blood once the body was recovered. The ceremony cemented an alliance between the Republic and the local forces.

Operator 901 has proven himself to be the kind of officer I have always attempted to be. Given the nature of the non-traditional operations our command engages in, I highly recommend him for advanced training, and eventual command as my replacement, once I am promoted.

LTC Ajax
Commander, Operation Cavalier

21

Rechs made his way back through the burning wreckage, wandering the ruined streets for several hours in the long march back to the *Crow*. His ancient armor was covered in so much ashy grit and black soot, scorched by the blast, that it seemed none of the survivors he passed thought of him as anything more than a legionnaire who had somehow survived the destruction. Or maybe just a lucky bounty hunter who'd managed not to get killed in the shootout between rampaging mech and everyone else.

Rechs listened in to L-comm chatter, switching channels until he found some high-level intel. Taijing's Legion commander, along with a special Dark Ops shot caller running a pair of kill teams, were putting the pieces together, based largely on data provided to them by drones. The Dragon, it seemed, had ejected just before the mech detonated. At first there was some debate over whether he survived, but about an hour after the explosion, a Legion squad reported visual confirmation of the Dragon, under heavy fire, boarding a fast freighter bearing Kungaloorian ident codes. The ship blasted out of the port and jumped from low altitude. That took some stones—atmospheric jumps were always a tricky proposition. Unless you could afford a solid beacon via hyper-comm constantly updating the necessary calculations, it was a good way to get yourself killed.

Rechs had a pretty good idea where the Dragon was headed. It was a place that didn't exist, officially, on any of the stellar charts.

Shangri-La.

And therein lay the problem. No one knew where that fabled planet really was. There were rumors, but the galaxy was big enough to get lost in for a very long time if your only option was running down the whisper of a rumor.

Rechs needed hard intel. Someone had to confirm where Shangri-La was and how to access it. He would need to stick around on Taijing longer than he'd anticipated.

As soon as he'd made it back to the docking bays, Rechs found a local supervisor and bribed him to move the *Obsidian Crow* down into the delayed freight storage sections of the massive dock system burrowed into the side of the coastal mountain range, and to keep it off the records. Rechs waited on board his ship as preparations were made.

The smart play is to get in the air and clear out of Taijing, he told himself. The Republic was about to get even more interested in this place than before, after the rampage and detonation of the Sinasian Samurai mech. A weapons system that wasn't supposed to exist anymore.

And if the clandestine search for the Dragon had seemed chaotic and overwhelming, what would come now that the House of Reason had a public excuse to go after the operator... well, it would be nigh-impossible to keep in front of. The Republic would be swarming all over this planet in search of a very definite lead on their number one target.

And with all those extra eyes, someone was sure to score a sighting of the galaxy's *second*-most-wanted man.

Still, with the *Crow* hidden from anyone checking docking registrations for a medium freighter, Rechs had a little bit of room to maneuver. He only needed to stay out of sight, and he'd remain out of the Republic's mind so long as the Dragon occupied its interest. Besides, he wouldn't be here long—just long enough to find out how to follow the Dragon's ship.

A tug came into the bay on repulsors, tractored the *Crow,* and began the deep and dark journey into the freight levels. Eventually the ship was hidden behind a large wall of Duranium-loaded shipping containers awaiting verified transport.

Rechs racked his battered armor and treated his wounds—of which the blaster graze on his arm was the worst. Once everything was cleaned, sterilized, and bandaged, he took a good look at the armor. Its nano-systems would repair given time, but right now it was pretty much shot to hell.

Rechs's stomach had been empty and complaining ever since his adrenaline levels had died down during the march through the city. He now devoured two steaks out of the meat locker and then forced himself to eat some vegetables. Sated, he swallowed a tranquilizer and passed out.

Eighteen hours later, he came to.

Someone was banging on the outer hatch of the supposedly hidden and untraceable *Obsidian Crow.*

***

Captain Jacobson was standing at the top of the boarding ramp. For a moment Rechs just watched her, still rubbing the sleep out of his eyes.

Then he opened the external hatch comm. "What?"

"He's not dead," she said rather stridently. Like somehow it was Rechs's fault.

"And?" grumbled Rechs.

He debated whether he should just start the engines, clear her off, taxi to the main exit tube the big freight lifters used, and make the jump. If she knew he was here, hiding down in stores, then who else knew?

"I haven't told anyone you're here, General," she said as if reading his mind from the other side of the lock.

Rechs didn't like that. How she called him *General*. She didn't know him. Didn't serve with him. It was a manipulative piece of work—using a title of intimacy to make their relationship seem like it was deeper than it actually was. But he was too busy trying to clear the cobwebs from a mind mummified by sleep to point out that he wasn't *her* general.

"Who is she?" asked Lyra quietly. Ethereal and present all at once on Rechs's side of the hatch.

"Nobody," muttered Rechs, ignoring the complications that seemed to be multiplying by the second.

He hadn't even had his coffee yet.

He decided to open the lock and let the Nether Ops captain in.

A few minutes later, over steaming cups of instant coffee in a lounge nearly overtaken by the sprawl of

Rechs's weapons and special projects, Captain Jacobson sat studying Rechs from above the rim of her cup.

Lyra had been silent since the pretty blonde had come aboard.

"So the legends are true," she remarked, looking Rechs up and down. This was her first time seeing him in the flesh sans the Mark I armor. "You look like a perfectly fit middle-aged man. Or do you prefer... man of a certain age?"

Rechs raised his eyes from his coffee, hoping to convey how stupid and silly he felt the comment was.

"Is it always so dark in here?" she asked, changing the subject. Trying to start over.

"Yeah," said Rechs. Dark was how he liked it.

That ended the small talk.

But this wasn't just Rechs being his usual laconic self. Jacobson knew something, and Rechs didn't completely trust her. Sometimes, he had found, going silent caused people to spill what they knew out of sheer nervousness. Out of some need to fill up the very silence Rechs so preferred with the noise, chatter, and constant babble of galactic civilization.

"I guess... Shangri-La?" Jacobson said.

Rechs wondered how much she knew about the lost, supposedly mythical Sinasian world. Fantastic temples and actual dragons. Mist-shrouded mountaintop fortresses and rivers of death where legendary, mystical lotus grew. A place supposedly protected by the Sinasians and never touched by the Republic.

Anyone in the Sinasian government in a position to know always laughed off questions about Shangri-La. Like it was a running joke and they were playing their part yukking it up for political good will. Operating from a desire to be viewed as relatable. Down to earth.

But the rumors persisted. Lingered. Had never really gone away.

She was betting that Rechs knew about Shangri-La, too. And that the knowledge of such a place might make them unlikely partners in finding the Dragon. The question for Rechs was how much he was willing to give away.

He sat stoically, almost defiantly, as she watched him, taking occasional sips of her coffee. Her sculpted eyebrows and model good looks made her innately enigmatic. She looked like the movie version of how everyone thought a spy should look. Beautiful, cagey, intelligent.

In reality, the best spies always looked ordinary. That had been Rechs's experience. The kind of person who wouldn't make you think to take a second look. Those were the ones who had done the most damage.

"Why there?" grunted Rechs, draining his mug. He got up to make another cup.

"Where else?" Jacobson asked, rising to follow. "Six months ago, the Dragon got involved in a local dispute and killed half the local police force on some backwater planet. He'd been out for a year by that time, just… wandering."

"Huh," Rechs grunted noncommittally. Like none of this mattered to him.

"But he surfaced enough to provide us with enough reports to keep tabs on him. Our liaisons at the House told us he would be needed for something big in the near future involving the zhee. A counterinsurgency to turn all four tribes against each other for good. Let them wipe each other out and stop blowing up legionnaires. They thought the Dragon was the one to do it for them. He certainly had the track record."

She held out an empty cup to be refilled. She was standing close to Rechs, still wearing her black tactical LCE, cargo pants, boots, and a tight tank top. The cap and sunglasses were back on the table where she'd been sitting. The wicked little Python was on her shapely yet narrow hip.

She's dangerous, Rechs told himself. The old bounty hunter had been around long enough to spot the type. *In more ways than one.*

With weapons, for sure. But also with the beauty she knew she had. That much was obvious from the way she'd approached him, a sort of sultry walk that promised romantic sparks—a physical closeness not warranted for a simple refill of coffee.

Except Rechs was thinking about Lyra. He didn't want to hurt her. And he knew how crazy that sounded. He didn't want to hurt his AI.

You spend too much time with too many machines.

Rechs stepped away, leaving her holding her empty mug in an outstretched hand. He moved to the table and picked up a Maas subcompact auto-mag used for assault operations. He didn't like the weapon all that much. It burned through a charge pack in about thirty seconds of high-cycle fire, it sprayed wildly, and barrel control was impossible. But in a pinch, it would keep everyone's heads down long enough to take control of a situation and move to Plan B. Plus, he could use two, one in each hand, if he needed to clear a room. And they were extremely lightweight.

"General?"

Rechs looked back at Jacobson and set the weapon down. He picked up his coffee and took a fresh sip. "Sorry."

"That's why they were keeping him around," she continued. "They wanted to kick off something big."

"Okay."

She sighed. Took a deep breath and drank some of her coffee, wrinkling her nose at either the temperature or the strength of it.

"That's about the time when his old group leader got involved. Colonel Ajax. Man's the real deal. Don't get me wrong, he's not a... superhero like you or the Dragon. But he's a real operator from the Darks Ops glory days not long after you... disappeared."

Rechs waited, sure that the whole backstory was coming.

"This is the part almost no one on the hunt for the Dragon knows: Ajax busted him out of a Republic prison vessel on its way to Herbeer."

"They had him?" This surprised Rechs. He'd assumed the Dragon had been untouchable this entire time. To know that the Republic had once succeeded in capturing the man... Rechs was impressed.

"Oh, I see you've decided to come out of your shell. Yeah. They sentenced him to twenty years for wiping out half that security force I told you about—though from what I've gathered, he was justified. The hicks on that backwater got in over their head and pissed off the wrong drifter; the Dragon was just passing through. Security just happened to try and strong-arm the sort of guy who was especially skilled at giving people a hard time."

"So I've seen," mumbled Rechs and drank more coffee.

"Anyway, Ajax busts him out. And Dark Ops is waiting for about two weeks for them to show up back together."

"So he wasn't acting rogue in breaking him free?"

"We didn't think so. Not at first, anyway."

"But you do now." Rechs shrugged. "It happens."

He raised his eyebrows when she stopped and just stared at him. As if, to her, it was impossible that anyone would ever do such a thing. Betray their orders. Not show up for duty. Walk away from the Republic. The Legion. Everything that really meant anything.

"Well," she finally whispered. "They became ghosts."

They fall silent. Both content to think and finish their beverages.

But not for long. G232 scuttled into the lounge. Rechs was surprised it took the bot this long to interject himself into things.

"Oh!" G232 flailed awkwardly, as though startled to see the pretty blonde talking to Rechs. It seemed to be caught between fleeing toward the flight deck and backing away toward the engine room. "I am sorry to interrupt, master. How dreadful of me to have happened upon this intimate moment in your life."

Rechs waved a hand and the bot went off, looking awkwardly over its shoulder for a first, second, and third glance.

Captain Jacobson took the bot's appearance as a cue to restart the conversation. "We went digging into Ajax's background. He had a whole other life. He was very dissatisfied with how the Legion was running its operations—a real hawk. Thought the Legion commander should have gone Legion on more of its enemies. Accused the Republic of rot.

"I have unconfirmed intel that he's actually active with the mid-core rebels. The long story made short is that he thinks the Republic is weak. That we're open to the threat of external invasion from an extra-galactic entity. Crazy, I know. And now he's been working with the Divine Hand, a Sinasian freedom group, that wants to turn on the old war machine and liberate Sinasia and, according to what we were able to dig out of some of his contacts, replace the Republic with a benevolent dictator, someone like the Dragon, if not the actual Dragon.

"He saw his protégé… the Dragon… as the kid that could make this happen. A half-Sinasian orphan who had no real connection to the worlds other than a big blank space inside himself he was trying to find his identity in."

"You knew he was coming here all along?" asked Rechs, sure that she did.

"*I* knew it," she said, shaking her head. "Everyone else thought he was just on the run, wanting to disappear. I felt like he wasn't finished with something."

That was a lie, but Rechs didn't say anything. If the Republic thought the kid only wanted to disappear, then why would they bother with the massive bounty and a spot as the galaxy's most-wanted high-value target?

"But you don't think he's dangerous."

"Oh, no." Jacobson's eyes went wide. "I do. I think he's very dangerous. But that doesn't mean we kill him. It means we bring him in, treat him, and put him somewhere where he can be free to live out the rest of his life. That's the least we owe him, General."

There was that undeserved familiarity again. Rechs held back a snarl.

The captain continued. "Not a bolt in the back of the head because we're afraid the monster we created might use his skills against us. My reports—what I submitted to the committee involved at the highest levels on this—all place the blame on Ajax. The colonel is a like a father to the Dragon. After that little science project that was Project Phoenix—and I wish I knew more about that, whatever that was—after Legion Basic and some time in the One Thirty-First, it was Colonel Ajax who made him into what he is now.

"Ajax has power and control over our best infiltration and killing machine. A machine that doesn't merely kill but teaches others how to kill. The Dragon makes armies. That's what makes him so dangerous. Especially to the House of Reason. They want him dead right now because they are well and truly afraid of him. Justifiably."

Rechs nodded. "And you?"

"I want to save him. Give him a chance to be someone besides the Dragon. Grow old. Have a family. Die in peace."

Rechs watched her eyes.

She'd switched over from being a high-speed low-drag Nether Ops killer to... someone who cared for the Dragon. That was plain.

"The reports?" he asked.

She blinked. Came to herself. Put her coffee down and took a deep breath. "My background is psyops and profiling. They brought me in, gave me the parts of his file that hadn't been redacted, and asked me what I thought. I told them about Ajax, and not a single person believed me." She flicked the side of her mug, making a *tink* sound with her manicured fingernail. "But lo and behold, we're here with a division of legionnaires and a super-destroyer plus escort in orbit. I'd bet my captain's bars that ship is on standby for planet-wide orbital bombardment just in case. If they'd thought for a second this shot at the Dragon was all they were going to get, they'd have razed the entire city. They're that serious, believe me."

After what Rechs had seen... he didn't blame them.

"And in spite of everything that's happened, you still think you can get to him, clean up his mind, and disappear him?"

Jacobson stared at Rechs—wide-eyed but looking inward. "No. Not now. I thought that at first, back when I pulled every string to get attached to this expedition. Thought I could somehow change the course of events. But not after what he did to that city down there. No. I don't think I can rescue him. But you... you can. If anyone can... it's probably you. You're his only hope."

She paused.

"General—Rechs—I'm pretty sure that super-destroyer has a crustbuster planet-killer on board. And if they find the Dragon, they're gonna crack whatever planet he's on from orbit. Just to be sure."

22

RECHS AND CAPTAIN JACOBSON MADE THEIR WAY OUT into the Taijing afternoon. From the top of the docking levels, high up alongside the mountains that overlooked the port, they could see an almost perfect circle of black—the blast radius where the Samurai mech had detonated.

Much of the Legion base had been wrecked, as had the bridge leading to it. Luckily—amazingly—the city of ten thousand lily pads was still mostly intact, except for the large new pools where several had been damaged and sunk. And already those spaces were swiftly under reconstruction. Life on Taijing didn't seem to have much room to spare. One person's tragedy was someone else's opportunity.

Republic dropships crisscrossed the skies, ferrying legionnaires, supplies, and wounded to and fro within the city. The super-destroyer had moved down out of orbit and now hung over the city like an ominous cloud.

Jacobson's brow furrowed under the shadow of the massive warship. She turned to Rechs. "According to our intel, there's a Sinasian freighter pilot on Taijing who may know a route to Shangri-La. A smuggler's run. If he wasn't killed, maybe he can get us there, for a price."

That didn't seem like much of a starting point. "I wasn't aware there was a smuggler's run. And seems like anyone who knows it would already be rich enough to scoff at your price."

"The very few smugglers who know the way are understandably tight-lipped about it. And Nether Ops has more ways to convince people to do what we want than credits… if that's what it comes down to."

They started down the escalator to the first tram level. Rechs indicated with a silent flick of his eyes a legionnaire patrol stationed at the platform they were headed toward. Glass that had once formed the roof of the terminal had been blown out by the mech's blast.

"They're looking for the Dragon," observed Jacobson.

"Yeah."

They passed the squad without incident and took another tram down to the base of the mountain.

"Transfer here," Captain Jacobson said, and they stepped on yet another mover, which carried them along the bay to an old fishing village along the outer coast.

Here, away from the city, the locals seemed rougher and more suspicious, watching the outsiders with wary eyes and little chatter. The coastal sea had turned rough from an offshore depression, and rain came down in brief spasms.

Jacobson led Rechs into an old waterfront bar decorated in neon and fishing tackle. The bar area was half-crowded by obvious out-of-town types, whereas the locals dominated a terrace that hung out over the water. Evidently this was where they'd find the smuggler. They took a seat, and a Sinasian girl with painted eyes and a smoldering glare came over to take their order.

"You drinking?" she practically barked.

"Two beers," said Rechs.

"I don't like beer," Jacobson said once the waitress had gone.

"You'll learn," said Rechs.

He felt that to order anything fancier would only draw more unwanted attention, given how the server had been eyeing them.

A twin-hulled freighter, rust-red and white, roared off and out to sea, rattling the establishment's roof as it went. Two Lancers were escorting it away. For a moment the howling wake of the freighter and the fighters washed over the bar. Someone turned up the local pop, a whiny keening kind of dance beat, to full blast.

"They're verifying all freight traffic and escorting every ship leaving here," Jacobson whispered as the roar of the starships faded. "That'll be hard for your ship to get through."

Rechs said nothing.

"Beer," said the returning server, slamming two bottles down sloppily. She also threw down a greasy basket of hot and salty fried pork chips and a local hot sauce before departing, yelling something in Sinasian through a kitchen reach-through.

Rechs took a long pull on the ice-cold beer, then used his fingertip to push the wet ring of condensation it left on the table into dents and grooves along its surface. The beer tasted good. Maybe it was the sweltering heat. The rain. The smell of fish frying. Or of the pungent salty dipping sauce the locals liked with it. But that icy first swallow cleared the dust from his throat.

"You're Tyrus Rechs!" screamed a big Drusic from the shadows of the bar, its chair and table skidding across the room as it abruptly stood.

The bar got real quiet. Only the sound of frying fish and that annoying whiny pop playing on some device with a blown speaker. Everyone had heard the Drusic shout the bounty hunter's name, and everyone froze.

Rechs had been in situations like this more than once. But usually when he was in his armor. This one might be a bit trickier. Either way, he knew what to do next: say nothing and move his weapon hand as close to the blaster strapped on his thigh as he could get it. Because shooting was about to become the only option.

Someone thought they'd just hit the lottery.

Someone who wanted to get rich and didn't realize they were about to die trying.

"I know you from Noonidaar," the Drusic said, taking heavy footsteps toward Rechs. "There was a big fight there. You brought in Suba da-Tai. Nasty gangster who killed for Ozmodi and his boys? You were hit in your helmet and took it off right before you shot down Suba. Yeah, I know your face *real* well, Tyrus Rechs."

Rechs's fingertips brushed against his blaster. He glanced up at the speaker, giving the big Drusic a dismissive once-over, then lowered his eyes. His ears would tell him if the big alien moved in the least. Especially if he decided to pull.

"You got a problem with that?" asked Rechs. Except it didn't sound like a question. More like a statement. Or an accusation that was going to get someone in a lot of trouble.

Rechs had seen plenty of people back down when he put it that way.

The Drusic chose to stand. He had two blasters over his wide simian chest. No armor because there just wasn't any made to fit a species that size—unless it had the money for a custom job. Rechs had once seen a Drusic rip a man in half with his bare hands.

And they were fast. Fast enough that Rechs didn't chance a pull. Not yet.

Because they could be reckless.

Because everyone inside the cantina was in the way. Someone was going to get hit if blaster bolts started flying.

And, more than anything else, because that was going to draw the Legion. Rechs didn't need for them to become aware of the fact that Tyrus Rechs was planetside.

So he held off on settling accounts.

"Yeah, I have a problem!" roared the big ape, fangs bared. "Suba was *my* bounty. Worked on it for weeks, then you come in and kill everyone. You stole my contract!"

There was a longer story, one that the Drusic might have appreciated. But Rechs didn't think this was the time or place. Or that the big ape was a listener.

At that moment, the door to the bar swung open and in walked a human in a grease-stained tropical shirt, a leather coat, olive green cargo pants, and sports shoes.

"That's our pilot," Jacobson whispered, and for some reason Rechs would yell at himself about later, he took his eyes off the ape who was about to kill him and checked the newcomer.

What he saw was the clueless pilot now stopped dead in his tracks. Without prompting, the pilot raised his hands over his head. When Rechs looked back at the Drusic, he understood why.

Both of the alien's blasters were pointed right at Rechs's chest.

"Now I'm gonna shoot down the famous Tyrus Rechs and collect a nice big bounty."

Everyone in the bar was *real* interested now. Rechs watched as several hands went to several blasters. Everyone seemed to be feeling very lucky. Or at least… they thought they were.

"Get the pilot out of the bar when it starts," Rechs whispered to Jacobson.

"When what—" She stopped herself. She must have figured it out. He saw her nod through his periphery.

"What you say?" roared the Drusic to Jacobson.

The little exchange seemed to enrage the simianoid even more.

"Easy," Rechs soothed. He muttered to Jacobson out of the side of his mouth, "Get ready."

There was electricity in the air. Like a thunderstorm in summer. To his credit, the pilot merely stood there, apparently convinced that immobility was his best and only defense with so many blaster selector switches being gently flipped from secure to make-your-play.

"*Those* guys are the ones you should be worried about," said Rechs as he indicated with his eyes the locals on the terrace. It was funny how these things worked out. At first, Rechs had been intent on saving them some trouble. Now that they'd gone to their blasters to show their true colors, Rechs would use them all up.

The beast spun and unloaded with both barrels, sending a furious blaster barrage at the customers along the terrace. Not all Drusics are so easy to manipulate, but Rechs could tell that this one was amped up on a cocktail of adrenaline and testosterone from its many gonads.

Those on the terrace who had foolishly drawn their weapons—blasters they did not make a living with;

weapons they liked to wave around for show or were somehow comforted by—were taken down with an economy of shots that was stunning given the rage with which the Drusic bellowed while firing. The simian's blaster bolts tore into the patrons' chests regardless of whether they tried to fire back, drop for cover, or even dive over the terrace rail into the cobalt-blue waters out here along the coast.

Rechs used this opportunity to shoot the Drusic in the back of the head, trusting only his hand cannon for the job. Best to be sure when it came to Drusics. The shot exploded the thing's skull, and the big monster went down.

Its blasters were still firing. The bitter waitress was grazed. Fishing gear caught fire. One shot smashed something in the kitchen that knocked the frying oil over onto open flame.

So much for avoiding the kind of scene that would draw the attention of the Legion. Or worse... a Nether Ops kill team.

23

"CAPTAIN HESS."

The comm interrupted the badly scarred, one-eyed officer whose career had once been destined for the heights of the House of Reason.

He was leading his men in a physical training run down the length of the ship, part of a grueling session that had started on the hangar deck with a hundred burpees, then cleans with interceptor tow bars the Navy chiefs had laughingly provided until they saw what they assumed to be a squad of Dark Ops leejes actually repping them out. That was followed by a duck-walk with their N-4s over their heads the length of the flight deck, which was down for maintenance rotation.

This brisk run down the massive ship—and not the direct route down the central spine transportation corridor, but a route with as many stairs, ladders, and tubes as possible—was intended to be the cooldown.

His Nether Ops squad didn't call him Hardcore Hess merely because he'd taken to beating the crud out of everyone in weekly hand-to-hand sessions. They called him that because of the way he was always at the front of torturous sessions like this one. They called him that and other, less polite names, because he was a driven man. Fanatically determined to cleanse some unit weakness that only he could see. As if through pain, drilling, and training he would purify them all so they could purify the galaxy.

"Go for Hess," the captain responded, activating a sweat-soaked comm.

"Sir, we have a possible sighting on your tango by a local on the payroll. A bar in Dom Kay. Little fishing village along the coast outside the main lagoon. Prepping your dropship now."

Hess swore. They were way down-spine. Even taking a speedlift, it would be ten minutes before they could gear up, another five to make the ship, and fifteen to reach the target.

Hess called a halt and told them what needed to happen.

"On my mark, you sprint your sorry asses back to the ready room and gear up. Board the drop. First man in the bird gets a promotion and thirty days leave."

Hess had barely finished before the first man in the column just turned and ran off. He hadn't even dismissed them. The others caught on and followed, pouring it on and clubbing the front-runners to get ahead of them.

Hess liked that kind of motivation and initiative. With such men he could conquer the galaxy.

By the time the bird lifted off the pad, the men were bruised and cruising on adrenaline, but locked and loaded.

Thirteen minutes.

The dropship cleared the portside hangar deck of the super-destroyer *Vigilant* to begin the drop for the landing zone.

And Tyrus Rechs.

***

Greasy flames raced across the weathered, dry wood of the bar. Crawling like greedy hands, they caught the nets, burned blue from the spilt booze, and generally roared inside the kitchen where they had gotten their start.

Captain Jacobson had tackled the pilot as he'd turned to run. Rechs had flipped a table and was now caught in a firefight with some of the other patrons. It turned out they weren't all just gaping fools wanting to look tough. Some of them were legit hired blasters, and it seemed likely that at least one or two were low-level bounty hunters running down leads on the Dragon.

Now all of them had collectively decided to kill Tyrus Rechs.

Jacobson dragged the pilot to his feet and fled out the door, having to push the smuggler through like he was drunk. Rechs used his blaster on high cycle, burning through a charge pack just to lay down enough cover fire for the two of them to get out. He squatted back down behind his overturned table and swapped charge packs as blaster bolts slammed into his cover and the wall behind him. Three charge packs left. And a knife. He pulled the blade, reversed it over his firearm, and duck-walked for cover behind another table.

No one seemed interested in charging Rechs, even though it was the move with the best chance of succeeding. A fearsome reputation had its advantages. Instead, they seemed content to shoot the tables he used for cover to pieces.

Rechs chanced a blind shot from around a corner, hoping to burn a smoking hole in someone's head.

"Rigo's down!" someone shouted from that side of the bar.

"Who shot him?" someone else bellowed. And then, "Hey! Don't shoot us until we get him!"

Now what? wondered Rechs.

He crawled on his belly for a set of stairs that led down. Maybe to a storage cellar, or maybe to the water itself—the bar hung out over the water. As blaster bolts sizzled around him, Rechs threw himself into the darkness of the stairs.

He smashed against the wall of a landing midway down, pushed off, and tumbled down the rest of the way. He could hear boots pounding on the wooden floorboards overhead like a herd of jauntas rushing at the scent of blood.

They were coming after him.

Rechs fired into the ceiling, blowing smoking holes into the hardwood. Showers of displaced dust trickled down into his eyes, causing them to water and flutter. Hopefully he'd hit someone in the foot. Or at least kept their pursuit back for a second.

At the bottom of the stairs, a supply dock bobbed in the dark water. Two boats sat beside crustacean cages, old nets, and gear. One was a thin paddle boat used for fishing. The other was a high-powered hoverboat, no doubt used for smuggling.

Rechs jumped aboard the smuggler's boat and tapped the power display. A passkey screen came up, and he fished out a small device from the pocket of his coat. He adhered it to the screen and aimed his pistol at the stairs.

The first guy down the steps took a bolt in the chest that sat him straight down, temporarily blocking the stairs for the rest. But his friends were set on coming. They crushed the hapless man beneath their boots just to get off a shot at Rechs. The bounty hunter sent a flurry of bolts into the stairwell, hoping his charge pack would last long enough for the device to get him past the boat's defenses.

A small chirp indicated the lock breaker had bypassed the security key. Rechs tapped in the commands to fire up the twin turbines the slick little boat used for engines.

Attempting to swap out charge packs with one hand, Rechs had to duck as those intent on collecting his bounty burst through the stairwell. Hand on the throttle, he slammed it full forward. The craft lurched, still moored to the dock, mooring lines straining, causing a small tidal wave of water to splash up, obscuring the blaster shots of Rechs's pursuers. A moment later the craft ripped free of the lines, rending the dock and sending the would-be bounty hunters into the water as it spat off into the ocean.

Rechs tapped his comm as he rose up to take the controls, scanning the waters around the boat. The twin turbines howled like tormented phantoms out over the waters beyond the fishing village.

"Jacobson!" he yelled over the spray of water and the ominous moan of the engines.

"Here," came the reply over the comm he wore in his ear. "Extracting the pilot. We're halfway down the street. Where to?"

"Give me the location of his ship. Tell him we need to depart now."

There was a pause. Rechs checked the skies above, expecting to see shuttles or dropships from an interested Republic.

"He says he's not sure he can make the jump with this much heat in the sky."

"Doesn't matter," shouted Rechs over the engines. "His ship is jumping for Shangri-La in the next thirty minutes. And he'll be onboard."

The comm went silent.

Rechs could see a Legion patrol pointing at him from the beach. They were doing a sweep. And no doubt calling in a sitrep. A firefight. A fleeing boat. And those on the street mentioning the name "Tyrus Rechs."

"Roger," Jacobson finally responded. "He's open to trying it. But he wants credits. A lot of them."

"Not a problem," said Rechs as he yanked the boat hard to port and rounded the point.

But still nagging him was why this Sinasian smuggler who knew the location of a planet without a confirmed existence, a fabled rumor, would be willing to give it up for the promise of mere credits. More likely, he was stalling.

Rechs made for the entrance of the lagoon where the city of ten thousand lily pads floated before the Taijing docks. It was the only way back now. If the smuggler's ship was in the docking bays, then Rechs was going to need to get back into the main lagoon, through the lily pads, and onto the mountainside tram.

It wouldn't be easy.

Nothing ever was.

"Ship got a name?"

"*Shurrigan's Goose*," Jacobson replied. "Bay two twenty-one."

Not easy, but not impossible, thought Rechs. Second level. Low down the mountainside.

"I'll meet you there. Have the engines fired up."

Overhead, a dropship exited the super-destroyer. Rechs watched its course and speed. They were definitely coming in toward the now-burning bar.

They were coming for him.

Rechs throttled up and entered the lagoon at full speed.

24

THE JET-POWERED HOVERBOAT HANDLED LIGHT AND fast. She had to if she was going to outrun Republic interdictors on the high seas that surrounded Taijing.

But—and this was surprising to Rechs—she didn't have any weapons. And all Rechs had were the rounds left in his hand cannon, a blaster with two charge packs, and a knife.

He aimed the howling boat at a flotsam-filled waterway that led into the canals that surrounded the central hub of the city. He kept the throttle at full forward and held on to the wheel, the near-entirety of his focus on keeping the speeding boat off the ramshackle walls of the canal.

The dropship had changed course. Someone must have fed it intel that Rechs was no longer at the burning bar, but on the speeding watercraft. But it didn't immediately open up its guns, even as it got low and close. Rechs chanced a look over his shoulder during a straightaway through a small waterside market that seemed to be doing a brisk business in fish and vegetables despite the detonation of the mech yesterday.

He saw leejes in charcoal-dusted gray armor, legs hanging over the edges of the fat ship. The pilot rapidly dropped altitude and began to crab the ship, craning his neck to see below as the aircraft flew a straight line, diagonally oriented toward the ground. This brought the door gunner into view and offered an excellent opportunity for the swing-mounted N-50 to open up.

But at just that moment, through no planning of Rechs's, the boat crossed under a series of narrow bridges. The gunner was either told to hold fire or hesitated on his own accord as the speeding boat disappeared underneath walkways laden with people and market goods.

Looking to lose the dropship, Rechs scanned for any alternate routes along the intersections of waterways. He spotted an extremely narrow canal that seemed dark enough to go nowhere but a dead end.

But maybe not.

Without thinking too much about it, he jerked the speedboat into a sharp turn and launched its pointy bow, riding high and arrogantly in the brackish green water, into the tight press of buildings. As he disappeared down the shadowy stretch, he again looked behind him.

The dropship banked hard to follow, and the gunner sent a burst from the N-50. High-powered blaster shots in rapid succession chewed up the water in front of the hoverboat, soaking Rechs as the plumes came crashing down inside the speeding vessel. The old bounty hunter weaved the boat back and forth, trying to make it harder for them to range and hit him.

Ahead, the dead end he'd feared loomed. Or so it seemed at first. As he streaked toward what looked like a solid wall that was the edge of the old astrodrome, Rechs saw that the channel dog-legged hard right to run parallel with the wall.

Easing back off the throttle and throwing on the reversers, Rechs barely made the turn. And not without eating some of the wall. He was jolted, struggling to keep his footing as he heard a wicked scrape followed by an ominous hull thump. If that wasn't the hull cracking apart, Rechs didn't know what it was.

Except the boat didn't begin to sink. Yet. Its repulsors kept the thing above the water line.

The dropship's door gunner opened up afresh. Blaster fire smashed down into the astrodrome walls, sending duracrete in every direction. Rechs flinched as the dusty spray smashed into the tiny windshield that protected the controls where he stood. More plumes of water erupted like sudden geysers in front of the speeding boat as the gunner found his range.

Rechs throttled up, and the hoverboat surged forward, racing through the pillars of water. He hoped that his change in speed would make the gunner have to readjust his sight picture to lead the ship.

Within seconds the canal ran out—a docking ramp marked the end of the line. Rechs had no choice but to take it.

The boat surged out of the water and up the ramp, launching itself into the air like a daredevil jumping a desert canyon. The craft landed hard, its repulsors unable to keep the bottom from slamming hard into the street before scraping through a crowded central square filled with market stalls selling everything from bootlegged holo-chits to roasted reptiles.

For a moment, Rechs considered rolling out from the boat and losing himself in the crowd. But the chances were that he was being pursued by a kill team that would have facial recognition IDs. They could scan the crowd and pick him out in short order until Rechs had the chance to turn loose another worm in their system to destroy any captured data—a trick he'd been pulling for some time to remain anonymous.

"Bad news, General," said Jacobson in a small voice over the comm. "The docks are crawling with legionnaires."

Rechs could hear another voice in the background talking about getting out of there fast. Probably the pilot.

"What's your ETA?" Jacobson asked. "We can make it to the ship in about ten."

The dropship came in low and off to the side of the still-speeding boat. Rechs found that he could still steer the thing, but not as tightly as when they were in the water. He smashed into kiosks and brushed against shops of all kinds as everyone on the ground ran pell-mell to get away from the speeding craft and the thundering dropship dripping with deadly Republican legionnaires.

The dropship's gunner swiveled his N-50, and the legionnaires hanging out the cargo door likewise raised their weapons to engage.

Rechs stomped on the rudder and yanked the wheel hard over in their direction. The speeding boat shot straight at the level dropship. The legionnaires' blaster fire went high and wide. The pilot pulled back hard on the stick and added thrust as the dropship climbed to avoid Rechs's desperate kamikaze attack.

Then the boat flew off the edge of the lily pad trade market built beside the repurposed astrodrome. Rechs hovered like a seabird and watched the waters come up to greet him.

The weight of the boat, even with the repulsors engaged to full hover, pushed it down into the choppy water. One engine flamed out as the craft bobbed up from the wallow of sloshing foam and floating garbage before shooting forth once more.

"Rechs, are you there?" asked Jacobson. "What's your ETA? We can't sit here forever."

"I'm coming. Hang on."

Rechs had wanted to make it back to the *Crow* before boarding the smuggler's ship. He needed the Mark I armor—broken or not, it was better than running around in his civvies. And he could use some additional weapons and charge packs. There was no telling what he'd find on Shangri-La. Other than the Dragon. Plus, he'd dropped a request for Chappy and Doc to tell him what, if anything, they knew about Captain Jacobson.

But getting back to the *Crow* wasn't going to be an option. He'd be going to Shangri-La aboard another ship with few weapons and no armor.

And that kid, the Dragon, had been better than all of the weapons that had been used against him so far. Which included several dropships and squads of legionnaires.

And you.

Rechs tapped the ignition switch for the failed engine, hoping to bring it back to life. He was rewarded with a half-hearted *whump.* Like some fire had caught and blown itself out in the same instant. The hoverboat raced over the waves of a small manmade lagoon within the center of the city. High above, the dropship was circling, looking for a new angle of attack.

Rechs tapped his comm. "Nine minutes. Fire up the engines. I've got company!"

He spun the wheel, throwing up a great rooster tail of water. The boat sped into a series of stilt houses built along the water's edge. There was no finesse in what Rechs planned next. This was a bull-in-a-china-shop maneuver.

The speeding hoverboat snaked between the long-legged stilts, its stern slapping against the rotting wood like a great fish whipping its tail around. Some of the stilts collapsed, causing the newly unsupported houses to tumble with their occupants into the lagoon.

The dropship opened up with everything it had. Auto-blaster pods hanging off the stubby wings of the craft spooled to life and spat fire across the landscape, ripping the water and stilt houses to shreds. Shacks were holed and exploded. The side gunners added to the mayhem by sending short bursts into the rooster tail that marked Rechs's destructive wake.

***

Captain Hess watched as the wake of the speedboat carrying Tyrus Rechs ceased. The boat was down there, under the stilt houses, but it had stopped moving, and a plume of smoke was rolling out. They'd got him.

The dropship shot overhead.

"I want *visual* confirmation of a kill right-damn-now!" he screamed.

"Can't confirm visuals, Captain," responded the door gunner. "Sorry."

"Captain Hess," called out one of his leejes. "Let us toss some fraggers down. That'll take care of it."

His kill team were a grim lot.

The dropship orbited the wreck of the hoverboat in tight circles, searching for some sign of Tyrus Rechs.

"Yeah," chimed in another legionnaire. "Best case, they get a kill or wound him if he's below the surface. Worst case, we dust some fish or Sins." Sinasians—Sins to the legionnaires—were considered acceptable losses.

But Hess was convinced that either Rechs was dead at the bottom of the lagoon or, more likely, he was making his way through the warren of passages within the stilt houses.

"I want teams of two dropped in a radius that covers every access point to and from this area!" Hess barked into the dropship comm. "He's out there, without armor, and we're going to finish the bastard."

Tyrus Rechs. No armor, no gear. This encounter was the first time Hess hadn't seen the bounty hunter open fire at his men. He was operating without a plan and on the run. It was exactly how Hess had always imagined—fantasized about, really—Rechs's final moments.

Desperate and totally at Hess's mercy.

25

"CAPTAIN HESS, WHAT IF HE WENT DEEP?" ASKED A Nether Ops kill team member after twenty minutes of fruitless searching.

Hess heard the comment on the channel, but didn't bother to respond. He was too busy attempting to get more assets in the area. And the super-destroyer's captain was fighting with him over it. They were there to get the Dragon, full stop. It didn't matter who else might be here. The Dragon was everything.

At least until Hess mentioned his connections to some of the more powerful members of the House of Reason. Until he mentioned how, in Nether Ops, he had the freedom to check up on the family members and backgrounds of those unwilling to help in the Republic's larger efforts against traitors.

When he mentioned those things, available marines were quickly found and reallocated to Hess's search.

"Been thinkin' the same thing," said Sergeant Brian Schmidt, the senior NCO in charge of the kill team. He had shadowed Hess in an element performing a grid search through the area they thought was the most likely one Rechs would have fled into.

The high-powered hoverboat the bounty hunter had stolen had sunk. Two legionnaires had gone down to the bottom to check the craft. No body.

"Will you two shut up and let me think?" Hess realized with growing horror, one he was not willing to admit to anyone, that Rechs had slipped the leash.

***

Schmidt silently questioned yet again his decision to leave the Legion for Nether Ops. For all the recruitment bluster about it being a place where things got done, in reality it involved a thousand competing fiefdoms all doing what they decided was best and with no regard for the consequences. He should have hung in there and waited for an invitation to Dark Ops.

For now, he was cleaning up Hess's sloppy search and destroy. Which wasn't typical. Hess knew what he was doing, but something about *this* target, Tyrus Rechs, made him distracted. The captain had exposed his men to whatever the bounty hunter might have left in his flight—IEDs, auto-turrets, you name it. And it was up to Schmidt to make sure none of his boys ended up dusted because of it.

And then he saw it: two of his boys' vitals suddenly went offline, causing his HUD to flash an alert.

***

"Captain Hess, what if he went deep?"

Just as Rechs surfaced, he heard the Dark Ops leej utter the prophetic words. The bounty hunter quietly climbed up a small dock and approached the legionnaire from behind. He thrust his combat knife into the leej's kidney while simultaneously darting his hand between the helmet and chest plate to crush the man's windpipe.

The legionnaire was bleeding out and choking at the same moment as Rechs rushed his buddy, curling his arm around his throat and pulling him down into the water. The bounty hunter plunged the knife into every gap in the armor he knew, sending the blade up and down like a piston. In the hurl and toss of the water, he struck armor a few times, chipping off the tip of his knife, but he scored more hits than misses, and the water snaked red with blood until Rechs released his victim and plunged the blade into the man's throat. The legionnaire sank fast, drowning through the new opening in his neck.

Rechs swam through the pink water and climbed back onto the dock. He stripped the bucket off the dead legionnaire still topside, then pulled out the comm. More would be coming soon. More than he could handle at the moment.

He took the kid's N-4 and as many charge packs, bangers, and fraggers as he could stuff in his cargo pockets.

Rechs had ditched his jacket back when he first bailed from his boat after it caught fire beneath the stilts. The remaining good engine had exploded after being hit, and the craft no doubt sank quickly after that. But by then Rechs was beneath the water in the dark stilt forest.

He surfaced for air only briefly and sporadically in small, dark pockets beneath the stilt houses. He'd suck in a lungful, then dive right back down into the dark water and swim for the next protected pocket, never really sure where he might find it. He'd made it to the outer edge of the security cordon when he spotted the two leejes on the narrow little dock above him. He could have bypassed them and swam on, but he needed a weapon.

And now he also had a comm synced to the Nether Ops kill team, for however long it lasted before they did a frequency switch.

Rechs kept the N-4 down along his dripping pant leg and threw himself into a crowd. He put the leej's comm piece in his other ear and listened in on the kill team's channel.

The commander's tag was Cobra Six. The guy seemed like a real petulant piece of work who led through bullying, intimidation, and humiliation. He spoke with a nasal whine. As Rechs cycled through the other comms, it didn't take him long to figure out that this Cobra Six was a captain named Hess.

They knew he'd iced the two legionnaires, but no one seemed all that broken up about it. Tyrus Rechs expected nothing else from Nether Ops.

He quickened his pace.

Ahead was a makeshift pontoon bridge Republic engineers had thrown out from the port to the city of ten thousand lily pads. Republic marines, sent down from the big super-destroyer no doubt, guarded the bridge from small, modular bunkers and amphibious assault sleds.

"Jacobson," said Rechs, careful to be sure he was speaking into the correct comm. "What's your status and location?"

The reply was a little slow in coming.

"We're aboard the pilot's ship. There's more to this than I thought."

"Like what?"

Rechs hurried to catch up with a large group of refugees making their way across the bridge, hoping to blend in. Sinasian faces cast bitter glances at him as he fell into their midst. That seemed to be the most they were inclined to do about his presence, though.

"The good news is it's a short trip," Jacobson said. "A half-hour jump. Bad news is it's a blind jump based on a secret hypercomm channel beacon. That's why no one ever found the planet by accident. It's hidden inside the Suwaru Nebula."

"There in five," Rechs grunted.

He kept his head down and his rifle as concealed and close to his wet clothes as he could. But he had that sixth sense that told him when someone was watching him—always had—and right now he felt it. Sure enough, when he looked up, he saw someone staring right at him. The mounted gun operator of an amphib assault vehicle at the far end of the bridge. Though the gunner's weapon was pointed off into the sky.

The marine looked just like every other kid who'd ever joined to go exciting places and kill exotic people. But the squint in his eye told Rechs that while he might not be putting all the pieces together, something was bothering him. Probably the fact that Rechs looked nothing like the other refugees. Or maybe the kid was picking up on all the passive-aggressive Sinasian contempt being directed toward Rechs from those around him.

Maybe, thought Rechs as he watched awareness dawn in the marine's eyes, *the kid won't put it all together before I'm clear.*

He kept walking toward the far end of the pontoon bridge with all the other refugees. But the kid's suspicious look had Rechs picking up the pace. The old bounty hunter was so close to the end of the bridge that he allowed himself to think he was going to make it without incident.

But then the kid pulled back the charging handle on the mounted N-50 and swung its long barrel right at the crowd of Sinasians surrounding Rechs.

In a blur, Rechs brought his N-4 to bear and shot the kid in the chest, shouting "Down!" as he did so. The marine slumped in his gun emplacement, and Rechs shot him again. Served the kid right for thinking he was going to unload on a crowd of innocent bystanders.

Is that why? the voice asked. *Or do you really mean that it serves the kid right for wanting to take down Tyrus Rechs?*

Rechs broke into a sprint as the rest of the Repub marines sprang to life. Some seemed to have only a vague sense of what had just happened, but others had seen it all, and opened fire on the man responsible. Their blaster bolts chased Rechs as he scrambled behind a parked command sled that had been left by the side of the bridge. He still had another hundred meters to cross before reaching the entrance to the escalator terminal up to the docking bays.

Rechs weighed whether to return fire or get ready to boogie for more cover.

Time was running out.

Two marines appeared at the terminal entrance, drawn by the action, already snapping their rifles up to fire. It was a clear shot, so Rechs's decision was made. He moved immediately, barely avoiding a slew of shots that slammed into the space he'd just occupied.

Rather than fire back, Rechs dashed toward a small building that would protect him from their fire, but unfortunately not that of the marines he'd first come in contact with. Their plan seemed to hinge on getting the amphibious assault vehicle into the game. The thing's repulsors kicked in, sending up a spray of dirt and grit. Marines crawled along its compartmented hull to pull the dead gunner out of the mounted blaster hatch.

Seeing the start of a death trap, Rechs rolled out from his cover and engaged the two marines at the terminal, moving straight for them.

Both were busy swapping out charge packs at the same time. They'd managed to use up an entire pack apiece in the burst that had chased Rechs to the building.

They're new, decided Rechs. *New with no NCO to guide them, and amped up by the unexpected firefight.*

Something paternal—and maybe a feeling of guilt for icing the kid back there—prevented Rechs from shooting at the green kids as he moved along the portico that fronted the terminal, using blaster-pockmarked columns for cover.

Only after the marines had swapped their charge packs did they cover behind a small duracrete wall that fronted the plaza before the escalator terminal.

Rechs couldn't help but think their NCO would die of embarrassment at how these two pups were handling what was most likely their first real firefight.

And he knew right then and there that killing them wouldn't be a hard thing. This was the galaxy, after all. A galaxy where men carried blasters. Where they shot at each other. Killed each other. A thing Rechs did especially well.

But only when he felt he had to.

Right now, he didn't have to.

He cooked one of the bangers he'd taken off the leej back inside Hess's cordon and tossed it at the terminal entrance. The second it went off, Rechs sprinted forward, knowing the two marines would be down on the ground wondering if they'd ever hear again and whether the world would ever stop spinning.

Behind him, Rechs could hear the amphib coming. As the replacement gunner shouted, "Engaging!" Rechs vaulted the steps into the terminal and threw himself down on a floor covered with shattered glass, likely from the previous day's mayhem.

The weapon opened up, sending hot, short bursts into the front of the building. Blaster fire careened off the face of the transportation terminal and slammed into the duracrete wall.

Rechs waited, readying himself for his next move.

And then he caught a break.

"Pack's dead!" shouted the gunner. He raised the N-50 to pull back and link to a new charge pack. That was bad luck for them—a faulty charge pack hard-mounted in the bowels of the amphib.

But Rechs would take it.

He heaved himself off the ground and sprinted for the escalator amid a flurry of small-arms fire. The amphib roared forward, right into the terminal, firing once more, but by then Rechs was already moving up the escalator toward the second level.

Marines dismounted to give chase.

At the top of the escalator, legs pumping, arms pulling, Rechs ran.

Blaster fire chased him down the vast passage that fronted the bays. The blast doors of bay 221 were wide open, and *Shurrigan's Goose* was ready for departure.

Whether it was spaceworthy or not was another story. It was an old Arcturian raider, still sporting the classic Arcturian design—a crescent with the curved edge forward, four massive landing gears splayed out from the belly of the crescent. But it looked like it had been converted to freight hauler years before, and a job badly done at that. The pilot's cupola was mounted along the portside edge of the crescent, while the rest of the ship had been modified to hold modular storage blisters, which were scattered about in a slapdash, haphazard fashion, resembling nothing so much as overgrown barnacles. In short, a once elegant and graceful ship, one that had probably participated in the wars between Arcturus and her rival trading enemy Maelstrom Fringe, now looked like a gypsy caravan come in to trade. Possibly after having a complete breakdown and then remaining derelict for twenty years.

Rechs saw Jacobson waving from inside the illuminated, bulbous pilot's canopy. "Hurry up and get inside!" she demanded over the comm.

He pounded across the docking hangar, his body threatening to crash on him. He'd been running on pure adrenaline since the shootout in the oceanside bar. Now it was fading, and every limb felt like it was turning into duracrete as he pushed himself toward the boarding ramp.

The old freighter's engines screeched to life in a perfect hum reminiscent of the latest military interceptors. *Shurrigan's Goose* didn't look like much, but it sounded wicked.

The marines reached the massive blast doors that opened up onto the hangar, and to their credit, they shot to disable the light freighter. Rechs sent a few unaimed shots their way just to distract them. Who knew what they could break on the junky old ship?

As if on cue, blaster fire hit something beneath the ship, sending sparks flying and smoke gushing from one of the landing gears.

From the sound of the spooling engines, Rechs knew the ship was leaving with or without him. The pilot didn't want a pile of credits bad enough to stick around and get hauled in by the marines.

Rechs fired once more from the boarding ramp as it retracted into the belly of the crazy freighter... and then it pulled him inside and sealed behind him. He felt that sudden shift from natural gravity to artificial as the ship lifted off the dock, drew up her gears, pivoted for departure, and went to engines full amid a hail of blaster fire.

26

Inside the light freighter, everything was util-
itarian and well-used. Almost nothing was new. Every
hatch rattled, as did the internal walls as the ship climbed
like a banshee through the atmosphere. Rechs had moved
forward to where he thought he'd find the flight deck
when he heard the telltale shriek of starfighter blaster fire
above the screaming engines of the freighter.

Jacobson and the pilot were busy on the flight deck
when Rechs found them.

The Nether Ops captain was re-angling the deflector shields to meet the interceptor threat while the
pilot swam his long fingers across the control panel and
watched the canopy and digital feedback like a H8 junkie
staring glassy-eyed into oblivion.

Rechs had only been able to give the pilot a cursory
glance in the bar seconds before the blaster fight had
erupted. Now that he got a longer look, he saw a tall,
gangly, bug-eyed man with a giant Adam's apple and tremendous teeth.

The ship shuddered from a strafe by a Lancer. As
the Lancer overtook them and sped past, Jacobson looked

down at her controls with a puzzled look. "Hit... but not bad."

"That's good," said the pilot.

The Lancer swung around for another run.

"Interceptors," Rechs called out. When working with others, he found it was best to call out the obvious until he was sure of everyone's capabilities.

"No bunga, my man," shouted the pilot. Though he wasn't really shouting. He just had one of those voices. Loud. And like he always spoke from the back of his throat with a serious sinus condition. "You have well and truly karballed my livelihood in the Sinasian smuggled goods trade, mate."

More shots raced across the deflectors. Rechs's eyes went to the damage readout. Superficial. Again.

"It'll be a good long time before they'll let me do the run now that the Republic's all over our back," the pilot moaned.

Rechs had the feeling that he was protesting too much. "This is supposed to be a beacon jump? How much longer until we go to light speed? Your ship won't stand up against these interceptors."

"It's a beacon jump, my man," the pilot said. "Problem is I need a nice long straightaway to match the jump calc to the beacon's last updated signal. She updates every twenty minutes. Normally we do this jump in the dead of night out along the Darshell Reefs in the southern continent where the Repub could care less what goes on. Now, with interceptors all over me, it's proving a bit hard to match course and calc."

That's not how Rechs knew beacon jumps to work. He quietly thumbed the selector on his N-4.

The pilot brought the old freighter through a full yaw rotation until the sky was the ground and the ground the sky, then the ship dove for the wide ocean and a small island chain. In that world-spinning moment, Rechs saw at least a full squadron of fighters. And directly in front of them, streaking to intercept, was the super-destroyer.

"Not to worry, my man," announced the pilot to some question he'd thought was most likely plaguing Rechs or Captain Jacobson. "I'm full of all kinds of tricks."

In seconds the freighter was down, skimming above the ocean and speeding directly into a chain of volcanic islands. Some of which were active. Dancing among the volcanos might allow them to pull away from the less-maneuverable Lancers, but they were still on a direct course for the super-destroyer.

"If your big trick is going real fast," said Jacobson as she tightened herself in the navigator's chair, "then you might want to think up some new ones. They've got us in the next thirty seconds."

But the craft kept its course, moving inevitably closer to the super-destroyer. Rechs crept up behind the pilot and pressed the barrel of his N-4 against the back of the man's head. "Get us out of here. Now."

"What are you doing?" shouted Jacobson.

"He's not taking us to the beacon. He's setting us up for capture by that super-destroyer. Aren't you?"

Beads of perspiration formed on the pilot's lip. "Listen… I can't just give up the location of Shangri-La. I can't just take you there because you have credits. You don't have enough credits to ever pay for something like that."

Rechs pushed the barrel harder against the man's head. "How many credits is your life worth? Do we have enough credits for that? Because if you don't get us out of here right now, your head is getting splattered all over this Arcturian console."

The pilot seemed to weigh just how much Shangri-La, a bounty on Tyrus Rechs, and his life were worth. He decided that living beat out all. "All right, all right. But when we get there we make a point of saying you forced it on me. And I still get paid."

"Fine."

The pilot changed course, flying straight into the face of a tropical volcano before rolling the ship over on her starboard axis at the last second and pulling up hard to fly along the steep face of the cone. The two closest pursing Lancers couldn't make the turn and dashed themselves into the volcano. But the rest, a veritable swarm of angry hornets, backed off their speed, pulled hard, and rolled out on their new course heading aft of the freighter's tail.

"Better," Rechs muttered.

"Ain't seen nothin' yet, my man," bragged the pilot in his swallowed yet loud voice.

Streaking along the face of the tropical paradise, rolling sporadically but still following the same course heading, the freighter found a crack in the line of small mountains that fell away from the volcano and dove into it. The gap widened into a narrow canyon that ran off toward the island's interior.

Jacobson checked the back-scan sensors and remarked less than enthusiastically, "Still on us."

"Not for long," said the pilot. He swiveled away from the controls and turned his attention to an ancient nav comp that had been jury-rigged to a dish-assisted hyper-comm. "Now for the finishing touch."

Blaster fire rocked the hull of the ancient ship. The deflectors collapsed, and more blaster fire raked the engines. The faux pursuit of moments earlier had ended; now they were shooting for real.

"Never mind that, folks," said the pilot distractedly as he brought in the automated damage control systems. "All part of the show…"

"They're closing," said Jacobson, the fear of being shot down in the next ten seconds evident in her voice. "Do something. It's now or never, flyboy!"

Rechs turned around, studying the various control panels along the side of the cockpit. He'd removed the N-4's barrel from the pilot's head, but still had it on him. And probably would for the rest of the flight.

The pilot cast a quick, worrying glance at the bounty hunter, and then down to the rifle. Despite his assurances, he seemed to be out of tricks as the freighter shot down the tight length of the canyon.

Rechs spotted a U-handle release marked "WARNING: Cargo Disconnect." He slammed it from the lock position and up to release.

A normal freighter would've never had such a simple system so lacking in redundant safety features. A smuggler, on the other hand…

"What're you doing, mate?" shrieked the pilot—knowing full well what Rechs had just done.

"Saving our lives and your ship," grunted Rechs. He pounded a green-lit contact button on the panel.

"No! Not that…" whined the pilot forlornly.

There was a series of loud thumps and bumps as the ship suddenly accelerated forward. Cargo modules along her upper hull came loose and flew into the face of the fighter swarm closing in for the kill. Some Lancers slammed into the sides of the canyon while trying to avoid the loose cargo modules. Other fighters crashed into one another. Others still collided with the modules at full force, their forward deflectors quickly overpowered.

No one was shooting at the freighter now.

As Rechs had anticipated, the nav comp beeped and then turned over to a steady tone indicating the jump solution was as good as it was going to get.

The pilot looked like he'd lost a small fortune in abandoned cargo. "Toranga's not gonna like that even a little bit." He reached forward and moved the jump throttles to full. "Well... here comes nothing... literally."

And then the old freighter was gone, leaving the few still-trailing fighters nothing to follow but blue sky.

27

"What's Shangri-La like?" asked Jacobson. "And no more tricks."

"What's it like, mate?" repeated the pilot. "It's crazy pants. It's Sinasia five hundred years ago and yesterday. It's half circus of freaks and carnival of nightmares, and half... I don't know. Something out of our shared history from way back. Earth. If you believe that place ever existed."

The pilot held out a hand. "I'm Shurrigan. Hence the name of the ship. It's my goose. I'm also a businessman and occasional raconteur when stories are needed."

"And someone I can't trust," Rechs said, gripping his rifle. He'd relaxed to the ready position, no longer aiming the weapon at Shurrigan's head, but that was as far as he would go.

The pilot winked, which surprised Rechs. "You kidnap me and try to justify it by offering me far too few credits to give up Shangri-La. I try to turn you in to the Repub for a bounty. I'd say we've canceled each other out."

Jacobson leaned back in her seat. "Getting to Shangri-La was too important to take no for an answer."

"Well, we're on our way there now," said the pilot, sounding like he'd adjusted to the situation.

Rechs didn't figure the pilot would risk crossing him again. That would be an instant death warrant.

He got down to business. "We need to get on-planet without being noticed."

"Oh, *trust* me, I have no intention of letting *anyone* know that I brought you there."

"And we need to know what the situation is like on the ground."

"The trick is this. There's only one field I'm allowed to set down on. And that's the only one I'd chance. What's going on right now? I don't know. I've seen things. Things out there in the mist. But... ah... that doesn't mean I know what's going on."

"Explain," said Jacobson.

The pilot rubbed his stubbly, nobby chin, then massaged his gangly neck with long, piano player's fingers. "How about I tell you a story."

Rechs sighed. But he shrugged and indicated the pilot should proceed.

"Follow me," said Shurrigan. "Lounge is more comfortable."

Jacobson led the way, blocking the pilot's path should he want to make any sudden breaks. Rechs followed behind with his blaster rifle ready.

"It's like this..." Shurrigan began, spinning around to look at Rechs and alternating between walking backward, forward, and sideways as they moved toward the lounge. "About five years ago there was this bigwig hotshot pilot who had the exclusive deal on running out the best shipments to Shangri-La. Ebaar Hum. A Tarrakoan with a real nice ship. One of those Bendetto blockade-runners with big holds and all the gear and tricks. He was bringing back sled loads of jade lotus. The pure uncut stuff that usually only sees the inside of the party palaces around Utopion. Illegal for the rest of us, look the other way for them. Makes ya think when I put it that way, don't it?

"Anyway, he was the guy who had the main contract. The rest of us only got called out for special runs. No return cargo, but sometimes, if you were really lucky, they'd load you with black lotus. Which is really no favor because of the Sinasian locals who make that weird place their home. If they caught you distributing anywhere but the landing site... then it's an immediate death sentence."

Shurrigan found a seat and leaned back, kicking his long legs up onto a power converter. He seemed to be warming to his tale and enjoyed being listened to. Rechs preferred the quiet type of freighter pilot. The kind who felt that hauling the space lanes was a lonely business and preferred it that way.

Shurrigan was the opposite.

"Ebaar somehow made contact with a different group on Shangri-La promising him more if he would be willing to violate the established protocol." Shurrigan wagged his finger as if warning Rechs and Jacobson. "Now let me tell you something... that's like candy to a smuggler. We can't resist an opportunity like that. I mean... c'mon. It's what we do. We smuggle. We go where we're not supposed to be, for more money. Easy, right? Anyway, so Ebaar makes the run, and he's never seen or heard from again. In the flesh, I mean."

Shurrigan looked toward the ceiling of the lounge. He cocked an ear and listened to something, though Rechs didn't hear anything in particular. Probably the absence of some sound the ancient ship was *supposed* to be making that only the pilot knew to listen for.

The pilot continued. "About six months later at a bar in Rice Town, an old man shows up. Typical papa-san. Wooden sandals. Robe. Wide, flat, woven hat to keep the sun off. Gnarled staff. Me and the other pilots who've managed to make the runs in and out of Taijing without attracting too much Repub attention, we had a little chess club going on there back then. Now, Ebaar was always the big fish. That was because he was so in with 'em and all. That jade lotus is powerful stuff if you ever get a taste. But as they say, once and you're hooked. You're hooked for life. Never touch it m'self. Maybe if I get some horrible disease or I've gone off the charts and my engines have died and it doesn't look like I'm getting rescued. Because you see, that's the thing about smugglin'… no one knows where you are. Has to be that way. But what happens if ya get in trouble and you're all out there on your lonesome? Huh? What happens then?"

He drew a long finger across his throat and made a sound with the side of his mouth.

Rechs clenched his jaw and indicated the pilot should return to his original narrative.

"Yeah," agreed the pilot, though it was clear he would have been more than happy to continue talking about the dangers of space travel. "So, we're sittin' there on a dark and stormy night playing hyperchess, and I'd just lost my tyrannasquid to a cheap shot from a Basudi pawn, when in walks this old papa-san holding a basket in one hand and a cane in the other. I'll spare you the imitation, but long story short, he tells us this: an opportunity to do 'grand things for the Throne of the Emerald Dragon' has opened up.

"Then he gives us a lecture about doing what one is told to do and doing it precisely. Some story about a kid who was fishing and a talking donkey who granted magical wishes. Can't remember, but I got the gist all the same. Do what they said to do and only that. Rewards for obedience. And rewards of another sort for disobedience. And then he reaches in his basket and pulls out Ebaar's head."

This was the big moment in the story. You could tell that Shurrigan had spun this tale before, and he'd been rather proud of the reactions he'd gotten from past listeners at this particular point.

Rechs wasn't bothered by the head in the basket, and Jacobson didn't seem to be either.

Shurrigan went for it once more, repeating the line like he'd probably done it a hundred times before. The reaction was the same.

Looking slightly crestfallen, Shurrigan shrugged and continued. "Now you might be thinking that's just what happens to an old smuggler who'd done double-crossed the wrong people…"

"I know the type," Jacobson scoffed.

"Yeah," Shurrigan said, eyes darting from side to side. "Anyway, y'know… you might be thinkin' fat and bloody head, eyes rolled up and staring, or seeming to, at some dark eternity unfolding. A silent scream forming at the mouth within the yellowish embalming fluid or what have you. That's what you might be thinking, and you would be wrong. This wasn't that kind of head.

"This head was inside a crystal ball. Swimming in a shimmering, almost iridescent electrical solution. And the eyes were *seeing* us. Mouth screaming in horror. Silently, on account of it being encased in the crystal. And it probably didn't have no vocal cords."

Shurrigan paused for effect, threw open his bird-like hands to full span, and exclaimed, "In other words, he was *alive*. Aware and bodiless inside that crystal ball the old papa-san had plunked down on the table. He told us this was the fate of any who did not follow the rules required of a smuggler who served the Throne of the Emerald Dragon."

Shurrigan paused again, and frowned at his stoic listeners.

"Then he offered us jobs. There were twenty of us there. Only three of us agreed to fly the runs. One got caught by the Republic about a year ago and killed himself rather than talk. He didn't want to take the chance the old papa-san, or whoever, would crystal ball his head for a thousand or more years. Safer to just go ahead an' off yourself if you got caught, musta been his thinking."

A silence fell over the lounge. And Rechs imagined, upon listening to the ghostly hum of hyperspace beyond the hull, that Shurrigan was hoping that the pause would allow for some reflection. The pilot was facing some bad results for rolling over on Shangri-La.

But Rechs didn't particularly care. Shurrigan was lucky to still be alive.

"So what it all boils down to is, the landing zone is the landing zone, mate. I'm probably in big trouble already, but after just barely escaping the Repub, I'm done with Sinasian runs. I'll drop you, then I'm gonna disappear out toward the edge for a while. I'm fond of my head right where it is, and its presence atop my neck is in serious jeopardy now that you two dragged me into all this."

28

Ironically, Shurrigan's head was right where it was supposed to be now that he was dead. The thing that was out of place was the massive shrapnel wound in his chest from the shattered canopy. The wound was unexpected and fatal. The disbelieving look in the pilot's eyes, rolled up at the control panels above, seemed to indicate that he was the most stunned of all.

And his ship, which he'd lovingly called his goose, was in a dead spin over Shangri-La. They were at thirty thousand and dropping fast into the green-mist atmosphere. Distant, colossal mountains poked through other fogs, making it look as though the ship was dropping into some vast primordial lake of haze and mist.

"Rechs!" shouted Jacobson hoarsely from the navigator's chair. She'd strapped in as they'd begun their approach to the mysterious and forbidden world of Shangri-La.

As the wounded ship fell, spinning out of control, centrifugal force was crushing both her and Rechs into their seats, preventing them from moving. They were helpless. A tornado of wind rushed through the shattered canopy, gale force and almost freezing. Jagged pieces of the canopy that hadn't been torn away in the initial explosion whipped away from their tentative hold on the impervisteel-latticed viewing ports, cutting Rechs and Jacobson wickedly.

Altimeter, overspeed, and every other warning system that still worked shrieked violently for attention. An automated voice, that of the ship's extremely primitive AI, kept announcing that a catastrophic structure malfunction had occurred.

Rechs wanted the thing to shut up and stop stating the obvious. But that wasn't the real problem. The immediate threat—aside from the ground racing up at them from below—was the three interceptors that had jumped them on approach through the upper altitudes of mysterious Shangri-La.

All three were advanced tactical interceptors that Rechs had never seen before in all his years and crossings of the galaxy, and they had come out of nowhere, invisible to all sensors like a Republic stealth shuttle. There had been no hail, no warning. They had started firing immediately.

Each ship had a central pilot pod and three shaped panels that seemed to act as both thrusters and deflectors. The little crafts reminded Rechs of the shadow warriors of Katar. Nimble, dancing, everywhere at once, cutting until you bled out. He had a memory of such a fight and wondered if hypoxia wasn't making his mind go all over the place.

And why deflectors? his mind asked, rather than trying to focus on something that might save them from smashing into the planet below.

"Warning!" bellowed the ship's low-level AI.

Maybe there had been a higher-functioning AI that had been destroyed when the three interceptors started shooting up the hull, causing the rupture on the flight deck that had killed Shurrigan. The windstorm rushing through the smashed cockpit shifted the pilot's body, flopping his head over to look at Rechs with that horrified *I-can't-believe-I'm-dead* expression. Staring accusingly at Rechs as though somehow, everything was Rechs's fault.

Because it is.

"Warning! Catastrophic structural damage has occurred. Abandon ship."

Some large section of the ship ripped away with a tremendous groan. Jacobson may have briefly screamed. Rechs couldn't be sure he heard her over the shrieking wind.

"Ship!" shouted Rechs.

Nothing.

Rechs sucked in what little air there was and shouted again. This time he got a response from the automated AI. "How may I help?"

"Access the flight controls!"

The AI's tone bordered on cheerful. "I'm afraid I can't help you with that. But we're always working to improve my capabilities!"

The ship began to tumble, and the spin revolutions were so violent that a black cloud had begun to form at the edges of Rechs's vision. In seconds he would pass out.

"Do it!"

Rechs was looking at the world through a tiny pinpoint of light.

"I'm sorry..." began the ship's AI from down some distant hallway that Rechs was only distantly aware of. His body was held by gravity—pinned, really.

He was thinking about the little boy in the forest when he passed out.

***

"Ball, Papa."

Ball.

Papa.

Except "Papa" wasn't right. It had never been used. Just that one word. *Ball.*

Rechs remembered nodding and saying "ball." His voice catching in his throat. The sound it made was a dry croak on a dark rainy afternoon on a planet called Raven where the children were like those forlorn, ever-watchful birds.

And then he had… kicked—gently—the ball to the strange boy in the forest.

The boy had smiled and run off to tell the other birds, the other boys, about the strange man in the woods.

And that had left Rechs with such a profound sadness. Like nothing he'd ever known in his life. A lonely life of lonely crossings and last man standings on all the worlds that had ever known war.

Rechs had been there.

Buried the dead.

Seen the field of corpses.

Added to their number.

But nothing, no feeling he could remember… or rather no failure… was like the boy in the forest dark. Hearing the word…

Ball.

Ball.

Ball.

Over and over, again and again.

Failure.

Rechs forced himself to surface from that black forest. That black lagoon of mind and memories.

Ball. Papa.

What he saw was the fog racing up at the ship. The spin had stopped. The yaw reversers had kicked in and stabilized rotation. But they were well below the ring of mountain teeth. Lower than the snow-covered conical fangs of their uppermost peaks.

What? wondered Rechs. Trying to figure out the altitude. Under twelve thousand at best.

The air wasn't as thin as it had been.

"Ship!" croaked Rechs. "Engage reversers to full. Bring the repulsors online."

There was no response but the sound of the wind screaming across the ripped fuselage.

He looked over to see that Jacobson had passed out. Her chin was down on her chest, and her hair was flying about her head. At least she didn't have to sit there knowing that they were about to die, smashing into the planet below.

Rechs realized that he'd been able to move his head to see Jacobson. And then he fought to move his arm. He searched for the controls in front of him. The reversers were there, all linked by bar handle.

He grasped the thrust reverser bar and pushed forward.

A second later there was a loud bang as the engines exploded, sending a soul-crushing shudder through the ship. Rechs could see the readouts indicating the damage.

It was bad.

The ship fell down into the mist bank that lay across the surface of the world like some lake. The soft green blanket of nothing seemed even to absorb the sound of the engines.

And of course, thought Rechs, *the repulsors won't come online because they're slaved to the engines on an old rig like this.*

Shurrigan's Goose was in free fall. It would drop like a rock straight down until it hit the side of a mountain or a valley floor and just disintegrated into a million pieces. Along with Rechs and Jacobson.

The interceptors must have left them for dead. Rechs would've preferred that they'd vaporized him instead of leaving him to this death.

The old bounty hunter looked around from the co-pilot's chair. Maybe there was something he could still do. Craning his neck, he saw a red metal tag that read, "Emergency Landing System." Below it was a covered switch.

As Rechs flipped open the cover, the tag raced away in the wind, tumbling end over end back into the ship. Rechs pushed the switch—with no small effort—and heard a series of small explosions across the hull. The sound of a kite, or a parachute, rippling in the wind, an old and familiar sound to Rechs, could be heard repeatedly, big and booming like sail canvas.

And then the ship was floating, slowly, softly, down through the fog. Quiet. Silent. It came to rest in a small hidden lake. An ancient and forgotten-looking temple sat along the shore.

Maybe it was a good thing those pilots hadn't vaped them after all.

29

THE OLD FREIGHTER HAD FINALLY COME TO REST IN HER last berth and was now sinking into the peaceful mire of the twilight lake. Green mists wandered over its battered and dingy surface as it slowly surrendered to the dark, murky waters.

Rechs had revived Jacobson, checked her for injuries, unharnessed her, and led her in a mad flight with whatever gear was at hand out through the flight deck's only emergency hatch.

Jacobson had had the wherewithal to keep her tactical ruck near her person, and Rechs still had the little he'd brought with him: his knife, the blaster pistol, the N-4 he'd taken off the leej, the fraggers in his pocket, and one banger. Not a bad haul considering how much everything had whirled and whipped about in the cockpit during the fall. But his slug thrower was gone, which was too bad. Rechs liked that gun.

The escape hatch had a spot for an emergency life raft, but when Rechs popped open its compartment, he found nothing but empty space. Rechs figured the smuggler had most likely ditched the raft long before so he could carry more contraband.

The pair dropped down into the dark, cold waters of the alien world. They swam for the shoreline and the old temple.

What they experienced of the world of Shangri-La was silent. An eerie quiet devoid of wind, animals, civilization—any of the things that Rechs was accustomed to in the galaxy. Only the sounds of their splashing strokes and breathing could be heard in all of the lake's vastness.

It's this mist, Rechs told himself. *Smothering everything to death.*

Indeed, the ever-present jade fog had settled everywhere, making the temple seem like the spire of a lost city and the trees like strange monsters wandering nearby.

The steps of the temple descended into the waters, and soon Rechs and Jacobson were able to eschew swimming for a dripping-wet climb, darkening the ancient gray stones with each droplet of water that fell from them.

Just outside the ancient temple, Rechs sat down and began to disassemble his N-4. Ideally he'd like to dry it as well, but the wan sunlight wasn't enough to do that job. The damp pall that surrounded them was too oppressive.

"N-4s can be submerged," said Captain Jacobson.

Rechs, straining for any sounds beyond the spy's voice—which was like a shout amid the stillness—shook his head. "Maybe. Used to be, anyway. But with the way the House of Reason has slashed the Legion's budget…"

Jacobson shrugged and removed her blaster from her waterproof ruck. She strapped it to her thigh. "I'm going to the top to get a better look. Here—you can dry your weapon with this." She pulled a T-shirt from her ruck and tossed it to him.

Rechs caught it and nodded his thanks. He disconnected the upper and lower receivers of the N-4 and quickly dried the parts. With Jacobson gone, he heard only his own breath in the silence of Shangri-La, and he felt more and more with each passing second that there should have been, within the soundscape, some lonely and forlorn cry, perhaps from a bird haunting the vine-draped jungle's depths.

But there was nothing.

Jacobson returned with the same observation. "Ghost town," she whispered breathily, crouching down next to Rechs. She pulled out nutrition bars and water, and shared what she had.

They ate and drank in silence, the sound of their chewing and swallowing seeming obnoxiously loud. Both paused as the lake let loose a distant, explosive hiss. It had swallowed the last of *Shurrigan's Goose* with a great gusty slop.

"There goes Shurrigan," Jacobson said, watching as the main engine housing slunk beneath the water. "Down into Davy Jones's locker."

"Heh," Rechs replied, surprised at himself for laughing. He appreciated the old archaic phrases. Even when those uttering them didn't understand what they meant. Especially then.

The lake had returned to its still, mirrored bliss by the time the two were done with their refueling.

"This place is a temple," said Jacobson. "Definitely Sinasian."

"Who else would it be?"

"The Ancients?"

Rechs shrugged and took the last swig of water from Jacobson's canteen before refilling it by the lake. The canteen would be able to filter the water into something safe to drink by the time they needed it next.

"It's got all the signs of Sinasian architecture," Jacobson said. "Dragons, big dogs with their tongues out. Gray stone. Village beyond. Incense burning."

"Thought you said it was a ghost town."

"It is now. But someone was here recently." Jacobson scanned the mists. "Maybe a few days ago. Or maybe a few hours. Hard to say. This place has that kind of feel like... something sudden can happen."

Rechs put the finishing touches on the N-4 and did a systems check. A small green light indicated that the weapon would fire if the trigger was pulled. But again... who knew?

"Well then," Jacobson said, "what next?"

Rechs thought about that as he gathered himself up, staring at the serene waters. He didn't answer right away, preferring to think and put all the pieces together in the same slow, relentless way he did when running down bounties.

"Something big was going down on Taijing," he began. It always helped him to hash out what intel was known. "But Shangri-La is where the Sinasian tribes will gather, because it's where the Republic can't find them."

Jacobson was bent over, tying her boots. "If the House of Reason knew about this place, they'd order the Navy to nuke it from orbit."

Rechs nodded. "If the Dragon made the case, back at Chung's Pit, to be the Sinasians' new khan and war leader, then this is where he gets to do it. He needs a place to arm, organize, and launch from. If we're going to stop him before things get out of hand... then it has to be here."

Jacobson looked up at Rechs sharply. "Is that what we're here to do? Stop him?"

Rechs said nothing, checking his knife, fraggers, and charge packs instead.

Jacobson grew heated. "Because I came here to *save* him. And I thought you did too, General. Or are you just pure bounty hunter now?"

Rechs hoisted his N-4 and rested it on his shoulder. "Ready to go?"

"No. I'm not. And since we're on the subject of who you were, General, and what you've become, *Tyrus Rechs*... what was the Phoenix Project?"

Rechs turned and began to head up the wide stone steps into the temple proper.

Jacobson followed. So did her questions.

"Because I've seen the files. Read between the lines on the redacted sections. Your name is never brought up except right at the beginning, but clearly the project is about you somehow. How?"

The temple was square, open on all four sides, and here at the top of the steps, Rechs could see the strange mecha idol within and the abandoned village beyond. Small joss sticks still whispered and slithered within the darkness like eyes of a thousand predators in the dark of night, their smoldering stubs nearly extinguished.

"You've had no problem pressing *me* for intel," Jacobson said, "but now that I ask, you've got nothing to say?"

Rechs didn't. And he wasn't about to begin. But the shadow he saw moving quickly between buildings made that moot.

Jacobson continued on, apparently unaware that they were surrounded and being watched. "Unbelievable. Fine. Play the tough guy silent type. Or just admit that you're out of your element and you have no idea what—"

Rechs tuned the Nether Ops captain out as he considered his next move. They needed intel, and getting his hands on whoever these shadows were might lead him straight to the Dragon. Should he alert Jacobson? He decided against it. The shadows might vanish if they noticed her noticing them.

Rechs crossed through the temple dark, smelling the thick and heady scent of jasmine burning on the small two-legged central pod mecha the village had deified.

Jacobson followed. "He's had this life forced on him, Rechs. At the end of the day, that's all that should matter."

Rechs exited from the other side of the temple and started down toward the silent village, walking right into the trap only he could see forming all about them. For a Nether Ops operative, Jacobson wasn't picking up on much. Maybe her emotions were blinding her. Maybe...

"So that's it then, is it?" she practically shouted at him, following Rechs down a small narrow lane between old wooden huts. "You're just gonna kill him after I got you all the way out here. A planet no one else can find. It's really all about the bounty, isn't it? You're—"

Rechs pushed her hard into the darkness of one of the huts. He'd seen a blur of motion; something was flying at them incredibly fast. Something that became a swarm of small, shining, metallic objects spreading out to catch them like the cone of a silent shotgun blast.

With Jacobson tumbling into the cover of the hut, the old bounty hunter threw himself to the hard-packed dirt of the lane, smelling the fertile dark loam in the split second before he sprang back up and brought his blaster to bear.

"Ambush!" he shouted, pulling the trigger of his N-4 as a black-hooded figure charged at him, pulling two swords from sheaths crisscrossed on his back. Some minor angel of avenging death come for his next victim.

The N-4 shorted its charge pack, causing thin tendrils of smoke to rise from its barrel. Rechs cycled the pack, aimed for center mass, and pulled again.

He'd drop this ninja.

Ninja.

That was a word Rechs hadn't heard for an extremely long time.

Jacobson would probably have been happy to shoot Rechs after the argument and his shoving her. But seeing the danger, she fired her blaster pistol at the closing figure. Three bursts of fire—one from her and two from Rechs—and the figure broke off his attack with a sudden, cartwheeling change of direction.

Rechs was dazzled by the maneuver. It was like seeing the fabric of the universe open and close.

"More of them!" he shouted. He drew his knife and reversed it into a carry position as he discarded the N-4. It wasn't sighted correctly, and he didn't have time to fix it now. He pulled his remaining blaster pistol, ready to deal out damage.

A noose dropped around his neck from above and constricted almost instantly. Rechs fought the instinct to move away from it and thereby accelerate his strangulation. Instead he reversed his direction with a roundhouse kick, bringing his booted foot down hard on the light rope. The man who held it failed to let go of it in time, and was pulled down from the roof. He landed on his feet next to Rechs.

The bounty hunter wasted precious little time. He took a swipe at this second ninja's chest with his combat knife. The hooded figure danced lightly back and then threw his weight into a fancy backflip that further removed him from Rechs's reach.

But Tyrus Rechs still had his blaster. He aimed and pulled the trigger in one practiced motion, sending a blue bolt into the ninja's chest, knocking him to the ground dead. The green mists seemed to greedily consume him as he lay in the mud.

A blur of motion came from every corner of the village. Up until that point Rechs hadn't been sure how many he was dealing with. Now it seemed there were far too many.

Jacobson was sending more blaster fire down the lane, giving Rechs an opportunity to scramble for cover. He rushed into the same hut he'd thrown her into, joining the captain inside. Return fire smashed into the hut's wall, snapping ancient boards in sudden dry explosions that left flaming holes in their wake.

"I guess only the first two relied on swords," Jacobson said almost indignantly as she shifted to her knees, and fired at someone beyond the door.

Between blaster reports Rechs listened for the sound of movement. Stuck inside the hut, they were practically blind—and without his armor, the bounty hunter didn't feel like risking a peek from any of the windows. There was probably a sniper with eyes on the hut, and Rechs wasn't going to give him an easy kill.

So instead he started popping fraggers and tossing them out the hut's door and windows.

Explosions rocked the nearby dwellings, sending shards of wood and shrapnel to rattle against the hut they'd chosen to cover in.

"Last one," Rechs announced. "Then we go out shooting. Take the left. I'll take the right. It's our best chance."

The dysfunction of their relationship in the moments right before the battle was gone. Jacobson nodded in quick agreement, and Rechs tossed the last grenade—the banger—out into the now-burning village.

Then they went out shooting.

Flames from the fraggers and errant blaster bolts quickly consumed the dry sides of the old wooden huts and ignited thatched roofs. Gray smoke intermingled with the mist.

But that was all there was to see. Everything else was gone. No attackers. No bodies left behind.

It was as if they'd been fighting ghosts.

30

Rechs bent low, beneath the drifting smoke, and made his way farther into the village, Jacobson on his six.

"What is going on?" the captain asked no one in particular.

Among the last huts, Rechs found a trail of dark blood spray. Someone was badly hurt. Rechs guessed perhaps it was an artery slashed by debris, given the color and sheer volume of blood. A comrade carried away from the carnage of the battle amid Rechs's fragger bombardment.

Jacobson didn't speak a word as they followed the trail of blood out of the village and into the rainforest. But there was another sound on this planet of misty silence: rushing water. Rapids. A dull, steady hum of water throwing itself against rocks in furiously roaring abandon.

As the blood began to thin and the trail grew more difficult to track, Rechs found himself wishing it hadn't been an artery that was bleeding. The victim was running out. And the trail of the man carrying the victim was also hard to follow—even for a bounty hunter whose life was built on following trails of one sort or another.

Whoever they were following, this person knew what they were doing.

What Rechs needed most of all right now—aside from his armor or a reliable weapons suite—was a hypercomm. There hadn't been time to use one back on *Shurrigan's Goose*, and given the damage the craft's onboard systems had suffered in the fall, the ship's hypercomm was probably non-operational long before it sank to the bottom of the lake.

But with a hypercomm, Rechs could get the *Crow* here. Finding one, however, was going to be a real trick. Shangri-La didn't officially exist, and you didn't stay hidden by setting up comm stations. This was a comm-dark world.

Which means, thought Rechs as he worked the trail, *the only way out of here involves hijacking another ship.*

Given his paucity of weapons, stealthily stealing a ship was probably the easier option.

The blood trail was now little more than a few droplets spattered along moist leaves. They were hard to spot without his bucket, and Rechs began to realize just how much he'd come to rely on that suit.

They reached the thundering river. Water crashed among large gray tumbled stones, dense green moss and bamboo, and the jade mist. And on the opposite bank was movement.

Rechs and Jacobson got low and crawled to the edge of the trees, water-saturated moss squelching beneath them, soaking their knees and elbows like wet sponges.

"Is that a ship?" whispered Jacobson, peering across the river.

Despite being right next to her, Rechs barely heard her over the water's roar. "No. Speeder. Old one."

It was a Tadashuo ATS—an all-terrain speeder. Like the Samurai mech on Taijing, this was a thing from the Sinasian past. A vehicle that wasn't supposed to exist any longer, much like the world it now prepared to speed through.

One of the shrouded and hooded fingers was gingerly placing the body of the most likely dead man in the passenger seat with a sort of protective reverence. That his clothing was dry despite crossing the river spoke to the person's capabilities. The rocks jutting out of those rapids were not closely spaced, and they looked wet and slick. That must have been quite a series of jumps from one bank to the other, particularly while carrying a body.

There were no other attackers—just these two. The ninjas at the village had probably approached the crash site on separate speeders in two-man teams. Maybe this was Shangri-La's version of a quick reaction force following up on the crash after the interceptors shot the freighter down.

"We need him alive," Rechs whispered. He pointed a finger down to indicate that Jacobson should wait where they were, ready to disable the speeder with her blaster if it attempted to escape.

Rechs slithered through the underbrush at the river's edge, un-nesting a family of water spiders, each the size of a family pet. They scurried into the trees that hung above the river, and Rechs slipped into the rapids, the swirling waters betraying no trace of his passage.

To stay beneath the water that tried to push him downstream, Rechs pulled himself along the slimy, rocky bed, moving from handhold to handhold, his feet caught in the current so that his body was parallel with the river's flow. Each new handhold required a fight against the current and a blind search that threatened to use up all his oxygen and force him to surface. And that would be disastrous.

But his lungs held out, and soon he emerged on the opposite riverbank, wallowing in mud. Well below the speeder's line of sight, Rechs risked poking his head upward.

The survivor was mounting the speeder and reaching for the controls.

Jacobson should be acting soon.

The old-model repulsors fired up, making a noise that rivaled that of the river. Refusing to risk the speeder's escape, Rechs made a snap decision to charge. He sprang up from the bank, lunged forward, and flung himself at the speeder, jumping on just behind the driver. His knife was out and at the man's throat.

"You make this bike move a centimeter and I'll start carving you up so bad that every leaf in this forest will wear your blood."

The repulsors shut down.

Jacobson stood up from the other side of the river. Something in her face let Rechs know that she was less than happy with the way he'd thrown out the plan by jumping into her line of fire. But scoring the survivor *and* the speeder was worth the risk.

While Jacobson tried to find a crossing, Rechs pulled the ninja off the sled. He removed the man's mask, only to find him frantically working his tongue inside his mouth.

"No you don't!" Rechs clamped down on the man's jaw with an iron grip, holding his knife out as if he was going to use it to pry his teeth open.

Forcing open the man's mouth, Rechs fished inside with his muddy fingers and found a pill—no doubt some kind of necrotic suicide caplet. He flicked the blue suicide caplet onto the ground and crushed it with his boot.

The ninja took the opportunity to bite down viciously on Rechs's pinky finger, which had lingered too close to the ninja's mouth.

With a low growl of rage, Rechs sent a knee into the guy's stomach, doubling him over. He followed up his gut shot with a swift punch to the back of the captive's head, sending him sprawling onto his stomach.

Jacobson arrived—surprisingly quickly. Perhaps the crossing wasn't as difficult as Rechs had imagined. Then again, one of her pant legs was soaked to well above the knee. "What's going on?" she said.

"Nothing."

Jacobson pulled netting off the back of the speeder and tied the captive down. "Watch him," she said to Rechs. She took off her ruck and extracted a small clamshell case. It popped open with a pneumatic hiss, and she took out a gleaming injector. "This'll make him talk," she said in a business-like tone. A tone that revealed just how deep into Nether Ops she really was. "And it might kill him too."

Rechs nodded. They were running out of time. And with the way his finger throbbed from the bite, he didn't much care if the bastard lived or died.

The man struggled, but Rechs pinned him down as the Nether Ops captain knelt and deployed the injector into the ninja's neck. She tossed the spent needle and cartridge into the jungle. The man's eyelids fluttered, and he promptly passed out.

"Takes about twenty minutes to work," Jacobson said. "He'll go into a deep sleep that will lower his defenses to suggestion. When he comes out, he'll think he's having a nightmare. He'll tell us everything. We'll be the embodiment of his worst fears."

"This is something you've done before, I take it."

"And had done to me. It's a trip."

Rechs moved to search the speeder for weapons. Some of the ninjas from the village had had blasters. But apparently not these two. He found nothing more advanced than the swords each man carried.

Jacobson came over, arms folded. He already knew what she was going to say. He'd ignored her questions back in the village. But they hadn't gone away.

"I need to know where your head's at in this, Rechs. And I need to know now before I can go any further with you. Are we working together, or am I working against you?"

Rechs pushed the dead ninja—it was a laceration across his throat that had done him in—off the speeder with an unceremonious thump in order to get at some drinking water. He wiped the sweat off his face and sighed.

There was still some time before the other guy came out of whatever dreamland Nether Ops had put him into. So Rechs was going to have to deal with this now.

He took a drink first.

"For about two years I was dead."

The hard stare Jacobson had been giving him turned to a look of confusion, then to something else. A willingness to listen, perhaps. To maybe hear the whole story.

"The Savages found a strange world in an uncharted area of space way out beyond the frontier. What we call the edge today. It wasn't really a world, though."

"What was it?"

"A gateway. A gateway to another dimension."

He took another drink, giving that outlandish statement—one he wouldn't have believed if he hadn't lived it—time to sink in. When Jacobson didn't protest, he continued.

"We called it *Diablo's Durance*. Actually, it was some navigator on a scout frigate who came up with the name and recorded it in his journal. That's the only reason we knew about it in the first place. We found that frigate drifting in Repub space after being lost for a couple of years. Crew wasn't dead… more like puppets. The Savages liked to experiment."

Jacobson didn't say anything. But Rechs could tell that she was starting to view him as a crazy old man. A legend, maybe, but a crazy one.

Still, she was listening.

"So they sent me in with a task force to investigate this 'Durance.' And… we got wiped out."

Rechs let that hang like it was the entire story. Even though in his mind he was seeing every battle, the entire campaign, and then the two years he'd spent in that… other place. That other hell.

Or maybe it was the real deal.

"How did you…?"

"Escape?" Rechs shook his head. "That's not the story I'm trying to tell. Not trying to relive my glory days. That's just the, uh, what do they call it? The backstory. To the Phoenix Project. How it came about."

Jacobson knelt down and checked the ninja's pulse. "Still a few more minutes."

Rechs knelt next to her, wanting to be ready for when their source of intel woke up. And wanting to look Jacobson in the eye.

"We were losing on all fronts in those years. And I wasn't the first to go into the Durance. We'd lost two expeditionary teams before that. A pair of naval strike forces made up of several ships from a fleet that couldn't spare them. We weren't about to lose a third, but we couldn't leave it alone, either. So in went a brigade of the Legion's best, supported by assault carriers... the works."

Rechs looked away, lost in a gripping and horrible haze of war from long ago. "Lost a lot of men. Seventy percent just in the initial invasion. Just to get a foothold."

"I'm sorry."

"Yeah. The House of Reason was called the House of Justice back then. And they didn't want me to go on what they considered a suicide mission. Said I was too important to the war. But I couldn't keep sending men to die there without seeing it myself. So I threatened to resign. And I got my way."

Rechs realized he was rambling. But there was a part of him that felt... relieved to tell someone about the long-ago times. "The part that concerns us right now, is what came after. Project Phoenix."

Rechs sighed. He didn't know if what was coming next made him feel embarrassed or ashamed. It made him feel uncomfortable, if nothing else.

"Some scientists wanted to clone me and raise a group of... children under the same set of circumstances I was raised under. Like back on Earth when I was their age. Except this would be controlled and, according to them, improved upon."

Now Jacobson *definitely* thought he was a crazy old man. "Earth, General?"

"I'm very, very old. Most people today—Nether Ops and the House of Reason included—have no idea. But back then, some people did. Because everything was on the table. All the secrets. Defeating the Savages required it.

"Anyway, if I didn't make it back from the Durance, this was going to be the final line of defense, or perhaps a recovery option, should the Republic be overrun. If the Legion were broken."

Rechs looked earnestly at Jacobson. "At the time, that seemed like a real possibility."

"That's what I've always heard."

"So every human culture, along with some compatible non-human ones, had someone raised with my DNA. Someone who could, supposedly, survive despite the odds. *That* was the Phoenix Project."

Jacobson stared at him with her mouth slightly open. "But the Savages were defeated. So what happened to these… children?"

"I'm not…" Rechs paused. "I don't know. According to the Republic, for about two years, I died on Durance. And when I came back I was… let's just say my bell had been pretty thoroughly rung. It took years for my mind to recall the project again. And when at last I did, and I tried to gain access to it, everyone involved felt that I would be a corrupting influence on the test subjects. I'd violate the purity of data by introducing myself to, for all intents and purposes… myself."

Test subjects.

Ball.

"So I had to forget about them."

"And did you?"

Rechs nodded. He was still struggling with that fact. He forced himself not to look away, even though he knew his shame was written all over his face.

"You're his… father?" Jacobson asked.

For a long moment Rechs didn't answer. He finally shook his head. "No. We have the same DNA, but that doesn't make me his father. But maybe... maybe I'm all he's got right now. Maybe he needs me and doesn't know it. So I'm here. And you're right. We need to try and get him out of this. If we can. If that's possible."

31

THE NINJA, OR WHATEVER HE WAS, CAME AROUND. Jacobson had implanted a biometric nanite in his wrist and laid out more syringes. She didn't need them. The first dose had been more than enough.

He thought he was talking to two demons from what he called "the underworld of a thousand hells." He blubbered like a little boy. Said he was sorry for all the wrongs he'd done. Especially the murders. He named several he'd committed.

Jacobson encouraged him to focus on his more immediate sins, and from there he told them everything of what he knew.

For hundreds of years, Shangri-La had chosen to live according to the old ways, reflecting the time before the rise of the Republic as a galactic culture. But then the Divine Hand, the secretive group behind Sinasia's latest independence movement, took control of the planet. It was the Divine Hand who brought back the old Sinasian tech from the Savage Wars, found by their agents—like the ninja—throughout the galaxy and smuggled in by carefully vetted freighter pilots and crew.

This was something Jacobson confessed Nether Ops had no idea about.

For years, the elders of Shangri-La—monks living in a retreat on a mountain farther up the river, a mountain whose Sinasian name translated to *White Plum*—insisted that the Sinasians return to their old customs. Content to be blissfully lost among the stellar dark.

The Divine Hand, through assassination and intimidation, annihilated the monks. And now they had built a formidable base beneath White Plum, along with the arsenal necessary to reclaim Sinasia.

As the ninja continued to talk, his mental state deteriorated rapidly. He wailed as if he were being consumed eternally by living fire. Through gritted teeth he choked out: "The Guy-Wu has done this to us. I see the end now. All is fire. And death for those who have chosen to follow Guy-Wu."

He released a screeching, panicked scream, the desperate cry of a man descending into madness. And then he froze in place—and keeled over. Stone dead, just like that. Heart attack. Or maybe a stroke.

"Galaxy's a better place," Rechs remarked when the biometric nanite read back a flat line.

But the Nether Ops captain seemed to have already forgotten the ninja. "Who is Guy-Wu?"

Rechs could tell she wasn't asking him.

Jacobson pulled out her datapad and tapped a few screens. "Okay. Here we are." She showed it to Rechs. On screen was what looked to be a transcript of the interrogation, and Jacobson was running it through a translator app. "Most likely he used the word... *Guàiwù*. It means... Ogre."

***

White Plum was thirty kilometers away, but the old speeder made the trek a manageable one. Like everything else on the old vehicle, its navigational software was slow and outdated, designed to rely on satellite mapping, and since Shangri-La had no satellites in orbit, its screen was a blank canvas. Until Rechs pulled up a folder containing past routes. Red lines appeared, showing the last thirty routes the speeder had taken.

It had been to the mountain frequently.

Rechs didn't follow any of the routes directly, preferring instead to forge a new route to the same destination. It was safer, though it required dodging more rocks and trees.

After the speeder jumped a brook and scraped bottom in a thicket, he turned to Jacobson. "You okay?"

"Yeah. But there goes the trade-in value."

White Plum wasn't so much a mountain as a massive rock wedged in the middle of a depression teeming with greenery. Rechs figured it was likely some asteroid that had smashed into the primordial landscape and stuck there centuries before.

A narrow staircase had been cut into the rock, climbing three thousand feet to a temple at the top. The former home of the monks. The bottom of the mountain was shrouded in mist, but they knew it provided access to the Divine Hand's subterranean bunkers. That was where their tortured captive had told them the "Samurais slept."

It hadn't escaped Rechs's or Jacobson's notice that a plural was used.

Samurais.

It made sense. How else to take back Sinasia?

The Samurais carried a variety of weapons systems that could decimate ground troops at division strength as easily as they could take out low-orbit capital ships.

Rechs had no armor, one working blaster, a few charge packs, and a knife.

Even for the bounty hunter, those odds were not to be dismissed.

"How do we know he's there?" Jacobson asked. She sounded almost desperate. The odds seemed to be weighing against her better instincts, too.

"We don't," Rechs replied. "Not until we get visual on him. But I think this is the big game. And I think whoever this Ogre is… he's the one driving the Dragon. The one who's put all the pieces in play. This isn't the Dragon's show. It's his."

"Ajax."

Rechs nodded as he drove the speeder.

"Okay," she said after a long moment. "Then how do we get in?"

Rechs had been thinking about that. He *wanted* to barge in right through the front door. Once inside, he'd try to get his hands on some decent weapons. Then he'd kill his way all the way to the Dragon. Odds be damned.

He liked that approach. It was his specialty.

And it gave him the best chance of getting his hands on a hypercomm. If the Sinasians had been smuggling tech the size of Samurais onto Shangri-La, then they'd have to be using at least a few big ships. Heavy freighters with room to haul the mech's larger assemblies. No way were they running an operation like this on a planet that was comm-dark. They had hypercomms. Rechs just had to find out where.

Then he could call Lyra, get her to dust off from Taijing and jump the *Crow* to him at full speed. Hopefully she could avoid the interceptors better than Shurrigan had. If she violated all the safety parameters… the *Crow* could be here in thirty minutes. And once he got into his armor—which should be in much better shape now, thanks to its repair nanites, plus whatever the bots were able to accomplish—the odds might shift enough to effect a rescue of the Dragon.

That plan would settle the issue quickly, one way or another. Either he and Jacobson would do a lot of quick killing, or they would quickly be killed themselves.

But as much as Rechs liked that plan, he opted for an alternate approach. One he figured had a higher chance of success in the long run.

"I'll climb the stairs up the side of the mountain, to the temple at the top. With all the monks slaughtered, chances are the temple will either be abandoned or repurposed."

"And what about me?" asked Jacobson.

"Try the front door if you don't hear from me in six hours. Try to sneak into the hangar and find a hypercomm to call in your pals in Nether Ops and tell them to take out the base. Kill the Dragon if they have to. Otherwise it's war."

"So you're back to that?" she said angrily.

"Captain," Rechs began, then stopped. "Wendy. Ask yourself: is one person worth all the dead a war with the Republic will cost? If we can't save him… that's the price the rest of the galaxy will have to pay. The galaxy has seen enough war. It shouldn't have to foot that bill again."

***

A peaceful stream encircled the massive, oblong granite that was White Plum. From this vantage, the uppermost regions of the rock were swallowed up by the mist, but the base came into view between patches of green fog.

"There's the main blast doors," Jacobson said, pointing. A small army of sentries patrolled the powerful doors, which were cut right into the mountain. Defensive towers rose up from the mist, guarding the pathway to the door every forty meters.

"Six hours," said Rechs. "And then you know what you have to do. Take my blaster and charge packs. My way is stealth... yours will probably require a fight."

Jacobson didn't respond, and Rechs left not knowing if she would do what it took—what the galaxy needed—if it came down to it.

The only way this wasn't going to end badly was if Rechs could get to the Dragon with the *Crow* already inbound for an extraction. Then, either he would convince the kid to spare the galaxy another conflict that would kill millions if not billions, or he'd try to subdue him long enough to get him on the ship and off the grid until the kid's mind was right. The Dragon had been conditioned to behave the way he was behaving now. Rechs felt like, given time, he could decondition him.

Or you could just kill him, said that other voice. *Because you know that has to be an option. If you can't reason with him or take him alive... then you know you have to.*

Rechs waded through the stream and crept out on its far side beneath the shadow of White Plum. The mist was coming in stronger now, fighting to remove even the limited visibility that Rechs had enjoyed just minutes before. It looked as though a blanket were being draped over the mountain, swallowing the mountain's stone pathway, hiding rickety-looking bridges that crossed over cracks and fissures. Covering the sheer faces where no visible path could be observed. But Rechs could still see the base of the steps, carved into the stone not far from where he stood.

I must focus on this, he told himself, pushing out thoughts about the Dragon. He didn't know how long it had been since the monks had been purged, or if anyone had stepped up to maintain the trails after they were gone. It wasn't a large mountain, but what he'd seen of the path didn't inspire confidence. And it was certainly tall enough for a fall to be fatal.

He climbed, his body adapting to the air while protesting the exertion. It had been a rough few days for Tyrus Rechs, and he needed more rest than he'd gotten. He reached a curve in the cleft where the stairs turned almost vertical, forcing him to hug the rock with barely any room to stand on. But it afforded him the chance to scan the rainforest to see how Jacobson was holding up.

His eyesight was excellent. Always had been. Even before the Savages experimented on him. At first he thought the mists were too dense, and he was about to move on. But then he spotted her. She'd moved from their initial observation point and was crouched at the base of a tree, hidden from the main blast doors but not from Rechs.

She was talking on a device that looked to Rechs a lot like a mobile hypercomm.

She's sold you out.

32

Lʏʀᴀ ᴄᴀʟʟᴇᴅ ᴏᴜᴛ ꜰᴏʀ G232 ꜰʀᴏᴍ ᴡɪᴛʜɪɴ ᴛʜᴇ ᴄᴏɴ-fined and empty vastness of a silent *Obsidian Crow*. It was just a freighter, but without Rechs around, quiet as he was, it felt to the AI like a country unto itself.

"I am here, miss," answered the admin and protocol bot. It was seated next to the nav computer, where it had been conversing with the system about minutiae regarding anomalies of certain celestial bodies where the ruins of the Ancients had been found.

In Digita, of course.

Lyra wanted to run something by the bot, ostensibly to get its opinion, but primarily to have someone to talk to. "My passive sensors are detecting the super-destroyer is powering up her main jump reactor. Do you calculate they are leaving soon?"

G232 had been monitoring the comm traffic ever since the master's escape. The Republic seemed intent on finding the location of that smuggler's freighter. They had assessed—correctly, so far as G232 knew—that the master was on the trail of an individual known as the Dragon. Thus finding Tyrus Rechs was supposed to lead the Republic to the Dragon, or so most of the commanders involved in the operation surmised.

And G232 had listened to their every word.

"If our navigational tracking was unable to establish the master's course, I do not believe the super-destroyer will be able to do better."

Lyra sighed. She'd had this discussion with the bot before. And while G232 didn't seem to tire of repeating itself, she longed for something new. Something more substantial. "The nature of Tyrus's departure and the high alert of all forces in the sector in the aftermath of the mech's rampage would have allowed the gathering of enough data to provide likely jump solutions." The AI was quick to add, "Not for one hundred percent certainty, of course."

"The master and his… acquaintance could be off on a wild goose chase, miss," G232 reminded her, with no small amount of sobriety.

They had discussed this possibility and many others in the hours after Rechs's escape. Lyra was concerned for her captain. He had departed the ship without his usual array of weapons and without any of his armor, the latter of which the little Nubarian bot had fawned over while attempting some sort of repairs.

"In my experience with the master…" G232 stopped itself. "I mean the *captain*, I have found that it is best to simply do as he says. It is undeniable that he attracts a high volume of blaster fire and animosity. The likelihood of him being in a blaster fight at any given moment is far above that of an average humanoid. However, once that fight begins, I assure you the math is quite in our master's favor."

"I believe he is in danger, G232," said Lyra. "We have the tools he needs. I believe that in our service to him it is advisable that we power up in time to leave storage and follow the super-destroyer to its destination. I contend that in so doing, we will likely find Captain Rechs."

G232 paused as if considering. "Ah, I see your point, miss. I find myself agreeing with your conclusion. However, should we get close to the... er, *captain*, the overwhelming firepower possessed by the Republic super-destroyer will surely be aimed at us. I am not programmed for combat. And I do not wish to be."

The engines of the souped-up old freighter began to hum to life.

G232 looked around as if this was a sound it had never heard before. "I see you've made your choice, miss," it said, rather morosely.

The bot leaned close to the nav computer and whispered, "One wonders why *we* weren't afforded a vote."

***

The first thousand feet up the side of the rock was a study in madness. The staircase got narrower and narrower until Rechs was literally inching his way up the curving face, following the hewn rock as it climbed steeply into the mist ahead. The swirling greens seemed to have followed him up—they were everywhere now—and Rechs found himself unable to see more than a few meters ahead.

Eventually the stairs widened, allowing Rechs to relax his cramped and tension-racked muscles. But with that relief came a new obstacle that almost made the bounty hunter long for more of the narrow stairs. What could only loosely be referred to as a bridge swung before him. Its ropes were frayed and mildewed, and its boards looked rotten and none too stable. But there was no other way to go besides down, and if Rechs was going to move in that direction, he might as well make the trip a fast one.

He started across the suspension bridge, hoping it would hold his weight at least long enough for him to leap across to the rock wall on the other side of the gap. But not ten feet out he was rewarded with the thunder-clapping snap of an ancient board giving beneath his boot. His stomach dropped as he held tightly to the two guide ropes and shifted his weight onto his back foot. He looked down in a vain attempt to watch the broken board tumble to the bottom, but though he heard it clattering against the mountainside, its descent was veiled by the mist.

And then the board he stood on—what he imagined to be the stronger board—snapped as well.

Rechs felt all of his weight go out from underneath him. He hung, suspended over the boiling cauldron of green mist, a hand gripping each rotting guideline. How well would these now hold him? His muscles began to tremble as his feet dangled in midair over a thousand-foot drop.

With a quiet creak, one of the ropes began to fray and unwind. The bridge dipped down several feet at once.

His heart racing, Rechs pulled himself forward. He planted a foot on the next ancient board just as the frayed rope gave out. The remaining guideline was far from sufficient to hold Rechs's weight on its own, and snapped in two behind him. Just like that the bridge split in half, and Rechs, gripping the ropes with all his might, flew down and toward the far wall of the gap as though swinging on vines between trees.

He turned his body so his shoulder slammed into the rock, but still the collision caused an agony of blunt pain. The ropes frayed further, dropping Rechs and causing his shoulder to scrape against the mountainside. His shirt tore, and blood trickled from scoured skin.

He scanned the rock face frantically. The ropes could not be relied on for more than a few seconds more. He spotted handholds in the rock and leapt to them just as the bridge lost its moorings and tumbled down into the misty depths.

Chest heaving, breath coming in gasps, Rechs clung to mist-moist granite. He needed to catch his breath. He was red-lining on fear and adrenaline. Though his fingers ached, in time his breathing stabilized, and he heard nothing but the soft sigh of the wind as it moved the mist along the rocks.

It was a lonely sound, made more so by the state Rechs found himself in. Clinging to the face of a massive rock, no trail in sight. But he knew which direction he needed to go.

Up.

He knew that much.

And then he heard the laughter, dry and smoky like the crackle of burning leaves in fall. It drifted down from high above the upper reaches of the jagged crevasse. And then it was gone.

Rechs craned his neck to look straight up. All he saw was mist.

Maybe that's for the best, he told himself. It meant that he was hidden from the laugher just as much as the laugher was hidden from him.

He didn't like the idea of someone waiting up there for him, but his body told him he couldn't hang on the side of the cliff face forever. It was time to move.

Shut up, I'm climbing, Rechs responded. Willing his body to fight past the pain and fatigue, he ascended.

It wasn't the worst climb he'd ever experienced. He'd done tougher. But as he worked the face from position to position, testing rocks and crevices to see if they would hold his weight as he levered himself up along the wall one hold at a time, he decided that it *was* the most ill-prepared he'd ever been for a climb. At least in those other experiences he'd had gear. Picks, carabiners... power armor. Even chalk. Free-climbing was a whole different animal. Just your fingers, boots, and the stone.

At last, breathing hard, he pulled himself up onto a ledge and just lay there. The mysterious laughter was in the back of his mind, telling him to be ready, because in this weakened condition, he could be undone. But the only sound in the deeps of the high misty canyon was his own panting breath. Still, he pushed himself to his knees and looked to see where he should go next.

It was apparent that the only way forward was going to require some faith. The side of the crevasse was devoid of any further handholds or fissures. It was as though the monks had specifically taken pains to remove anything that would aid a climber. At least, anything that would aid a normal climb.

What they *had* provided was a series of square-cut, horizontal pillars carved out of the mountainside. Rechs could jump from his ledge onto the first of these pillars, and then jump again to the next one, each pillar rising a little higher than the last. It was a trail meant more for a mountain goat than a man.

But Rechs had no other options.

He leapt to the first pillar, miscalculating how wet it was. He nearly slip-slided right over the far side, saving himself only by buckling his knees and falling straight on his rear. The pillar was perhaps a meter square, and Rechs sat at the very edge. Looking down, even with the mist below, was vertigo-inducing, so Rechs maintained his gaze on the next pillar.

He rose to his feet and made three more leaps, each larger than the last, before he needed to rest.

The canyon walls had come close enough together for Rechs to see that he was climbing up inside some kind of wide fissure. He'd lost all sense of measurement and had no idea how high he'd climbed. Or how far he would fall if he made even the slightest mistake.

And who was to say if he was even on the right track? What if he was just off climbing some natural phenomenon? Or an ancient trap in the course that had been laid out to deal with the un-enlightened?

Or simply a dead end?

A gust of wind carried away the gathered mist. Rechs heard the sound of canvas flapping in the breeze, recognizing its sudden drumbeat. The sound grew in frequency, if not intensity, as though more flags—or whatever they were—were being caught in the wind.

Rechs peered up into the thinning mist and spotted three dark figures, hooded and wearing robes like shrouds. They were coming down the mountain walls on ropes that looked to be little more than black and gray sheets tied together in knots. They were rappelling, bouncing down the rock face, with an ease that didn't seem possible. That seemed almost reckless.

Then, almost as though unrolling itself from some carpet, the lead figure came at Rechs, its line of rope flaring out like a tongue of black fire. The man looked to be in free fall.

He moved with such surprising speed that Rechs wasn't ready for the kick aimed at his face. The bounty hunter had to windmill his arms to keep from going over the edge. He grabbed his face and felt blood pooling in his mouth.

The attacker had already spun away, swung off to the opposite canyon wall, and was rebounding to come back in for another strike. Above, the other two were unfurling their scarf lines and dropping in fast.

Rechs leapt, forcing his powerful legs to elevate him above the first attacker. He took hold of the line, dangling above the man, and cut the rope with a savage yank.

The man fell into the fog below. He didn't scream as he was swallowed by the greedy mist, but his body sent up a resounding thump as it crashed against some hidden rock, a farewell before continuing its tumble to the bottom.

The other two, seeing what had happened, halted their descent by some unseen means and drew swords. It was clear to Rechs that they had decided to treat the bounty hunter to a taste of his own medicine by cutting the line he now swung from.

He planted his feet against the mist-slick side of the crevasse, but rather than pushing off to engage, he began to haul himself up hand over hand along the rope of scarves. The fiber they were made from felt unlike anything Rechs had ever experienced. Cool as silk, and tough as Legion cord, the rope glided through his hands as he raced to get ahead of the ninjas now swinging in.

The first one beat Rechs by a slim margin. He wrapped his arm in Rechs's rope and his leg in his own, then swung his gleaming, curved blade at the thread of life from which the bounty hunter dangled.

Knowing what came next, Rechs let go of the line and grabbed the man's free leg. Using his knife like a climbing hammer, he slammed it into the man repeatedly, pulling himself up with each strike as the ninja screamed. The attacker dropped his sword, and his limp body would have fallen to the bottom with Rechs along for the ride had he not wrapped his arm and leg in the ropes.

Rechs pulled himself over the dying man's shoulders, grabbing both ropes now. The ninja, pale from the blood-letting, could only feebly watch as Rechs cut him loose, sending him down into the fog to litter the bottom of White Plum.

The remaining ninja, on the other side of the crevasse, let go of his line and leapt like some fantastic puma for the wall above Rechs. Miraculously, he held on and began to inch along the wall toward Rechs's lines, his sword still on his back.

Rechs thought about how much easier this might have gone for him if he hadn't left Jacobson his blaster.

He pushed himself off the wall with both lines and swung back to the other side of the crevasse, only taking his eyes off the ninja above long enough to land with both boots. He was cold and tired and didn't feel like there was much left in him. But he ignored all the weakness his body screamed on about. He knew firsthand just how much farther he could go. There was no room for weakness up here on the rock, high above everything. There was no room for it in the galaxy.

When he looked up, the ninja was on his lines.

33

"Ball, old man?" asked the ninja above Tyrus Rechs, both lines in his hands.

Rechs hung there, completely at the mercy of the hooded man.

Ball.

"You're..." *The Dragon.*

"We knew you'd visited us," said the Dragon, his voice sounding clear above the mist, above Rechs's heavy breathing. "Not then, but later. Once they allowed us more access to the galaxy, to better become you. We understood then."

Rechs said nothing. If the Dragon wanted him dead, he'd be dead now. He might as well do what he could to find a handhold in the rock while he still had the chance. But there were none. So he began to climb the ropes, staying in the game until he was forced out of it.

"On that day," the Dragon continued, seemingly uninterested in Rechs's climb, "when I came into the forest to find the ball we were using for our game..."

Every time Rechs looked up, he seemed no closer to the Dragon. He was always the same distance away. The

Dragon was obviously climbing to stay above him, but was showing no signs of exertion.

"... I only wondered who the stranger was."

Rechs's fingers were cramped and numb, and a small dark cloud kept trying to push itself into his vision. He fought hard, controlling his mind and forcing himself not to look at the cloud. Because the cloud said...

Let go. Just drop and it'll all be over.

You can rest while you fall.

"Imagine my shock," the Dragon continued, almost conversationally, "when as a legionnaire in Basic, they taught us the history of the Legion. Y'know that one course where you learn about the battles and the dead who earned the Order of the Centurion. About the flags and their meanings. The hall with all the portraits of all the dead heroes. Imagine, General Rex, when I found out it was *you* in the forest that afternoon."

Rechs's arms shook uncontrollably. It took the last of his ebbing strength to keep his hands closed tight around the ropes.

Imagine, the raven whispered in his mind.

No, Rechs roared at himself. *Not a raven. The Dragon.*

Anger surged into him. Meaningless anger he had no right to. But it was what he needed if he was going to get off this rope and reach flat outcrop.

Ten more meters to go. Dig deep. Fight.

How dare this kid start another war!

"And with enough digging," the Dragon continued, "we figured it all out. The ones of us who were left at the time. There are even fewer now. But still... we figured it out, General. Who you were. Who we are."

Ball.

Papa.

Rechs had called his own father that long ago millennia before. Back on Earth, when such a place still existed.

"I was wrong," grunted Rechs as the final embers of his strength looked to be quenched and he had nothing left but all the old sins that had come to haunt him. "I should have fought them. I should have fought for you."

The Dragon.

Jacobson had called the kid… his son.

"Imagine that," said the Dragon, a definite chill in his voice.

Rechs's strength was gone. He could climb no more. All he could do now was hang on the lines. For a long moment he twisted there in the soft wind that had come up through the crevasse, pushing the fog around to curl and writhe along the face of the gray rock all about.

When he finally looked up, the Dragon was gone.

But Rechs heard his voice.

"Go home, old man. You were nothing to me then, and you're nothing to me now."

"Then," Rechs managed to croak out, "why?"

"I owe you enough to let you live. This one time. Go home. There *is* a war coming."

Rechs heard the padding of the Dragon's feet up the crevasse wall. And then it stopped. The Dragon called down, his voice much more distant now. "You should have fought for us, General. We would have loved you. We would have died for you."

And then Rechs hung there alone, drifting from side to side, gently swaying in the breeze as he waited for his strength to either return and save him… or forsake him as the Dragon had.

***

Rechs's comm chimed.

Jacobson was on the other end, able to reach him in a comm-to-comm transmission. "So that's him. Target confirmed."

"Yeah," grunted Rechs, still not feeling up to the climb.

"You've been a help to me, Tyrus." Rechs noted she wasn't calling him *General* anymore. "So I'm going to do you a favor in return. In about five minutes you're going to see a super-destroyer overhead. You should surrender when it arrives. And if you can convince the Dragon to do the same... so much the better."

"I knew you sold me out."

"I never bought in, Tyrus."

Rechs grunted.

"There's no way off this rock for either of you. But this can still happen the hard way if that's the way you want to go out. It'll end very badly for a lot of people, though."

She didn't know the half of it.

Rechs wanted to lower his head and lean it against the rope. Just swing for a little while, feeling sorry for himself. But there wasn't room in the galaxy for that kind of weakness. It would eat you up. So he started climbing.

"You called them in as soon as I started up," he grunted as he pulled.

"I did. I figured you were right that this was the place, so I took the chance of calling in the cavalry before I'd confirmed visual."

"Guess you made the right call."

"No hard feelings, okay, Tyrus? This is my job. My duty."

Rechs pulled himself farther up the ropes, grunting as he said, "So much for not all of Nether Ops being the bad guys."

"Let's just say… there are layers, Tyrus. And turning in the Dragon, with you to boot, is going to fund a lot of black book operations for us. We make a lot of trouble for the House of Reason's enemies."

"I make trouble back."

"Not for much longer," she replied. And then the comm went dead.

Rechs climbed, still expecting the rope to be cut at any moment by a Dragon who'd changed his mind. The sensation didn't leave him until he reached an overhang and saw the summit of White Plum mountain above. At this height, the mist was beginning to clear.

He pulled himself up onto solid ground. Someone had left a medium blaster and a ruck full of charge packs. But what looked even better than the weapon was the canteen full of water and a square of rice and fish wrapped in seaweed.

Rechs sat down tiredly. Every muscle in his back and arms screamed like rusty old tension wires at the verge of snapping. His hands were trembling as he shoved the sweet fish and rice into his mouth. His jaw shook so much that he practically had to bite down on the canteen as its cold water poured down his gullet.

He picked up the blaster and checked its charge pack. Ravens—the actual birds—would sometimes leave baubles and other prizes for those who took care of them in the wild.

Ball.

"Ball," said Rechs.

***

Rechs was refreshed and heading toward the summit. Shangri-La's sun turned everything gold as it penetrated the green, otherworldly mist. The old and broken trail Rechs followed led to a low, flat temple that seemed as old as the ruins of the Ancients.

There was a flash and then the sound of thunder, with more rolling claps following. Rechs looked up and saw the newly arrived super-destroyer moments after it jumped directly into the atmosphere, tearing apart the sky with the shock waves in her wake. It was a reckless maneuver, testifying to just how much the Republic wanted the Dragon.

He didn't know exactly how, but he was sure there was a way out of this that didn't involve the Dragon's death. And he would die trying, if he had to, to save...

He didn't finish the sentence.

To be worthy, he told himself.

As the bounty hunter began to jog toward the temple, up through the slop of scree and stone, Republic Lancers screamed out from the super-destroyer's hangar bays. By the time he reached the outer edge of the temple, the Lancers filled the sky above him.

The temple was built from ancient stone, and covered in runes that didn't look Sinasian. There were no dragons ornamenting the structure, but beasts of a lost and mythical age were depicted in carved relief on the crumbling gray stones.

Rechs ignored all this lore as he entered.

Lancers buzzed the temple, causing it to rumble. And then Rechs heard the engines of the strange interceptors that had shot him down on his arrival to Shangri-La, a lost planet now found. The telltale exchange of blaster fire followed, marking either a skirmish that would end today, or a second Sinasian Conflict that would plague the galaxy.

Rechs ran, blaster out, deeper into the massive open spaces of the temple. He came to a garden of stone and sand.

The sound of a gong—the thing must have been massive, judging by the sheer volume it produced—stopped Rechs in his tracks. It was low and ominous, rattling the very molars in his jaw. Surely even the ships in the sky above would've heard that.

A warning. A call. An alert.

An old man, fat and scarred, with wispy gray hair and wearing the robes of the Sinasians, though not Sinasian himself, waddled out from the darkness of the temple beyond the garden.

"General!" the old man bellowed gustily.

Rechs studied the person before him, recognition coming to him slowly. All the photos that had accompanied the redacted files he'd studied on the long flight out to Taijing...

"Colonel Ajax," said Tyrus Rechs.

"General, you have no need of that," Ajax said, gesturing to Rechs's blaster. The weapon was aimed at the colonel's chest.

Rechs didn't lower his blaster. He stared into the face of the man who was behind it all. The Ogre. The magician who'd focused the Dragon's abilities, twisted the Dragon's longing to be part of something more than the Legion, leveraged him to start a war.

A war that was supposed to right all the wrongs.

Rechs had seen a thousand petty tyrants playing for the big seat across all his years. They always thought they were the ones who knew the way forward. That their plan was the thing no one had ever thought of. That only they could save the galaxy.

"I served under you at Telos," crooned the old colonel. "Was a lieutenant back then. What a day when we took that cruiser!"

The old man smiled, leaning against a pillar. Rechs could see that he was holding a very long samurai sword. Not a katana—it was much longer than that—but Rechs had forgotten the exact name.

"Old times, General," guffawed Ajax as though there were nothing but sentimental memories between the two old warriors.

The battle in the sky raged on.

"There's still time to get the kid out of here, Ajax," said Rechs. "I can save him."

"Save him?" exclaimed the fat old man. "He's going to save all of us. Like *we* should have. After the Battle at Telos, the Republic needed us so badly that we could have invoked Article Nineteen and put the Legion in control of the galaxy. They would have welcomed it. Begged us for it! Remember?"

Rechs remained silent. Starfighter battle, a sea of screaming banshees going at each other hammer and tongs, filled the air with its chaotic ambiance. Dropships and some of the newer shuttles were deploying. Soon legionnaires and marines would be all over the place.

Time was running out for Tyrus Rechs. And the Dragon.

"I remember," said Rechs.

"It could've been different!" shouted Ajax, a hint of melancholy in his voice. "It *should've* been!"

"But it wasn't," Rechs replied simply.

Ajax seemed genuinely surprised by this response. Or at least that was the look he'd affected. The old, fat man walked out onto the sand of the garden, raked in smooth lines. He dragged the long sword after him like a forgotten thing. A vicious dog following its master no matter where he led it.

"Join him, General. With the two of you working together... we can rule the galaxy. You know it. I know it."

He was coming closer. Dragging that sword, making new lines in the raked sand.

Rechs didn't want to have to kill him.

"Where is he, Ajax? I'm getting him out of here. Someplace safe."

The old colonel laughed again. "There's no place safer in all the galaxy, General. Only your presence has made it otherwise. But even so, he's very safe here." Ajax squinted up to where the super-destroyer would be, as if he could see it through the roof of the temple. "None of them will survive Shangri-La!"

The colonel laughed again, but it was drowned out by other sounds. Two dropships coming in hard and fast. Quick ropes, and then the boots of legionnaires hitting the roof. A door gunner opening up his N-50 on unseen targets.

Ajax looked around, taking in the sounds, a certain crazed delight dancing in his eyes at the start of this sought-after war.

Rechs surged forward and knocked the old colonel to the sand.

The drowning ghost-howl of a Sinasian interceptor rattled the temple. The report of its blaster cannons
made the swirling lines in the sand vibrate. The fight was
right above them. One of the dropships exploded, crashing down onto the roof and causing several stone blocks
beside the sand garden to shift and partially collapse. But
the temple held.

"We'll fight them to the death, General!" screamed
Ajax from the sand. "We'll make things right this time.
First Sinasia… then the Republic!"

"That ship is carrying a crustbuster, you old fool!"
Rechs shouted at the raving old man. "They'll kill the
whole planet just to get him!"

Colonel Ajax, once a golden boy of Dark Ops, sat
up, the side of his jowly face covered in sand. "And *you*,
Rechs! They'll kill you, too!" The colonel snarled. "And
that's something you couldn't stand for, is it? That's why
you ran! Why you left the Legion. Left all of them! You're
the fool. One so blind that you don't realize they'll kill
anyone to get their way! When will you learn that lesson?
How many—"

Rechs jerked the colonel to his feet.

"Where is he?" he shouted above the blaster fire in
the sky above and now resounding out through the temple quarters.

"He's coming!" Ajax shouted, his eyes wild with
delight. "He's coming! He's coming!"

The entire mountain began to shake. The pillars
within the temple portico began to crumble. The rooftop
at the other end of garden slid over on itself and collapsed
across that section of the complex, kicking centuries of
dust into the air, making every breath a choking ordeal.

Ajax hooted and howled, screaming, "Here he comes!"

Through the holes in the roof, Rechs could now see the super-destroyer turn to port, bringing her powerful guns to bear on the top of the high rock temple. But the almost alien Sinasian interceptors, agile and fast, were getting the best of the outnumbered Lancer squadron. The Republic had walked into a hornet's nest.

The earth shook and the sand began to sink and fall away as the very ground split open. A massive, hidden blast door was opening. And from it, up rose a vision from Rechs's past. Real and horrible all at once in this present nightmare.

The Samurai mechs had been unholy terrors on that long-ago battlefield Rechs and the Legion had fought on. Rechs had seen the havoc they wreaked on divisions of unprotected legionnaires. They were like a hot knife slicing through butter. Even one Samurai on the battlefield was a game changer.

The mech paid no mind to Rex or Ajax. It simply tore down the roof and climbed to the top of the temple.

Rechs could now see the smoking trails of missile pods—enough of them to have been launched from dozens more mechs—rising toward the massive super-destroyer looming in the sky above. They slammed into the massive engine cowlings along the aft section of the Republic's premier combat vessel.

But the super-destroyer was not without its own response. Almost instantly her powerful blaster cannons—guns meant to disable other capital ships, or destroy planetary targets through orbital bombardment—were brought to bear. Their hot fire sizzled across the landscape, raising the surface temperature as the massive attack sheared through large sections of the temple. Several of the mechs must have been incinerated in the blast—Rechs heard them exploding across White Plum like massive bombs. The temple was rapidly becoming a death trap. Rechs couldn't stay here.

Some of the other Samurai mechs must have deployed some sort of advanced shielding, because although the super-destroyer's blasts sent the machines flying skyward, they remained operational, gathered themselves, and continued upward under their own power.

Smart move, thought Rechs, and not just because their leaving the temple likely saved his life. The destroyer's blaster cannons were not made for precision firing, and would have trouble tracking the airborne Samurais.

As the bounty hunter stared up at the brilliant battle overhead, Ajax repeated shouts of "Yes! Yes!"

In the melee, Rechs spied a Samurai that was larger than all the rest. And more heavily armed. It was leading the assault on the super-destroyer from the front.

The Dragon.

"Captain! Can you hear me?"

Rechs shook his head. "Lyra?"

A moment later the bounty hunter saw the *Obsidian Crow* streak past the super-destroyer, weaving through blaster fire meant for the incoming mechs.

"I'm tracking your comm signature, Captain. We will pick you up shortly."

That was the best news Rechs had heard all day.

The old man was raving like a lunatic at the unfolding spectacle. The Samurai mechs closed in on the warship, downing Lancers attempting to intercept and then firing everything they had into the super-destroyer's hull. Explosions rippled across several decks. The damage was devastating, and though it was nothing close to what was needed to actually bring a ship like that down, Rechs doubted that the destroyer's captain had ever been in a fight like this one before.

Which meant, and Rechs knew this deep down, that the destroyer was probably requesting clearance to use the crustbuster to end this before it got any further out of hand. A firing solution was probably being calculated even now.

"Lyra, I—"

Rechs was interrupted by legionnaires entering the temple. Looking to KTF, they engaged immediately. Two blaster bolts struck Ajax square in the chest while Rechs ducked for cover behind one of the few remaining pillars, leaning at a sharp angle from the toppled stone roof that had fallen all around it.

"Are you hurt?" called Lyra.

"I'm fine!" Rechs replied as he attempted to keep the legionnaires back with the blaster the Dragon had left for him. "Just get here as soon as you can!"

The *Crow* arrived, flaring her repulsors hard amid the battle and trying to pivot for landing. But there was too little space to put the ship down.

"Master," said G232 over the comm, "I hope we have not ruined your plans by arriving without your express consent. And on a side note… this is all quite thrilling."

"Tell the Nubarian to start firing!" shouted Rechs as he moved to a new column to get closer to the hovering ship.

"Oh!" exclaimed G232. "I have forbidden him to fire at anything unless we are in direct danger, Captain. I was attempting to minimize damage to your often complex and enigmatic mission plans."

Rechs sighted a moving legionnaire and dropped him with a single blast to the head. Above, his hovering ship was having a hard time getting in close due to the mass of the rubble from the super-destroyer's strike against the temple. Big, uneven mounds of stone slabs had Lyra constantly dancing to avoid slamming into them. She couldn't stay level long enough for Rechs to run on board.

"You *are* in direct danger, Three-Two. Tell him to *open up!*"

The admin and protocol bot came back over the comm. "Good heavens. Disabling his restrictors now."

A moment later the omni-cannon started firing wildly. At everything.

"Lyra, lower the boarding ramp. And hold position if you can!"

Rechs chanced a look as more blaster fire came at him from across the ruined garden. The legionnaires were advancing, passing Ajax's corpse, its bulging eyes staring sightlessly up at the sky battle.

Rechs ran. He jumped up onto a pillar that had fallen on its side and leapt for the boarding ramp, grabbing the ramp's edge. He barely held on as Lyra pivoted the ship and made to depart, everywhere legionnaire blaster bolts scoring hits where he'd just been, their aim thrown off by Lyra's erratic flying.

Rechs pulled himself up onto the ramp, putting it between him and the blaster fire. The ramp began to retract into the ship, and he had to quickly crawl forward. He just barely made it in before the ramp would have taken off his feet.

Panting, he lay on the rubberized walkway within the ship.

"Lyra…"

"Yes, Captain. Preparing to jump—"

"Negative. Evasive maneuvers. Stick close to that super-destroyer."

"Captain! I—"

"Do it."

Rechs pushed off from the floor and ran for his armory as the ship streaked across the battlescape.

THE LAST BATTLE

Rᴇᴄʜꜱ ᴘᴜᴛ ᴏɴ ʜɪꜱ ᴀʀᴍᴏʀ ꜰᴀꜱᴛᴇʀ ᴛʜᴀɴ ʜᴇ ᴇᴠᴇʀ ʜᴀᴅ before. And then he waited an interminable ten minutes as Lyra flew increasingly desperate maneuvers to get closer to the gigantic hull of the super-destroyer. G232 attempted to call out enemy movements, but with little to no military expertise, he might as well have kept silent.

Rechs scoured his workbench, grabbing his heaviest automatic blaster, the N-34, and a cutting torch. As he made his way to the boarding hatch, the *Obsidian Crow* jerked and jinked across the battle.

"Situation, Three-Two!" he barked.

Through the hull, the sound of ship-to-ship blaster fire and explosions roared and cascaded like it was the end of the galaxy.

The galaxy has to end someday, Rechs told himself. As do all things.

"Well, master, those rather large bots—what's left of them—are using their weapons. I'm not sure what one would call them, some kind of missile. They're firing them rather prodigiously along the upper hull of the wounded capital ship. Several of the bots have now gone

◆ 294 ◆

down inside the ship, while the large one you've tagged as 'Dragon' seems to be overseeing operations along the hull after disabling the nearby blaster cannons. The humans you've told me to refer to as 'marines' are attempting to fight off the machines on the hull. But I fear their efforts are in vain. Or so it appears."

"Lyra!" shouted Rechs, one gloved gauntlet raising the boarding hatch and lowering the door position. Below and beyond the hull he could see the battle underway. "The time is now!"

The super-destroyer was under reverse power, backing away from the planet and heading for the upper atmosphere. Protocols for releasing a crustbuster included a requirement for extra-orbital positioning, but with the ship being boarded by Samurais, the Repub commanders on scene weren't likely to wait for protocol if it seemed the ship was going down.

"Lyra, put me down on the hull, and watch out for those Samurais."

The *Crow* came in hard and fast over the white hull of the sprawling ship. Down here, close to the surface, it was large enough to have its own horizon. It looked like a city of towers and boxes in the sky.

A flaming Lancer slammed into the cockpit of a Samurai, causing the mech's magnetic system to fail. The starfighter and mech tumbled together toward the planet's surface, intertwined in death.

Rechs jumped and fired his jets to land on the super-destroyer's hull, as though he'd just taken a bounce on a trampoline.

"Get the ship clear, Lyra!"

He moved forward, dodging blaster fire from both marines and mechs who were engaged in the "valley" of the central transportation cargo rail that ran the length of the ship. The Dragon's forces had breached all along its length and were holding that position. Possibly fighting their way down into the main launch tubes to prevent the crustbuster from being fired.

That was assuming they even knew it was there. But that's what Rechs would do if he were in the Dragon's situation.

Marines were getting chewed up by the few mechs holding the breach. But they had no choice: it was very clearly a matter of stopping the monsters or having their ride go down hard. So they kept fighting for all they were worth. Rechs imagined the super-destroyer's Legion element was entirely on the ground, with perhaps a company held back to defend the ship. If so, that element would likely be fighting the mechs inside.

"Captain—er, master—no, captain was right," began G232 over the comm.

Rechs was engaging a detachment of marines who were out onto the hull with an MPRGS, a rail weapon system. An old-school guaranteed mech killer they'd most likely had to break out of stores. Rechs's N-34, a special Legion weapon he'd purchased on the black market, over-cycled into high-speed automatic fire. Blaster bolts blurred from its long barrel like streaking lightning and cut the marines down in an instant. Bodies tumbled off into the atmosphere or slid toward the outer edge of the hull, where they cartwheeled down to the planet below.

"Still monitoring transmission over the L-comm, and it seems the ship's personnel have lost the launch tube control room. Which would seem to be good news," said G232 triumphantly. "Alas, the command bridge now has fire control and will launch the weapon shortly. Shall we come pick you up now that all is lost, master? This is all getting rather hazardous, or so it would seem."

More MPRGS teams were coming out onto the hull. Soon those portable rail gun systems would make quick work of the remaining mechs.

Rechs used his jump jets to bump himself up to a destroyed air-defense turret. The ship's current elevation was twenty-eight thousand meters and climbing. Still too close to use that crustbuster safely.

If the captain still cared about being safe.

Rechs tagged the Dragon's mech with the laser comm. "It's over," he said. "They're going to fire. Come with me if you want to live. There's still time to get clear of this. You can live. Have a life. A family. All those…"

He trailed off.

All those things I never had. Or had… long ago.

The bounty hunter watched the battle along the valley of the main rail line. The marines were turning the tide, dwindling the Samurais down to four. The hull-busters closed in from all points.

"Can't," came back the voice of the Dragon over the comm. "They're determined to use it. I need to stop it."

The massive Samurai turned and boosted off toward the launch tubes at the bow of the ship. The Dragon's mech was holed and trailing debris from several internals.

Rechs boosted his jets, praying there was enough jump juice to keep up as he bounded after.

"Lyra…"

"Here, Tyrus!"

Not Captain.

Tyrus. Like she…

Rechs shook his head. No time for that. He raced for the retreating mech.

The marines dropped the remaining Samurais and began firing hopeful rail gun shots at the bounty hunter.

Altitude was now reading thirty-three hundred meters.

"Lyra, stay close to me. I might not have much time to get away."

The mech reached the bow and began to climb down the burning bridge stack. Initial missile assaults had ruined this section of the ship. Primary control was most likely coming from the auxiliary bridge.

"Captain!" called G232. "I think this is very important. The missile is in the tube. They're preparing to fire. Orders to go to jump upon weapon release are confirmed by engineering. I estimate this is not fruitful to your plans."

Rechs gave up almost all the jump juice he had to reach the burning bridge stack. The ship was on fire across massive sections and bellowing ominous black smoke from her portside hangars. The mech had disappeared, and was most likely climbing down to the tubes along the ruined face of the bow.

He's going to block the firing tube with his mech, thought Rechs.

The weapon would still detonate; they'd probably disarmed all the altitude safeties just to get it to fire this close to the planet. But it would detonate here, rather than on planet. The ship would be destroyed in that instant. The planet, and the Sinasians with it, would live another day.

How do you know he'll do that? asked that other voice.

Because, thought Rechs as he peered over the bow of the ship and saw the mech climbing down three decks below to cover the launch tubes with its bulk. *It's what I would do.*

Rechs climbed down after the Dragon. If he slipped, he'd fall right off the front of the ship. It was a long way down, and not even the old Mark I armor could stand up to that.

A moment later the missile appeared, slowly thrusting its way from the ship as if being birthed. The Dragon was too late to stop the launch.

But not too late to hitch a ride.

Rechs watched in horror as the missile began to streak away from the ship, with the Dragon holding on and trailing behind it. The bounty hunter used the last of his juice to fling himself from the ship after them, arching out into the void.

His gauntleted fingers caught hold of a coupling hose on the mech's leg.

It must have been quite a spectacle: Rechs clinging to a massive Samurai mech, which in turn was hanging on to the largest piece of ordnance the Repub Navy carried.

"What are you doing?" groaned the Dragon.

He's wounded, thought Rechs. *Badly, by the sound of it.*

"Can you disable it?" the bounty hunter asked.

"Trying…" grunted the Dragon. "Hydraulics are going. I can't do much else besides hold on. Attaching mag-grapples…" He cursed. "Hydraulics are dead. That's all I can do now."

The massive mech was spraying fluid everywhere. Debris was coming off of it in sections. The mag-grapples were locked on to the missile, ensuring the mech would be carried along with it. But the Dragon was helpless to do anything that might disable the Republic weapon.

Except…

"Setting the mech to detonate."

"Don't!" shouted Rechs.

"It's okay… don't think I'm going to make it."

Ball.

Rechs fought to think of something. Anything out of what was shaping up to be impossible.

"Sorry…" said the Dragon. "I think you're along… for the ride."

"Kid?" called Rechs.

There was no reply.

"Stay with me!" he shouted into the comm.

The weapon was picking up speed now. Boosting its engines to achieve relativistic speeds. Eventually it would activate a small charge that would micro-jump the weapon into an identified planetary fault line and destabilize the surface. For all intents and purposes, the planet would die as the crust popped and fractured. The ecological ruin would be immediate, and within hours the planet would probably tear itself apart through its own eruptions and the local effects of gravity violently trying to correct its established orbit. The clincher would come when the poles reversed, and the planet literally came apart in sections.

"Stay with me!" shouted Rechs again. His voice sounded frantic in his ears.

And in his heart… he knew the Dragon was gone.

But you don't know that! his mind screamed.

And the memory of some old NCO, some long-dead sergeant from way back on the Earth that no one believed in anymore, hectored Rechs.

You don't quit till I get tired.

Rechs pulled himself along the body of the mech, despite the storm of wind and speed buffeting his every movement, knowing that one missed handhold would tear him away from the streaking Samurai and cast him off into an oblivion from which he would never emerge.

"Captain Rechs," said G232 over the comm. "Lyra is detecting an energy surge within the mech you are currently... next to. She indicates it is highly likely that it will explode once its reactor reaches an uncoolable cascade."

Thus destroying the weapon and saving the planet, thought Rechs grimly.

He reached the pilot's smashed cupola and looked inside. The Dragon was there in a flight suit, bleeding out. He looked dead.

The weapon they rode streaked across the surface of the planet, thundering through the mist-green skies. The landscape raced by below, and Rechs knew they were homing in on the fissure the weapon had identified as most likely to destabilize the planet in the shortest amount of time.

"Lyra. I need you to fly the *Crow* right beneath us!"

He could feel her saying no. He could feel *himself* saying no, telling himself all the ways this wouldn't work. All the ways this would end badly.

But he heard the engines of his ship coming closer.

Dangerously close. If ship and missile connected, that would be the end right there.

Rechs magnetized his boots and pulled the cutting torch from off his back, forcing it through the windstorm and gripping the mech cockpit with his other gauntlet.

He had no free hand with which to switch it on.

"C'mon!" he shouted at no one.

He bashed his bucket into the start button.

The cutter spouted to life.

"Captain…" said Lyra in a warning tone. The *Crow*'s engines whined, and the ship suddenly dove lower in a jerky movement to get away from incoming blaster fire.

"What's going on?" asked Rechs as he began to make his cut lines in the mech's hatch.

"The weapon has started its descent, Captain," said G232 forlornly.

Rechs continued to cut. Time was running out. Growing thinner by the second. Either the mech would detonate very shortly, or the missile would find the fault that would destroy this world. Either way ended up with him being atomized.

Rechs cut fast and had the hatch half open when the storm of wind tore it away with an abrupt metallic groan. Within the cockpit lay the Dragon, lifeless and being thrown about in his straps by the gusty storm.

Rechs let go of the plate cutter, letting it disappear in the wind to fall thousands of feet below.

"Get in closer, Lyra!" he shouted over the comm. The wind was slamming his bucket from side to side as he struggled to get into the cockpit.

He could feel the missile descending. Its final flight path was established. He could hear a sort of hum, even through the wind. Was that the missile or the mech? Which would it be?

"Tyrus, it's almost impossible!" said Lyra quietly. Fear and frustration permeated the AI's voice. Something supposedly impossible and yet there.

"Lyra… you can do this. I need you to. Otherwise… I lose him."

And I'm not letting go, he thought as he reached into the cockpit and grabbed hold of a man with his DNA. A man Captain Jacobson referred to as his son. Rechs realized that the inference had found a place somewhere deep inside of him.

The Dragon was his son. Rechs was responsible for his being in the world.

I won't let go. Not now. Not ever.

The *Crow* came in, its hull just beside the missile, so close it seemed the two might touch. Lyra had deftly positioned the upper cargo access right below and a bit behind Rechs. Two meters distance at an altitude of twenty-one thousand meters moving fast across the sky.

There was no guarantee that they wouldn't just streak off beyond the hull, Rechs and the kid in his arms. Maybe bounce off the engines and begin the long fall to the planet below. But Rechs had to make the jump, with no jets to guide him.

He let go, holding on to the Dragon, holding on to his... son... as the galaxy tried to drag them away. He let go of everything that could happen and dove across the void between the two vehicles. The missile and the old freighter speeding at the edge of sanity.

Margin for error: none.

Possibility verging on the impossible.

But some poet Rechs had once read said, *Gravity is love in the swimming pool of the universe.*

Maybe that was true.

For a moment they hung between the missile that destroyed worlds and the hold of the *Obsidian Crow*. All things, all the horrible endings, were possible in that instant.

The mech blowing up and killing them all...

The missile jumping into the fault line, liquefying Rechs from the inside out just from the energy of the sudden acceleration...

Missing the cargo hatch and flying off into oblivion at this high altitude of mind-numbing insanity...

Or smashing into the inside of the cargo hold, holding your son and seeing the cargo hatch closing behind you...

Which was what Rechs saw. That and the evil shape of the crustbuster, firing its engines right beside the ship. Surging to ready for the micro-jump and final impact.

"Break off, Lyra!" shouted Rechs. "Close the hatch and climb for jump!"

The *Crow*'s engines howled in response, and the mech exploded a second later somewhere beyond the ship... sending the *Crow* into darkness.

The ship was falling. Unpowered and dead. All systems knocked out by the powerful effect of the mech's detonation.

In the dark of the hold Rechs held the Dragon, not knowing if he was dead, or alive, or just hovering between those worlds waiting to be greeted by what lay in the strange and undiscovered country.

Ball.

"Ball," whispered Rechs.

If death was coming for him now, after all these years, then this wasn't the worst way.

All was silent as the ship fell through the atmosphere. The explosion pulse seemed to have knocked all sound out of the galaxy.

Emergency lighting came online. The ship was shaking like it might throw itself apart. The squeal and whine of the engines roared to life as if that were the most natural, and yet unexpected, thing in the galaxy. And then the ship was boosting, climbing away from that world.

"We're clear, Tyrus!" said Lyra over the ship's internal comm. "I got you." And then the AI repeated herself like she hadn't believed it the first time.

"I got you."

You certainly did, thought Rechs. *You certainly did.*

"The weapon?" he asked. His voice was a dry croak. He pulled off his gauntlet and began to search his son for a pulse.

"Detonated. No harm to the planet. I got our deflectors up just before it went off."

"Well," said G232. "This is enough excitement for one bot's life. I thought for sure this was the end of our runtime."

Rechs searched the Dragon for a pulse. That blue hammer inside of all of us, pounding out life for as long as it can. That gift no matter the circumstances.

He found it.

It was weak. But it was there.

Refusing to stop.

EPILOGUE

Rᴇᴄʜs ᴛᴜʀɴᴇᴅ ᴛʜᴇ Dʀᴀɢᴏɴ ᴏᴠᴇʀ ᴛᴏ Dᴏᴄ ᴀɴᴅ Cʜᴀᴘᴘʏ. The two operators made sure the kid disappeared. Healed. Became human again.

The Dragon left behind what he had been made to be. A killing machine like his father.

In time he found a woman.

They left for the stars and founded a world, violent and hard. They made their home there. A place for family and tribe.

A place missing from the stellar charts.

Occasionally the old bounty hunter who never aged would come and stay for a meal. And look on all that they had done. And watch his son grow a family of his own.

***

The man is at the end. The dying has begun in earnest. Long his days have been after those events in the Sinasian worlds when he was known as the Dragon, among other names.

His loved ones gather at his last, weeping and begging him not to go.

To stay just a while more.

But death has made its appointment.

It is not the first time he has died. He has died before. As the Dragon he once was. He knows what dying is like, and he is not afraid of it. He has lived a better life than he deserved. He had a family. And a chance.

And that was all anyone might ever ask. Despite their circumstances. He has learned the wisdom of that.

But he waits for the stranger to come and have the last goodbye. He is waiting before he goes, and he is not altogether sure if the one he waits for will arrive.

The light fades. The sickness, a cancer really, that once kept him young and able to heal like General Rex—like his father—is what now destroys him. There is no more Colonel Ajax. No more Project Phoenix doctors to put him through the torturous process of being cured just so the dying can be pushed back again.

Is it afternoon or night?

It no longer matters. There will be no more days on this side.

He is going now. The lamentations of those who love him break his heart. And it is good, too, at the same time. He made something. A family, a life, a place. Instead of destruction.

But he fights and holds on. Just like he did when he was at… at… that place…

… that battle.

All those times that are gone now.

The family parts as the stranger in armor arrives. He removes his helmet. And there is the old man who never ages.

Tyrus Rechs comes to kneel down at his son's side.

The man who never ages holds the hand of his son and leans close.

"I won't let go," Rechs whispers, knowing that he's been forgetting so much as of late. So very much. His son is dying before him now.

Ball.

The Savages that Rechs destroyed so long ago have now been afforded the last laugh. The experiments they did on him, giving him a long and un-aging life, have also left their curses. And this is one.

Outliving those you love. The curse of such a thing. The mercy, too.

His son beckons him close before dying. He wants to whisper one last thing before he goes.

He can go now. The stranger has come.

Tyrus Rechs leans close and listens.

THE END

MORE GALAXY'S EDGE

If you're spooled up for more Tyrus Rechs, let us know. The next book, *Madame Guillotine*, is in the production queue. Your feedback can help jump it to the front.

HONOR ROLL

We would like to give our most sincere thanks and recognition to those who supported the creation of *Tyrus Rechs: Chasing the Dragon* by subscribing as a Galaxy's Edge Insider at GalacticOutlaws.com

Elias Aguilar
Tony Alvarez
Robert Anspach
Sean Averill
Russell Barker
Steven Beaulieu
John Bell
WJ Blood
Aaron Brooks
Brent Brown
Marion Buehring
Van Cammack
David Chor
Kyle Cobb
Alex Collins-Gauweiler
James Conyer
Robert Cosler
Andrew Craig
Adam Craig
Peter Davies
Nathan Davis
Tod Delaricheliere
Christopher DiNote
Matthew Dippel
Karol Doliński
Andreas Doncic

Noah Doyle
Lucas Eastridge
Stephane Escrig
Dalton Ferrari
Skyla Forster
Mark Franceschini
Richard Gallo
Christopher Gallo
Kyle Gannon
Robert Garcia
Michael Gardner
John Giorgis
Gordon Green
Tim Green
Shawn Greene
Michael Greenhill
Jose Enrique Guzman
Ronald Haulman
Joshua Hayes
Jason Henderson
Tyson Hopkins
Curtis Horton
Jeff Howard
Mike Hull
Wendy Jacobson
Paul Jarman

James Jeffers
James Johnson
Noah Kelly
Jesse Klein
Mathijs Kooij
Evan Kowalski
Mark Krafft
Byl Kravetz
Clay Lambert
Grant Lambert
Dave Lawrence
Paul Lizer
Richard Long
Oliver Longchamps
Richard Maier
Brian Mansur
Cory Marko
Pawel Martin
Trevor Martin
Lucas Martin
Tao Mason
Simon Mayeski
Brent McCarty
Matthew McDaniel
Joshua McMaster
Christopher Menkhaus
Jim Mern
Alex Morstadt
Daniel Mullen
Greg Nugent
David Parker
Eric Pastorek
Daniel Caires Pereira

Jeremiah Popp
Chris Pourteau
Eric Ritenour
Walt Robillard
Joyce Roth
David Sanford
Andrew Schmidt
Brian Schmidt
Christopher Shaw
Ryan Shaw
Glenn Shotton
Daniel Smith
Dustin Sprick
Joel Stacey
Maggie Stewart-Grant
John Stockley
Kevin Summers
Ernest Sumner
Travis TadeWaldt
Tim Taylor
Steven Thompson
Beverly Tierney
Tom Tousignant
Scott Tucker
Eric Turnbull
John Tuttle
Allan Valdes
Christopher Valin
Paden VanBuskirk
Andrew Ward
Jason Wright
Nathan Zoss

Jason Anspach and Nick Cole are a pair of west coast authors teaming up to write their science fiction dream series, Galaxy's Edge.

Jason Anspach is a best selling author living in Tacoma, Washington with his wife and their own legionnaire squad of seven (not a typo) children. In addition to science fiction, Jason is the author of the hit comedy-paranormal-historical-detective series, *'til Death*. Jason loves his family as well as hiking and camping throughout the beautiful Pacific Northwest. And Star Wars. He named as many of his kids after Obi Wan as possible, and knows that Han shot first.

Nick Cole is a dragon award winning author best known for *The Old Man and the Wasteland, CTRL ALT Revolt!*, and the Wyrd Saga. After serving in the United States Army, Nick moved to Hollywood to pursue a career in acting and writing. (Mostly) retired from the stage and screen, he resides with his wife, a professional opera singer, in Los Angeles, California.

Made in the USA
Middletown, DE
26 February 2020